A DIFFERENT
KIND OF LOVE

Recent Titles by Jean Saunders from Severn House

GOLDEN DESTINY
JOURNEY'S END
THE KISSING TIME
PARTNERS IN LOVE
TO LOVE AND HONOUR
WITH THIS RING

writing as Rowena Summers

ANGEL OF THE EVENING
BARGAIN BRIDE
ELLIE'S ISLAND
FAMILY SHADOWS
HIDDEN CURRENTS
HIGHLAND HERITAGE
KILLIGREW CLAY
PRIMMY'S DAUGHTER
SAVAGE MOON
THE SWEET RED EARTH
VELVET DAWN
A WOMAN OF PROPERTY

A DIFFERENT KIND OF LOVE

Jean Saunders

This first world edition published in Great Britain 1998 by
SEVERN HOUSE PUBLISHERS LTD of
9–15 High Street, Sutton, Surrey SM1 1DF.
This title first published in the U.S.A. 1998 by
SEVERN HOUSE PUBLISHERS INC of
595 Madison Avenue, New York, N.Y. 10022.

British Library Cataloguing in Publication Data

Saunders, Jean, 1932-
    A different kind of love
    1.   Love stories
    I.   Title
    823.9'14 [F]

    ISBN 0 7278 5307 4

Typeset by Hewer Text Composition Services Ltd,
Edinburgh, Scotland.
Printed and bound in Great Britain by
MPG Books Ltd, Bodmin, Cornwall.

Chapter One

The night before the wedding, Kate's mother drew her aside. The younger girls had already been put to bed, vainly trying to subdue their excitement at being bridesmaids tomorrow and the Sullivan men had gone to the pub to celebrate. The two women were temporarily alone in the cramped waterside cottage in the small village of Edgemoor that had seen six Sullivan children born, and four survive. Kate, the eldest girl, the beauty of the family, was the first to be married.

She eyed her mother uneasily now. Alice Sullivan bore the marks of a life with too many children and too little money, and a raucous Irish husband who could get roaringly drunk on occasions. In Alice's saner moments, despite her love for her man, she knew they were hopelessly mismatched. She was the product of a late Victorian background and had never been comfortable in the twentieth century. Despite the leaps and bounds of its first quarter, and the vicissitudes of the hideous war that was now thankfully well behind them, Alice still lived by the old standards. But she doggedly accepted that one of a mother's prime duties was to prepare a daughter for the intimacies of marriage, however embarrassing.

"Mother, we don't need to talk any more tonight," Kate said swiftly, sensing what was to come. "You're tired, and we both need a good night's sleep before tomorrow."

"Sleep can wait, Katherine. We have things to discuss," Alice said, her normally pale face already beetroot red.

Kate sighed, knowing there was no escape when her mother

reverted to using her full name. They sat by the fire that was always kept burning in the parlour, no matter what time of year. The gleaming hotplate alongside it was inevitably laden with pans of steaming water. It helped to save using the gas for heating all the water in the scullery for the never-ending washing Alice did for the better off. There was always plenty of driftwood to be collected by her father and brother Donal from the waters' edge, and bits of coal from the moors, so the fire never went out.

To Kate, the constantly burning cottage fire was a symbol of the survival of the Sullivans. Against all the odds of poverty, of war, of bereavements within their ranks, they survived. At that moment, knowing her mother's embarrassment at speaking of things normally far too personal to even hint at, Kate felt a fierce surge of love.

She loved the raggle-taggle lot of them, from her big, blustering father, and her tall handsome brother, to her two small sisters, so different in looks. One was thin and pasty from consumption, the other as round and plump as a rosy apple. The small twin boys were rarely mentioned now, with only a visit to the cemetery on the hill once a year to mark their birthday with a bunch of wild flowers.

Kate was brought out of her dreaming by her mother's uneasy throat-clearing. She glanced at Alice, and felt the colour steal into her own cheeks. For how could she know, this stoical woman, that Kate was already well aware of the intimacies she was about to try to convey? That Kate had already lain with a man, spread beneath him in wild abandon, crying out in ecstacy as Walter Radcliffe forged into her beneath the stars on the darkened hillside overlooking the village, or on the back seat of his splendid Rover motor car? What would she say, this Victorian-bred lady with the work-roughened hands, if she knew that Kate had already been "spoiled", as Alice always referred to it when mentioning some unfortunate girl who'd been caught by a man and was now in trouble . . . ?

2

"Are you listening to me, Kate?"

She jumped, realising her mother had already started speaking, and she hadn't heard a word so far.

"Of course. I didn't know I was meant to comment," she said, hoping this was a suitable reply.

Alice nodded grimly. "It will be a shock to you, girl, you not having seen a man's body before," she agreed. "If God had been willing to spare them, you'd have helped bath our wee small boys and known what to expect. But it's always been a rule in this house that a person's body is their private property, and not to be displayed lewdly or accidentally."

"I know that, Mother!" The females of the family were always kept strictly away from the parlour when her father or Donal took their weekly baths in the old cast-iron tub in front of the roaring fire. And Kate willed away the image of Walter's body, that she knew so well.

Alice didn't look at her now, keeping her eyes on a point above the chenille-fringed mantelpiece with its collection of shells and pebbles and sepia-tinted photographs.

"Remember it in your married life then. Your duty will be to please your husband, but you should always keep yourself decent and covered, and you'll not lose your dignity."

A vision of Walter opening her with his fingers, and hoarsely asking to look, to touch, to taste, surged into Kate's mind. What dignity had she had then – and what had it mattered, when she had been so abandoned in the fever of Walter's desire? Was she, after all, more worldly-wise than her own mother, or was it all so very wicked?

Kate didn't know, but there was always the saving grace that she had allowed herself to be so deliciously seduced by the promise of becoming Walter's wife. Besides, the brown paper-covered manual she had read beneath her bedclothes, loaned to her by Walter, had stated plainly that in marriage nothing was wrong between a man and woman who truly loved one another. And she had loved him so much.

3

She moved slightly away from the fire. Her skin was starting to tingle, and she didn't want to look blotchy in her wedding dress tomorrow. Her creamy-white dress that should in reality be pale brown, since she had already anticipated the vows she would make.

And, oh yes, the Catholic shame of it still persisted, despite all Walter's protestations that he loved her for eternity, and that it was a well-known fact that a woman could do her man considerable harm if she didn't ease the affliction of his erection. He always used such words at those times, as if they lessened his urgent male needs of the flesh.

"Do you realise what I'm trying to say, Katherine? When you and Walter go to that hotel in Bournemouth for a week, he'll expect more from you than a goodnight kiss."

"I know that, Mother! Please don't embarrass yourself any more. You forget I was doing odd jobs on Huggins' farm during the war, and I know very well how animals mate . . ."

She knew at once that she'd said the wrong thing. On a farm such things were taken for granted, even by the slick city girls who'd joined the Women's Land Army, and teased the young country girl about her childish questions. But in brusquely glossing over the obvious, Kate knew by her mother's scarlet face that she had only made things worse.

"If that's the way you view the act of creation, Katherine, it seems to me that working on a farm brought out the worst in you."

"I didn't mean that. I just meant – well, I know how it's done, that's all," she finished lamely.

Alice studied her silently, this slender, golden-haired girl who was nothing like the rest of her family, and whom her garrulous son Donal once said laughingly must have been painted from a heavenly artist's palette, with her delicate features and startlingly blue eyes.

"Knowing how a thing is done is not the same thing as

4

doing it," Alice said, forced into voicing an opinion that she found highly objectionable.

Kate moved to her side, putting her arms around the stiff-backed little figure in the flowered overall which Alice usually wore to keep her tidy clothes clean. Poor they might be, but Alice Sullivan always changed out of her workday clothes, at the end of each wearisome day, into a serviceable dress covered by a neatly-tied overall.

"Can't we leave this discussion now, Mother?" Kate pleaded. "You've always done your best for me, and you don't need to tell me anything about family duty, for I've got your example to follow. And I know Walter will always respect me."

She gave her mother a swift hug, not wanting to meet her eyes. For Walter had shown little respect for her feelings two months ago, when she'd faced him, white-faced and trembling at their special meeting place between the village and the nearby small town where she bicycled to work each mist-filled morning.

"Are you sure?" Walter said harshly in his nasal northern voice. "Have you seen a doctor?"

"Of course not," Kate mumbled, dry-mouthed. "What's the point in paying a doctor to tell me what I already know? He'd be down to the cottage in a minute, and my Dad would kill me – and you too!"

Walter flinched, his knuckles stretched tight, his hands clenched, his good-looking face strained.

"There's only one way out of this, lass, and you've got to face it. I know somebody in Bristol who'll do the job and keep his mouth shut. I'll take you there as soon as I can fix it, and he'll get rid of it."

Kate shook uncontrollably at his callous words, hardly recognising the ruthlessness in his face now.

"You can't mean it," she said, ashen. "You'd be prepared to kill our child? You know it would be a mortal sin, against the teachings of the Church. Walter, you've *got* to marry me.

My family's expecting it anyway, and we must do it as soon as possible."

She clung to him, her fingers digging deep into his flesh. She knew he hated her to mention the Church with all its doctrines and demands. But she had already been guilty of one terrible sin, and she could never commit this atrocity. Her father's was a lapsing Catholic faith that the young Sullivans had only ever followed in a token fashion. But for Kate, it was now the only stable thing in a world that had suddenly fallen apart.

Walter looked hunted, and Kate was terribly afraid.

"You do want to marry me, don't you, Walter?" she said, her voice cracking. "You promised me marriage, and you know I'd never have let you – you know I wouldn't . . ."

"All right, but for God's sake let me think," he said angrily. "First of all – have you told anyone else?"

She shook her head dumbly. She could hardly believe what was happening. A moment that should be so wonderful between two people, had become so ugly and sordid. Walter waited too long before he took her in his arms, where she stood rigidly, misery enveloping her.

"We'll be wed then, if that's what you want. Will that suit? Just a quiet affair, mind."

"Oh yes," Kate almost sobbed. "Just a quiet affair."

He hadn't said it was what *he* wanted, but her relief was too great to question it, with all her pride scattered in the wind like a dandelion clock. She'd be saved from disgrace. It was the only thing that had mattered – then.

And once the family had been told about the wedding, but not the baby, Kate was touched to discover how her mother had over the years scraped together her meagre savings for this very occasion. Enough to see her eldest daughter properly married by the priest, in church, wearing Alice's wedding dress and veil, and with a modest bite at the cottage afterwards.

Money wouldn't stretch to a grand affair, for the men had

always done casual labouring jobs, save for when Donal had
been in the army. There'd be no formal guests, for the Sullivans
were company enough, and all Kate knew of Walter's family
was that they lived somewhere in Yorkshire and wouldn't be
able to make the long journey to Somerset.

Soon after the arrangements had been made, miraculously
avoiding any suspicion in her parents' eyes in all the excitement,
Kate had felt a searing pain in her lower belly. She'd leant low
over the industrial sewing machine where she stitched together
sleeves and bodices for factory-made garments. Vi, the woman
who worked beside her, sent for the supervisor at once.

"You know what's wrong with you, don't you, my girl?" Vi
said shortly. "I'll lay odds on it that your fancy travelling man
has been getting into your knickers."

Kate felt her face burn with shame at the older woman's
knowing look.

"It's not like you think, Vi . . ."

"It never is. But I'll bet he didn't promise you marriage until
you put a shotgun to his head, did he? No wonder you ain't been
looking so bright-eyed lately, if he was pushed into it—"

"He wasn't. We love each other!"

But then the supervisor came storming up to see why two of
his machines were idle, and Vi explained that Kate had a bad
gastric attack and would probably throw up in her machine if
she didn't rest for a bit.

Jenkins grudgingly allowed her to lie down in the back room
for a while, docking her an hour's pay for the privilege, by
which time Kate knew there wasn't going to be any baby. Her
feelings were a bewildering mixture of bereavement and wild
relief. She felt almost compelled to confide in Vi.

"And I always thought you were such an innocent little cuss,
with them big baby-blue eyes of yours. But I daresay it was
always a fair bet that some smooth-talking chap was going to
put you in the club," she said with rough sympathy.

"Thanks," Kate muttered. "That makes me feel a deal better, I must say. Now I'm simple as well."

"No you ain't, just too affectionate and trusting. It don't do to trust any man, and if you've learned that much, then it ain't all been a waste of time."

Kate couldn't cope with such philosophy right then. The pains in her belly were still griping, and she felt as if her head was floating somewhere above her body as Vi argued with the supervisor on her behalf, until he grudgingly agreed that Kate could just sit at her machine for the rest of the day.

But by then, Kate was already wondering if she loved Walter Radcliffe half as much as she thought she had. His passion had waned with the threat of a marriage she suspected he didn't want, and hers had all but disappeared in the shame of what had happened, and Walter's reaction to it. Because of him, she had deceived her parents, and she had deceived herself in thinking Walter wanted anything more from her than a few quick thrusts on a hillside whenever he was in the neighbourhood. But in a kind of desperation Kate convinced herself that this lack of passion between them was only temporary, and that once they were married, all the old fire would return, for there was no getting out of it now.

All the arrangements had been made. The priest had spoken to them, and had seen the futility of trying to convert Walter to the faith. As for Kate, he'd mentally washed his hands of another of the irritating Sullivan family whose elder members had formed a frowned-upon mixed marriage in the first place. In Father Mulheeny's eyes it was never a good thing. Kate knew that if she changed her mind about the marriage now, too many seaching questions would be asked, and she was too vulnerable and bruised not to give everything away. Besides, she would be shamed if folk thought Walter had jilted her, or saw her as a flighty baggage who couldn't make up her own mind.

At least marriage meant security for the future. Walter had a good travelling salesman's job that took him all over the country, so Kate could still live at home for the time being, until they could decide on a proper base as he called it. She didn't mind that idea. She would be halfway between her old life and the new, and for all her bravado, at not yet twenty-one she knew in her heart she wasn't really ready for the commitment of marriage.

Her real self-guilt in the whole affair, though, was that she hadn't told Walter about the miscarriage. As far as he knew, she was still pregnant and it was still a shotgun wedding. Kate had no wish to face her father's roaring blasphemies, nor the sorrow and disbelief in her mother's eyes. Things were better left as they were, and she would have to pretend to Walter that the miscarriage happened soon after the honeymoon.

So many deceptions, Kate thought with a shiver, when she had been brought up to be so honest. She consoled herself that they'd have got married eventually anyway. And she refused to let herself question whether any good could come out of a marriage based on so many lies.

All the doubts had been smothered, and all the plans put into operation, and now the wedding was tomorrow. And the wedding-eve talk between Kate and her mother had finally dwindled to nothing.

"Goodnight, Mother," Kate said quickly. "Get a good night's sleep and be happy for me. When I get back in a week's time, everything will be as it is now, except that Walter will stay here when he's not travelling."

"Nothing will ever be the same once you're married, Katherine, and don't be so daft as to think it. And I'm still not sure I'll like having a stranger living in the house."

"Walter's not a stranger! And he was Donal's friend long before he was mine."

It was odd how that friendship had resulted in her and Walter meeting. Donal and Walter had been together at the Front in France for a brief time, and when they'd accidentally

met several years after the war ended, Donal had invited him
home to meet his family.

That was Kate's first encounter with the tall, arrogant,
fast-talking travelling salesman with a suitcase full of brushes
and an assortment of household goods, and a big car that
the small Sullivan girls had squealed over with excitement.
And Brogan Sullivan had seen a fine young fellow who'd be
quite a catch for his daughter, and encouraged the romance
to blossom.

Kate snuggled beneath the cold sheets in her own small room
that night, listening to the comfortably settling creaks of the old
cottage. And later, to the raucous singing that meant Brogan
and Donal Sullivan were finally weaving their way homewards.
She lay wide awake, trying to see into the future, and trying
even more desperately to conjure up the magic she had first
known with the man who was soon to be her husband.

"It's wedding nerves," Vi had told her positively when she'd
said she was getting jittery. "Everybody gets 'em, duck, but at
least you know what's comin' to you, if you get my meanin',"
she added with a sly chuckle.

Oh yes, she thought weakly, Walter could still make her
feel good – *so* good – there were still times when passion took
them somewhere among the stars, in a manner of speaking.

"But do I really love him?" she whispered into the dark.
She'd been so sure, and now she wasn't. And if she didn't
truly love him, then all tomorrow's vows would be lies.

With her nerves at fever pitch, and the recklessness of high
melodrama colouring her thoughts, she wondered if she should
solve all their problems by jumping into the fast-swirling tidal
river nearby, or walk straight into the deep grey waters of the
Bristol Channel. But sheer panic at the thought of that icy
water enveloping her made her discard such stupid thoughts.
And it would be even more of a sin to drown herself than to
marry a man she didn't love.

Anyway, she didn't want to die. She had prayed so often during the last year of the war for her brother Donal to survive his time in France, and her prayers had been answered. She'd heard enough about dying during those war years, and then had come the irony of the terrible influenza epidemic that followed, killing thousands more.

No, thought Kate. I certainly don't want to die! It was wicked to even think of it. She was almost twenty-one years old, and tomorrow she was going to be married to a good man. They had loved passionately once, and any lack of passion now was only a passing phase.

In her innocence, Kate was sure that love would grow again once they were man and wife.

She awoke to the sound of rain on her window pane. It wasn't a good omen; the last few days had been cooler than usual for early May. But by the time she had washed in the cold water in her basin, the sky had begun to look brighter. With luck, it would have cleared by noon, and Kate's heart began to lift.

Alice and the girls were to walk ahead to church, with Kate and her father coming last. Donal would have already gone to meet Walter there. The small Catholic church was only a short distance away, so there was no need for transport, although Walter would arrive in his Rover, and he and his bride would travel back to the cottage in style.

To his credit, he'd offered to pay for cars to take them all to church, but it was a tradition in Brogan's family that the bridal party walked to church and back again afterwards. The tradition went back to his years in Ireland, and if Kate sometimes thought it odd that he should want to recall those apparently headstrong days in less than savoury surroundings, she never bothered to question it.

Kate's sisters bounded into her room in their nightgowns, chattering like a pair of excited magpies. Maura was as pale and fragile as ever, while Aileen was ruddier than usual.

11

"When are we getting dressed, our Kate?"

"Not for hours yet," she told them. "Go down and have your breakfast and leave me some peace!"

"Our Kate's got the hump," they chanted in unison. "Our Kate's getting married to soppy old Walter . . ."

They ducked as Kate hurled a pillow at them, and went giggling out of the room. Kate got up and put her arms through the sleeves of her old dressing gown. There was a nicer one for her honeymoon, but it wasn't as exotic as she would have liked. Something that would make Walter's eyes gleam . . . She smiled ruefully. He usually couldn't wait to get her clothes off, so it hardly mattered what she wore.

She'd been allowed some pretty offcuts from the sweatshop and, being deft with her needle, it had been enough to make herself a primrose-coloured nightgown and several new frocks that wouldn't be out of place in a swish hotel. She'd begged the use of her machine in her five-minute breaks for the main seams, finishing off the rest at home.

She went downstairs, feeling strangely unreal; this was the last time she would do so as an unmarried girl. The whole family was sitting around the table. Her father had his head in his hands, her brother was unshaven and haggard, and her mother's silent disapproval at their drunken arrival home last night was punctuated by the banging down of the teapot making them both wince, and the relentless sawing of the bread-knife on the breakfast loaf.

"Here comes my princess," Brogan grunted, brightening a little as she appeared. "Will you please tell your mammie that it's only once that a daughter gets married, and if a father can't celebrate then, I don't know when he can. For pity's sake, Katie girl, tell her to have done with her shenanigans, for my head's near to splitting with it."

"Why don't you tell her yourself?" Kate said, not daring to laugh at the comical figure he made, all remorse and hang-dog, and obviously with a sizeable hangover. She guessed he'd already had plenty of tongue-pie that morning.

"Sure and I've done me best," Brogan said, sighing heavily. "But your mother's a very unforgiving woman, Katie."

"Leave them be, Kate," Donal advised with a weak grin. "This is your day, and you don't want to be getting caught up in any family squabbles that are not of your making."

"Then I'll just eat my breakfast instead, or my mother will be getting on at me too," she said, neatly avoiding arguments.

When would it ever be quite like this again, she wondered? The good-natured squabbles, the giggles, the roaring family arguments, the closeness, the good times and the bad times, and the frequently meagre times, that were all part and parcel of what the Sullivans were? All that would change when Walter Radcliffe moved into the cottage. They wouldn't be the same unit any more. Everything would change, and here she was mourning it as if it was the passing of an era – a very bad thought to be having on her wedding day, Kate told herself in panic.

"Are you all right, Kate?" her mother said sharply.

"Of course I am."

"Well, you don't look it. You're as pasty as our Maura, and it's no way to be looking on your wedding day."

"Leave the girl alone, missus," Brogan said, lazily cheerful now that the attention was off himself. "She'll just be having last-minute nerves like any decent girl would, goin' to her nuptials."

The children giggled at this, not understanding the word, but finding the sound of it vaguely wicked, and one to be chewed over at the village school next week. Their mother turned on them at once.

"Now then, get on with your bread and honey and stop looking so dippy, or I'll box your ears for you. A fine pair you'll look then, walking down the aisle behind our Kate with bruised heads."

Kate bit into her own hunk of home-baked bread, oozing with butter from Huggins' farm, and the sweet wild honey Donal collected from the moors. She supposed they didn't live too badly, considering ... considering that Walter had all but sneered at the fact that two grown men didn't have what he called regular jobs, and that Kate's mother had to take in washing to make ends meet. Kate had smarted at that, hating the superiority on his handsome face, and springing to her family's defence at once.

She wished she hadn't remembered that just now, when she was about to tie herself for life to this man whom she'd once wanted so wantonly. Yes, it must just be wedding-day nerves that was making her feel like this, she told herself desperately, trying to ignore how all her bones felt as though they were turning to water at her unbidden use of the past tense. She *had* loved him and she *did* love him. Of course she did.

By the time it was decided that the girls could get dressed in their Sunday frocks without messing them, they were nearly bursting with excitement. They were now adorned with circlets of ribbon-threaded flowers in their hair, which Kate had made for them, matching the posies they carried. Donal had already gone marching off across the fields to the church, his army training still squaring his shoulders and lifting his chin in a way that charmed plenty of the local girls.

Brogan had washed and shaved and was bellowing curses from his bedroom as he struggled with the unfamiliar necktie, and Alice began to help Kate into the soft, creamy-white folds of her own wedding gown.

"Such dreams went into this, Kate," Alice said, with a rare note of softness in her voice as she stroked the silky fabric. "My own mother made it for me, and her skill is where you get your own flair for the dressmaking."

"Granny had the right idea. I'd sooner be stitching by hand for someone I love than slaving over that old machine for

14

Granby's Garments," Kate said, not quite knowing what else to say, and feeling her hands as cold as her heart.

"I doubt you'll be doing that for much longer, once the babbies come along."

At Kate's small intake of breath at the words, Alice looked at her sharply. "You're not ailing today of all days, are you, our Kate?"

It was Alice's delicate way of referring to the monthly cramps, and Kate gave her a swift hug, feeling her eyes grow damp with the poignancy of her words. And if it was impossible for Alice to be more free with words or feelings, Kate herself had no such inhibitions.

"No, Mother. I'm sure it's just like me dad said – wedding-day nerves. I wouldn't be a proper bride without them, would I?"

But her fingers shook, knowing what would be expected of her on this night, and all the nights to come. If she couldn't love Walter in the way that a wife should, then this would be her penance for letting lust get the better of her.

For a moment she remembered a young girl in the village a few years ago who'd allowed her soldier boyfriend to have his way with her, and then found herself pregnant. There had been such a scandal, because the boy had been blown to bits in France, and the girl still bore the shame of it with her child, ostracised by people wherever she went. At least that wouldn't be Kate Sullivan's shame.

They both heard a loud commotion downstairs, and Kate adjusted the veil over her shoulders as her mother tut-tutted.

"That'll be your dad getting into a fine old stew because he still can't fasten that necktie. He'll be at the cider bottle to give him courage, and if I don't stop him right now he'll be weaving his way to church. Will you be all right?"

"Of course."

They looked at one another, not just mother and daughter then, but simply two women, following the same path in life.

Marriage and children ... continuing the great scheme of things, Kate thought, with another huge surge of emotion and affection for this care-worn woman who had never had the best of it, despite the love and loyalty she felt for her own man.

Theirs was a real marriage, for all its ups and downs, and Kate felt her throat tighten, knowing that hers was going to fall so far short of perfection.

"You'll do, our Kate," Alice said softly.

Kate's eyes prickled, knowing it was as fine a compliment as she would ever get from her mother, but it meant all the world to her. She gazed at the unfamiliar vision in the pitted looking-glass in her room, so beautiful and remote in her white gown, the heavy lace veil obscuring the bleakness in her lovely eyes. And the woman who looked back at her was a stranger who was about to live a lie.

She gladly answered the sudden hammering on her door, before her own thoughts completely demoralised her when she must try to look cool and serene. It would be the girls, preparing to ooh and aah over the way she looked. She turned to the door, fixing a smile on her lips, and lifting her chin to a determined tilt.

Donal came into the room, his good-looking face a furious, sickly white. In his hand he held a crumpled envelope. His Sunday boots, so recently blacked to a gleaming shine, were mud-stained and filthy now, as if he'd taken every short cut across the fields to get back here in double-quick time. He was breathing hard enough to bust a gut.

"The bloody swine's not coming, Kate," he burst out harshly, completely unable to soften the words. "He sent a young lad to the church to tell the priest, and he left this letter for you. If I could get my hands around his throat right now, I swear I'd gladly kill the bastard!"

Chapter Two

For a few minutes, Kate was totally unable to believe what she had heard. She felt the way that the penny dreadful novels always told you a drowning person was supposed to feel at such shocking moments – dizzy, sick and choked for breath, and as if the entire span of her life was passing in front of her eyes.

"Sit down, our Kate."

Donal's voice seemed to come through a thick fog. He hovered in front of her in a ghostly mist, and for a few fragmented seconds she wondered if she was going blind. Then he lifted the wedding veil from her face, and she drew a deep, shuddering breath.

Donal poured some water from the jug on her washstand into a glass, spilling it over the white dress, and pushing it against her lips. She drank automatically, feeling the icy chill of the water running down her throat.

"Sweet Jesus, you look like death," Donal said savagely. "I should never have have blurted it out like that, but I feel so God-awful guilty for bringing the bastard into the house in the first place. I wish the bugger had gone over the top and got blown to bits by the Kaiser's shells instead of coming back here to break your heart. You sit still, Katie love, and I'll get Mother up here before I send for the doctor."

She let out her breath in an explosive gasp. It felt as if she had been holding it for ever.

17

"*No*! I don't want anybody near me until I've read Walter's letter. Give it to me, Donal."

She was startled by the sound of her own reedy voice. She already knew what the doctor would say. She was in a state of shock. Of course she was as any bride who had been jilted on her wedding day had a perfect right to be. Of course she looked terrible, and from the coldness spreading through her entire body, she knew she'd probably lost all her colour.

But at the same time, deep down inside her there was a more private feeling that she couldn't share with anyone, least of all her protective, defensive family. Deep inside her, there was an invasive sense of the most tremendous, guilty relief at knowing she didn't have to marry Walter Radcliffe after all. She saw Donal move away as she slit open the flap of the envelope, keeping her eyes averted from his face.

In any case, after all the private traumas she had gone through, this was probably no more than an involuntary defensive reaction, and the real pain of Walter's betrayal was yet to come.

"I'm still fetching Mother," Donal said harshly. "I don't like the look of you at all, our Kate. You should be weeping and wailing, and I don't reckon you should be left alone . . ."

She hardly heard him leave the room. There was a letter written on thick notepaper, and a smaller, bulky envelope inside the larger one. She unfolded the letter and saw the page covered in Walter's small tight handwriting.

Never trust a man with cramped handwriting, she'd once been advised by a dour fortune-teller at a local fair. It indicates a man with a small mean nature.

Kate swallowed dryly as she began to read the letter. It was hard to focus on it properly, and she realised that tears had streaked her face without her even knowing it. No wonder Donal had been so alarmed . . . She concentrated on the letter.

18

Nothing in its contents was going to suprise her now – or so she thought. But a searing shock ran through her as she read Walter's words. For all his faults, she had never anticipated this. And she sensed that his words were carefully chosen, calculated not to make her think too badly of him – if that were possible, she thought bitterly.

My dear Kate,
By now you'll be thinking the worst of me, but believe me, it would have been even worse if we'd gone through with the wedding. I know things have been strained between us these past weeks. It's not because you mean any less to me than you ever did, but because I was torn between what I wanted to do and what I knew I should do.

In the end, I knew I couldn't go through with it. If I'd married you, lass, I risked a prison sentence. After that statement it seems ironic to tell you the reason is because I'm not free.

By now Kate was breathing erratically, her chest so tight it hurt to breathe at all, her hands clenched over the edges of the letter.

There's no way to soften this, so I'll say it outright. I already have a wife, Kate. She was my sweetheart before I volunteered for the army, but I never mentioned her to anybody while I was in France. I thought it was bad luck to keep talking about home. Now I wish to God I'd told Donal about her, and then this rotten mess would never have happened.

Kate's mouth shook at the crass insensitivity of having their relationship described as a rotten mess. But she was reading

19

more than the actual words in the letter now. She'd never thought of Walter as a supersitious man, and more cynical than of old, she could guess another reason why the dashing soldier hadn't mentioned his girl back home, even to his pals. He'd be too busy playing Jack-the-lad with the French mam'selles whenever he got the chance . . .

Dear Kate, I want you to know that I'm hellishly sorry for what's happened, and for leaving you in the lurch like this. I just couldn't see any other way out. You'll be feeling hurt and angry now, and rightly so, but I want you to know that the week at the Charlton Hotel in Bournemouth is all paid for, and I enclose money for your train fare if you want to take the small holiday as planned. In fact, I beg you to do so, as it will give you time to think, and to get away from prying eyes at home.

Kate felt her face burn with humiliation. Clearly, Walter expected her to fall apart, to be screaming out that she was pregnant, and that her menfolk must set the police after him at once for breach of promise. Just as clearly, Walter was desperate that she would do no such thing. It would be calamitous if his wife ever got to hear about all this. As always, Walter was only thinking of himself, despite all his protestations.

As for the other matter, let me know when the time comes, and I'll see you right, lass. I haven't had time to do anything yet, but I'll arrange a post office address where you can contact me any time, and I'll send it to your home as soon as possible. I'm also enclosing the ring I got for you, in case you feel the need to wear it.

That's about all there is to say, Katie lass. I don't expect your forgiveness, but I hope that in time you'll see that I did the only thing possible. You'd have been doubly disgraced

if it ever came out that you'd married a bigamist, so at least
I've spared you that.

Humbly,
Walter Radcliffe.

There was not a single word of love. Not even the pretence
of it. And by the end of the letter Kate was so incensed by
his blatant arrogance that she could only stare in disbelief at
his final sentences. He'd *spared* her indeed!

What he'd done was courted her and lusted after her and
seduced her, made her pregnant and turned her life upside
down. And now he had the almighty bloody gall to expect her
to be understanding because he'd *spared* her from marrying a
bigamist!

Kate could almost picture him preening in the word, for all
its criminal aspect. He'd think himself a real peacock of a
fellow, and if she'd had any semblance of love remaining in
her heart for him, he had just killed it stone dead.

She crushed the letter in her hand just as her mother tiptoed
into the room as if Kate were an invalid, her face as white as
her daughter's.

"Donal's told us what's happened, and he's gone off for
the doctor. The priest's downstairs and he wants to see you
directly to offer you comfort." She looked at Kate helplessly.
"I don't know what to say to you, girl, and that's the truth.
What does the letter tell you?"

Kate took a deep breath, hating Walter all the more at seeing
how he'd distressed her mother. Alice's eyes were dark with
tears. She had never cried in front of her daughter, and it was
Walter Radcliffe who had reduced her to this.

"Only that he's saved me from being married to a bigamist,
Mother, so we must all be thankful for that, musn't we?" she
said, her voice as brittle as glass.

She heard Alice gasp, and closed her eyes for a moment.
She didn't want to see her mother's anguish and misplaced

21

sympathy, but there was probably little hope of being left alone now. She didn't need a doctor, since she wasn't sick. She certainly didn't want the priest with all his pious words, nor could she think what comfort he might offer at a time like this.

Father Mulheeny would assuredly start thanking the Holy Mother that Kate Sullivan hadn't inadvertently committed a sin. For one wild instant Kate wondered about his apoplectic reaction if she were to give in to the temptation to shock him further, by saying it was probably divine intervention that the same Kate Sullivan hadn't been abandoned with a bastard child as well. She would never do such a thing, of course. She swallowed the lump that seemed intent on returning to her throat at every opportunity.

"I'm all right, Mother, really I am," she said huskily.

"Of course you're not all right! You expected to be married today, and the man didn't even have the decency to tell you to your face that he was already married. He's shamed us all, and we'll never be able to hold up our heads in the village again."

"Of course you will, Mother. And it's not your shame, nor anyone else's in this house," she said, more sharply.

Dear heaven, did everyone think only of their own feelings at times like these? Even Alice Sullivan? Kate began to feel that she was learning the entire range of human frailities in one fell swoop.

"You're still shocked," Alice stated, clearly refusing to believe that this young woman with the vulnerable, innocent looks of an angel – and the apparently iron-hard will – could be standing so straight and talking so calmly.

"You'll stay indoors for the week, Kate, and we'll let it be known about the village that it was your decision not to marry Mr Radcliffe. We'll say it was a bad case of nerves. It will salvage a bit of pride for us all, and anything's better than having it known that you were left at the altar."

Kate listened to her rambling words, feeling suddenly sorry for Alice and the dismal picture she felt obliged to paint for neighbours and acquaintances. Alice had always been a proud woman, and this would be cutting her deeply. But there were worse things than being left at the altar, she thought, more painfully knowledgeable than her mother in certain respects.

Kate's first instinct was not to touch any of the money Walter had sent in the small sealed envelope which she hadn't even opened yet. She was humiliated by his reference to the wedding ring, enclosed for her to wear should she feel the need, which, to him, would mean when her changing shape became obvious to the world, of course! She would throw it into the nearest ditch. She would certainly never travel to Bournemouth alone, nor set foot in an hotel unescorted, posing as the married woman she was not. And yet . . . as her mother prattled on, smothering her with plans to keep Kate coddled at all costs until she got over her humiliation, the logic of it all began to unfold in Kate's mind as if it was her destiny, pre-arranged and unalterable.

She hardly heard Alice's affronted words as her own thoughts raced ahead. If she went to Bournemouth, she certainly wouldn't demean herself by posing as a married woman whose husband had been unavoidably prevented from joining her. There were alternatives. She might be the widow of the gentleman who had booked the room. That way, no one would ask any questions and she would be left discreetly alone. In a way, she was as bereft as a widow, even if she didn't exactly feel the same kind of bereavement as the millions of women and girls, no older than herself, whose men had never come back from France.

Kate was well aware that only by occupying her mind in this way was she preventing the real shock from taking its effect. But remembering all those sad, lonely women made posing as a widow somehow shameful. So she could simply be a mystery woman, travelling on her own, with the added security and respectability of a wedding ring on her finger.

She had never been one to brood over things that couldn't

be changed, and for all her fragile air, she was stronger than she looked. She was already adjusting to the idea of a different future. As yet, Bournemouth wasn't a fully-formed part of it, but she could already envisage it as a kind of haven, a breathing-space. She knew she'd have to get away from the cloying love of her family, and unwittingly, Walter had provided her with the means and the way to do so.

But she couldn't say any of that to her mother just yet, especially when she was meant to be grieving and mortally upset at being jilted.

"What does my dad have to say about it all?" she managed to ask.

"He's gone off to get drunk," Alice said briefly. "And I wouldn't have stopped him, even if I could have done. He's got to work out his anger in his own way, and getting drunk at the pub's a sight better than breaking furniture in the cottage. Though I've instructed him to say what we agreed, that it was your decision not to get wed, and thank God I knew none of this other business before he went. Now, will you come downstairs to see the priest, or will I send him up to you?"

Kate drew a long breath. It was now or never, and there was no point in putting off her own decision.

"Neither," she said. "I don't need to be inspected by him or the doctor, and I won't be staying indoors for the week either. If Father Mulheeny wants to do something for me, he can take me in his car to the train station in Bristol as soon as I've changed out of this finery. My clothes are all packed, and I'm going to Bournemouth for the week, just like I expected to be doing."

It was almost comical to see the way her mother's mouth fell open. She was the one who was shocked now, and she blustered at once, trying to talk some sense into her daughter. But Kate was adamant. She had the means to travel, and the room was booked and paid for. She needed time to think, and she couldn't do it here, with her family fussing over her one

24

minute and afraid to look her in the eyes the next. She knew exactly how it would be, and she couldn't bear to hear the blatantly innocent questions from her little sisters.

"You can't possibly go away on your own, Katherine," Alice said, appalled. "What will people think?"

"Girls younger than me went away on their own all through the war, Mother. They went to France and saw horrible sights, and they faced death every day. If they could do that, I'm sure I'm capable of staying by myself for a week in a respectable Bournemouth hotel."

"Wartime is different," Alice said.

"I know it is, and women are more independent now because of it. A few hours ago you thought me old enough to be a married woman, so I don't see why you don't think me capable of managing perfectly well in an hotel where all my needs will be met. Good Lord, Mother, I'm not suggesting joining the Foreign Legion!"

She listened to herself speaking in this crisp, brittle manner in some amazement, as if she stood apart from this newly independent female. The initial shock of Walter's betrayal was receding a little, and now she was filled with a steely anger. As long as she held on to that anger she felt invincible, as brave as one of Mrs Pankhurst's suffragettes, standing tall against the world.

She was also astutue enough to guess that this was only a temporary defensive show of bravado. By this time tomorrow the reaction would have set in, and she would do all the weeping and wailing that everyone expected of her. But that was for tomorrow, and by then she intended to be quite alone to do it in private.

Father Mulheeny glanced repeatedly at the young woman sitting beside him in his battered old car. She sat as straight and still as if carved out of marble as they drove at a steady pace through the winding Somerset roads towards Bristol's great Temple Meads railway station.

Inwardly, he gave a great sigh. Such an asset to the church Kate Sullivan would have been, with her sweet voice and angelic face, but with far too much fire and temper for her own good, he amended sadly. There was too much of her father in her in that respect, so the way things had turned out might be for the best after all.

"Are you quite sure about this, Katherine?" he said for the third time, mindful of his saintly duty no matter what his own feelings on the matter were. "It's not too late to change your mind and go home. No one in the village will think badly of you, child."

She turned her luminous blue eyes towards him, and priest or no priest, he reminded himself to keep his attention on the road and not on the undoubted sensual allure of Kate Sullivan. The good Lord tested men severely, Father Mulheeny thought, just by putting such ravishing creatures on earth.

He'd been entrusted with the truth about Walter's marital state, and had shown all the indignation the situation deserved, but he was human enough to understand how any man would be entranced by one such as this. Perhaps it was as well for the sanity of all the lusty young men in the village that she was going away at this vulnerable time.

"Nothing you can say will make me change my mind, Father. I need to be by myself. You must see that."

"You may think you'll be by yourself, but you won't be, Katherine. God and Our Lady will be constantly by your side, and you'd do well to remember that and be comforted by it."

"I'll remember it, Father," she said stonily.

A swift image of herself and Walter Radcliffe joyously fornicating in the back of his Rover spun into her mind, and she could only hope that God and Our Lady hadn't been observing her then. She felt her cheeks burn at the blasphemy of the thought, and willed it away.

"And are you sure you'll be all right travelling on the train alone?" the priest went on, as if he thought she was on her way to damnation.

"Of course. As I told my mother, younger girls than myself went to France during the war, so it seems a very small thing for me to be doing, travelling to Bournemouth alone after all their courageous efforts."

At last she had found the means to silence him, knowing that memories of the war to end all wars were still vivid to older people, even though it had been over for more than six years now. Its aftermath was still strong in people's thoughts and actions. It was as if the war had become a focal point for whatever had happened in their lives, before, during and afterwards. Kate had been too young to take in the full horror of it at the time, but she knew well enough that everything changed after the war. Women found a new independence, working side by side with men, and taking over jobs that had been unthinkable for them to do. Even though the final glory of votes for women under the age of thirty hadn't yet been achieved, the war had emancipated them as much as all of Mrs Pankhurst's efforts. Kate had never considered herself an out and out feminist, but she believed in fair play for all.

She stirred herself out of her gloomy thoughts as the priest stopped the car at the entrance of the Gothic splendour of Brunel's Bristol railway station.

Kate was overawed by its cathedral-like magnificence. She had never gone farther than a radius of ten miles from home in her life before. This was an adventure she had expected to be sharing with her new husband, who would have taken care of her and pampered her, and now she was undertaking it alone. She swallowed dryly as they got out of the car, and Father Mulheeny handed her her small suitcase. He looked at her dubiously.

"You're quite sure now . . ."

"I'm sure, and thank you for everything, Father," Kate said swiftly before her nerve failed her completely, and she climbed straight back into the car again. "But I'd be glad if you'd call in on my mother when you have the time, as she'll be needing comfort."

He assured her that he would, though Alice Sullivan had never been one for inviting Catholic comforts, and had merely done her duty by her husband in seeing that his children attended the mother church in their early years. He knew it, and Kate knew it.

She turned away quickly, her knees shaking as she sought out a porter to enquire which was the right platform for the Bournemouth train.

Some hours later, having extravagantly taken a taxi from the railway station to the Charlton Hotel overlooking the cliffs at Bournemouth, Kate Sullivan let out her breath in an explosive little sound. She'd done it! She'd actually bloody well done it! She was here, in a room with a view, just as Walter had promised, with a little iron-railed balcony where she could lean out and breathe in the refreshing salt air.

Nobody had even raised an eyebrow when she'd explained in a dignified manner at the reception desk that she would be staying here alone for the week. It wasn't some seedy little hotel where they questioned guests' actions. At least Walter had booked them into a hotel of some standing, and she had already seen guests of all types. If she hadn't been made of stronger stuff, she would probably have turned turtle when she saw some of the toffs who'd obviously come down from London to take the sea air. She hadn't even had to explain about being a widow. She'd merely said her husband wasn't able to join her after all. The strain in her eyes, and the unconscious twisting of the unfamiliar wedding ring she'd remembered to wear at the last minute, had probably supplied the rest.

All that was behind her now, and she had taken the first steps back to normality – whatever that was. She had a week to be simply herself – whoever Kate Sullivan was. No, she was Mrs Kate Radcliffe, she reminded herself hastily.

That was the name she'd remembered just in time to sign on the hotel registration form. It would have been disastrous if she'd overlooked that – and at least it gave her dignity and status to be staying here by herself.

But once she was in the seclusion of her room, she wilted, and the sense of loneliness threatened to overwhelm her. Whatever Walter had done, however much of a rat he had turned out to be, she had loved him with a passion that she knew could never come again. Walter had spoiled her in more ways than one, she thought with a huge sense of loss and bitterness. He had taken her innocence and her trust, and she doubted that she could ever trust any man again.

She felt the tears on her cheeks without even knowing that they had fallen, and she wiped them away angrily. He wasn't worth it, she told herself furiously. He wasn't bloody well worth it, and she'd be cussed if she was going to spend the rest of her life mooning over him.

She opened the long French windows in her room and breathed in the fresh sea air. It was already early evening, and she wondered how late she could leave it before she went down for her evening meal to the splendid dining room she had been shown. She leaned out of her little balcony, trying to summon up that courage. At least she had clothes to wear that wouldn't mark her out as a country girl. Her skill with her needle had seen to that, and she would wear one of her new frocks this very night to give her confidence. It was clear that in the Charlton Hotel only the best would do. If she waited until the last minute of the allotted dinner time before leaving her room, maybe most of the other guests would have gone – because she wasn't all that brave yet.

"Hello," said a masculine voice right beside her. "Marvellous view, isn't it?"

Kate turned her head slowly, and looked straight into the

eyes of a tall man on the adjoining balcony. She guessed that he was about thirty years old. He was immaculately dressed for dinner. His dark hair was sleeked down, à la Rudolph Valentino, which didn't disguise the fact that it was thick and naturally wavy. His smile was wide and friendly, and it made Kate freeze instantly, because Walter's smile had been wide and friendly too. Two adjoining balconies were far too intimate for her liking.

"It's very nice, I'm sure," she said, keeping her voice distant, and turning back to admire the view rather than the handsome, assured man in the next room.

"You're not from London like most of the guests here, are you?" he said, his voice suddenly interested. "I love that accent. West Country, isn't it?"

She turned to face him again, ridiculously on the defensive and unable to stop her sharp reply.

"Where I come from, we think it's the folk who live in London who have the accents. Come to that, yours isn't exactly cut-glass, either."

She was immediately appalled that she had been so rude, and felt even more embarrassed at his indulgent smile.

"Oh, I assure you I didn't mean to criticise, and I apologise if that was the way it seemed. The way you speak is quite delightful," he said, as smooth as silk. "Shall we introduce ourselves?"

At this, Kate took fright. She didn't know how to behave in a hotel, and after Walter's betrayal, she didn't want to have even the remotest association with another man. That fact had been dawning on her all the way from Bristol, and she had looked on her week at the Charlton Hotel as something of a retreat, where she could become as anonymous as the wallpaper. She had been dismayed when the hotel receptionist had pointed out the board announcing all their social activities. There was dancing to a small band each evening, and various charabanc trips could be arranged by the management if sufficient guests were interested, and there was always a special banquet each Friday evening, "price extra" written in small letters underneath. And Kate wanted none of it.

"I don't think so," she answered the man on the balcony now. "If you'll excuse me, please, I'm finding it quite chilly out here."

But nothing like as chilly as the reaction he was getting from her, she said to herself, and a good job too. If he thought she was going to be friendly just because they were temporary neighbours, he could think again.

She went back inside her room and closed the windows, leaning against them for a moment, realising that her heart was pounding. Despite her determination to freeze any individual who attempted friendship, she was disgusted at herself, knowing she must have appeared naive and unsophisticated – which she was – in even refusing to let a gentleman introduce himself. What a simple country chick she must have seemed, and him so suave and gallant. So had Walter been, she reminded herself, and that had been the start of all her troubles.

She turned to her unpacking, her hands shaking. She hung the new frocks in the wardrobe, and for a moment she held the new nightgown to her face, breathing in the distinctive scent of soft new fabric which had so long been a part of her life. This particular garment had been stitched with so much love and hope. All her dreams had gone into it . . . Without warning, the tears came in a flood and she found herself lying face-down across the width of her bed as if in supplication, weeping as if her heart would break.

When the shaking finally stopped, she told herself furiously it was nothing but self-pity. She conjured up the brief sneaking feeling of relief she had felt, knowing she hadn't had to live a sham of a marriage, since she no longer loved Walter the way she once had. But it was his cruel deception that was still so hard to bear. And remembering how she had given herself to him so wantonly and freely . . . remembering all the things they had said, all the things they had done, filled her with shame.

Slowly, anger overcame everything else. A man like Walter Radcliffe wasn't worth wasting tears over, she told herself, and she had done with crying over a rotter. She got up from the bed, seeing how she had creased the lovely new nightgown she'd worked on so painstakingly, and she didn't even care. It was only a bit of cloth after all.

Chapter Three

Some time later, a paler Kate Radcliffe descended the curving staircase of the Charlton Hotel. She was more composed than an hour ago, and she wore the floaty chiffon frock with the handkerchief points at the hem that had been been intended for this first special evening of her married life.

She wore it defiantly, telling herself that nobody was going to take away the pleasure of knowing that she looked her absolute best in its shimmery soft hues of cream and gold, with a matching wisp of chiffon tucked inside the gold-coloured bangle on her upper arm.

The frock certainly did something for her waning self-esteem as she entered the dining room alone. She quailed for a moment, as people glanced her way, but she held her head high, trying not to guess at their speculation about her. Almost everyone else here seemed to be part of a couple or a group of people, and she had been told enough times by her parents that proper young ladies never stayed unaccompanied in an hotel. They had to be at least sixty years old to do so without inviting comment. There might be any number of reasons for a young girl to be travelling on her own, but people generally thought the worst. Especially if the girl held herself well and was reasonably good-looking. It was ironic that such a circumstance hadn't bothered too many people when those same young women were prepared to go to war alongside their men.

The maître d' hovered at her side, and Kate gave her name quickly, reminding herself that she had better remember her chosen persona of the young married mystery woman, Kate Radcliffe. It helped, in a way, even if she had no intention of sharing confidences with anyone else. But it was like playing a part in a play, and it somehow put a barrier between the old Kate and whatever the future held for her.

"Would madam like a window table, or one where she can hear the piano player?" the man said smoothly, his eyes noting everything about this golden-haired young woman.

"Neither, thank you," Kate said at once. "I'd like a quiet table where I can be quite alone."

"But there are much nicer tables where a lovely lady like yourself can be much admired—"

"Thank you, no," Kate said adamantly. "The one in the corner over there will suit me perfectly."

He sighed heavily as she indicated a table surrounded by potted palms, but Kate was more than content to merge into the background. But no matter how the buzz of genteel conversation went on around her, or the way the piano player occasionally directed his soulful music towards her, she had never felt quite so alone as she studied the dinner menu.

This night should have been so very different. Despite the anger she tried to keep uppermost in her mind, she could still feel the sharp pain of being jilted. Those who had never experienced it would never understand the sickness in the pit of her stomach whenever the shame of it hit her anew. Tonight should have begun so tenderly, and ended so lovingly. She should have been spending her first night as a married woman in her husband's arms.

"Has madam chosen?" said the waiter hovering at her side. She peered more carefully at the menu, dashing the hint of tears from her eyes. She had never eaten this well before, but since Walter's money was paying for it, she felt reckless.

"I'd like sliced duck, please, with a selection of vegetables in season."

"Certainly, madam. Would you care to see the wine list?"

She swallowed as she heard the words. What would this penguin-stiff waiter say if she requested a jug of foaming Somerset cider, which was the usual drink her father brought home at night! She had never tasted wine in her life . . . she caught sight of a familiar face across the dining room, and the man from the next room to hers raised his glass to her in a brief acknowledgement.

She turned away from his gaze, her cheeks burning, just as if he could have read her mind at that moment, and known what a hick she was.

"Just bring me whatever you recommend to accompany the duck," she said as coolly as she could to the waiter.

"Thank you, madam. Would you prefer a glass or a carafe?"

"Just a glass, please," Kate said, paling at this, and not having the slightest idea what a carafe meant.

That first evening was as much of an ordeal as Kate had expected. She stayed in the dining room for as long as possible, since the alternative was going back to her empty room and letting the misery take over. It wasn't *her* shame, but that made no difference to her feelings.

Long into the night, she could faintly hear the sounds of merriment from the hotel guests below and she wondered just what she was doing here at all. Yet the alternative to being among strangers was to brave the sympathy of those who knew her.

For the next two days she kept strictly to herself, spending the days striding into the wind along Bournemouth's blustery seashore; watching other families on holiday, the children digging up the sand and making sand-castles, or searching for shells to take home with them; watching couples, their arms linked, with eyes for no one but each other, and feeling the familiar pain in her throat.

On the third evening she was shown to her usual table for

dinner. By now the maître d' had developed quite a protective air towards the beautiful, sad-eyed young woman with the air of mystery about her, who always dined alone.

As he handed her the menu that evening, Kate noticed a card beside her table napkin. The name in gilt letters on it was Luke Halliday, and the address beneath was simply Dundry Mews, London. There was also a telephone number, and Kate thought immediately that it was the business card of someone who was either very arrogant or very well known. Kate had never heard of Luke Halliday, but that wasn't surprising. In her insular world, she knew nothing of London or its inhabitants.

"I think someone left this here by mistake," she said to the maître d'.

He shook his immaculately-coiffed head.

"There is no mistake, madam. The gentleman from Room 314 requests that you join him for dinner. If it is not your wish to do so, I will see to it for you."

Kate's heart jolted. Her room was 316 so 314 would be the one with the adjoining balcony where she had seen the man on her first evening here. She remembered Walter telling her that all the best rooms on the seaward side were even-numbered. While she was still thinking how to rebuff the invitation, she turned the card over, and saw the strong, masculine handwriting on the reverse side.

"Why don't you have second thoughts and join me?"

Her face flamed. The man had covered all eventualities, clearly having expected her refusal. And the maître d' was still awaiting her decision.

"I prefer to dine alone," she said at once.

"Then I will inform Mr Halliday that you don't wish to join him, madam."

But he didn't move away at once, as if he expected her to have the second thoughts just as Luke Halliday had suggested.

Kate looked beyond him to where Luke Halliday sat at a window table. She could see his reflection in the darkened window, as if there were two of him. He caught her glance and nodded briefly. She looked away, feeling gauche and nervous, because she simply didn't know to handle this situation. Almost at the same moment, she realised what a simpleton she must appear, to be thrown into such a panic at a perfectly civilised invitation in a respectable hotel.

"Mr Halliday is a much-respected client here, madam," the maître d' murmured discreetly, as if to reassure her. "He comes here frequently."

Kate took a deep breath. "Thank you. Then I shall be pleased to join Mr Halliday for dinner," she said.

Her legs were shaking slightly as she crossed the dining room behind the waiter. Luke Halliday stood up as she approached. She already knew he was tall, but she hadn't realised quite what a commanding figure he made as he held out his hand to take hers. She felt ridiculously, suddenly, afraid, as a frisson of something that was almost electric passed between them at the contact.

"I'm honoured that you agreed to join me, Mrs Radcliffe," he said gravely.

"Thank you, Mr Halliday," she said, confused at hearing such old-fashioned courtesy.

"Won't you please sit down?" he said.

She sank into the chair across the candle-lit table from him, her eyes lowered. Even so, his image was still in her head. He was ruggedly good-looking . . . but so had Walter been. And his words were bland, almost trite, the words of a stranger politely greeting a guest.

Won't you please sit down?

That was all he had said. But what Kate heard in her head was something different.

Won't you please come into my life?

As if he were the spider, and she the fly. Every instinct was telling her to say no. To turn and run now, before she began something else that would only end in unhappiness.

Kate knew she was being over sensitive, and that her nerves were still raw from Walter's deception and betrayal. But as she met the stranger's dark intense eyes which told her how much he liked what he saw, she couldn't rid herself of the eerie feeling that once destiny took a hand in your affairs, there was little you could do to stop it.

Luke Halliday hadn't been born into money. He had been brought up on the Kent coast in a family just nudging middle class, so he was well aware of its value, and the necessity of having something behind him. Something for a rainy day, as a doting great-aunt had often told him.

Then that same doting great-aunt had succumbed to the lethal flu epidemic that had ravaged the country the year after the war ended. She had left Luke a surprisingly large nest-egg, and he had known exactly what to do with it.

He wanted a place of his own for a start, and the maisonette in fashionable Dundry Mews in south London had been on the market at just the right time. Next, he needed a studio and darkroom, and all the more elaborate photographic equipment he had coveted and could now afford. He had always longed to delve into the mysteries of photography, and Great-aunt Min had given him the opportunity. Thirdly, the studio had to have a shop-window frontage where he could display, to his prospective clients, his portraits of weddings and babies and family occasions.

Once he felt he had become accomplished enough, Luke had advertised for clients by offering, for a limited time, to photograph men in uniform returning from the Front, at half-price, as a family keepsake. The idea was nothing short of inspirational. Having served in an infantry regiment in France himself, he knew how the folk back home would treasure such a memento . . . and from then on, he had never looked back. Orders had come pouring in, and when those same servicemen had married their sweethearts who promptly produced babies, they had remembered the keen young man with the ready smile and easy-going manner, and brought their custom to him. It was Luke's good fortune that it was becoming a national passion for families to have group portrait sittings at regular intervals.

His final flourish with Great-aunt Min's bequest and his new-found affluence, had been the swish dark green Bentley which now stood outside the Charlton Hotel attracting plenty of envious attention during that sunny May week in 1925.

By now, he was thinking of branching out into something new, and it was making his pulses race every time he thought about it. And the sight of this golden girl sitting reluctantly opposite him, as if she was ready to take flight at any moment, was exciting him even more.

"Please forgive me for staring at you so intently, Mrs Radcliffe," he said, realising he had been doing so for longer than good manners decreed. "But you know you've become something of an enigma these last few days."

At the unexpectedness of the remark, Kate felt a nervous twitch at the side of her mouth.

"I assure you there's nothing in the least odd about me," she said, not sure what the word meant.

"Forgive me for my crassness, dear lady. I merely meant that your air of mystery is most alluring," Luke said, not wanting to alarm her or to make her think that he was prying – which he most certainly was.

There was something endearing about the little nervous twitch at the corners of her mouth. He decided to be bold in his approach.

"For a start, where is the missing Mr Radcliffe, I wonder? And why does his lovely wife have such mauve shadows beneath her remarkable blue eyes? And even more intriguing – where does she go to every morning, when a lonely man such as myself is becoming exhausted from searching for her among the highways and byways of respectable Bournemouth?"

Despite herself, Kate laughed, albeit nervously, at his artless questions, and as she did so, she realised it was the first time she had half-relaxed her guard since arriving at the hotel.

Two days of wandering aimlessly about by herself had apparently made her ready for company after all. She knew that solitude didn't really suit her. She was too used to the boisterousness of her workmates, and the clattering and whine of the sweatshop machines where the women had to shout to be heard, to enjoy being alone for too long.

"Thank heavens for that," Luke Halliday said in a relieved voice. "I had begun to wonder if you could smile at all, and now that you have, it was worth the waiting."

It wasn't a gushing compliment, but it made her feel good. And before Kate could think of a suitable reply, if one were needed at all, Luke raised one finger to the waiter, and a bottle of wine, in a silver cooling jug on a stand, was brought to the side of their table.

The man poured out a glass of white wine for each of them, after giving Luke the cork to sniff and a taster in his glass, to which he nodded approvingly. It was all so suave and elegant, and Kate realised how little she knew of the social niceties.

The wine tasted cool and not too heavy, and she made no demur when he suggested he should order dinner for them both, unless she had any special preferences. She shook her head, thankful to have the decision made for her.

"Good," Luke said. "I'm sure you'll like my choice, so I thought we'd dispense with all that nonsense of going through the entire menu. So now tell me all about yourself."

"If there's anything more guaranteed to make a person tongue-tied, I don't know it," Kate said. "Anyway, there's nothing much to tell. I live in a small Somerset village, with the usual set of parents, an older brother and two young sisters. And me."

It sounded pathetic, and she was humiliated by her own ineptness. It seemed so dull, and so did she. She wasn't normally like this. It was Walter who had taken all the life and soul out of her. . . . Why couldn't she have invented something wildly glamorous about herself, to keep the interest of this intelligent man? And instantly, she knew why. She didn't want to interest him – at least, not in that way.

"You're very fortunate," Luke said, surprising her. "I no longer have the usual set of parents. And I never had any brothers or sisters."

"Well, they're probably not such an advantage," Kate said, and then felt awkward at her flippancy, as she suddenly remembered how some of the people in their village had laughed and cried and hugged one another, when any of their boys had come home from the war unscathed. And there had been many others who hadn't . . .

"Haven't you forgotten someone?" she heard Luke say.

She looked at him, puzzled, until she saw him glance at her left hand, and the wedding ring Walter had bought her. In her embarrassment she felt as though her face was scorched with heat.

"Mr Radcliffe is no longer with me," she said, as evenly as she could. "And I'd rather not talk about it."

Besides, she had no intention of adding to her humiliation by telling a stranger that she'd been jilted on her wedding day. It was still too new and too painful for her to be over it yet. There were moments when the pain became almost physical, and she wondered how she was ever going to face the people she knew again, especially her workmates who didn't even know that she wasn't a married woman after all.

Kate took a long drink of wine and felt her head spin as the cool taste of it ran down her throat.

"Fair enough," Luke said. "Then you must remain my mystery woman for the time begin. But am I not even permitted to know my lady's name?"

She wasn't his woman, nor his lady, and it was on the tip of her tongue to tell him so. But his eyes were frank and friendly and honest. She felt an unexpected little rush of gratitude that at least she wasn't entirely alone any more, and she was only just beginning to accept what an ordeal self-enforced loneliness had been until now.

"It's Kate. Katherine, really, but I much prefer Kate. It's what my parents and friends call me."

"Dare I be allowed to be included in that category?"

She smiled naturally at last. Their meeting might not have happened in the most normal way, but since nothing about this week was normal to Kate, this brief acquaintance merely fitted into the general pattern of things.

"If you like."

"And I'm Luke," he said.

He reached across the table, and his fingers enclosed hers for a moment. Kate felt the strength in them, and almost snatched her own away. The last time she had been enchanted by the touch of a man's hand was when she had been wantonly seduced by Walter Radcliffe.

She knew without being told that her face must have changed expression. From that small burst of pleasure at being in this man's company, she felt as though the strain was showing all over again. She felt remote, detached . . .

"I think the wine has gone to my head slightly," she murmured, seeing the puzzled look in her companion's eyes.

"But you've hardly touched it. How long is it since you've eaten?" he asked, brisk and authoritative.

Kate looked at him vaguely. "I'm not sure. I suppose it was this morning. Breakfast, I think."

The hotel didn't provide midday meals, and guests were expected to eat out. Kate couldn't remember eating anything, nor where she had been at midday, and she was suddenly alarmed at her own foolishness.

"That's far too long to go without food," Luke said. "I hope you're not one of these women who go in for this dieting fad."

Kate smiled faintly as he looked her over. No matter how

hard she tried, and however bust-flattening the current fashion for frocks, she couldn't hide her own curvaciousness.

"You obviously need someone to look out for your interests," Luke went on. "Where have you been all day?"

"Oh – on the beach, I think. Walking. Thinking. Nothing very exciting."

She stopped. She was probably giving him the impression of a madwoman. He'd soon be sorry he asked her to sit at his table and dine with him. It would undoubtedly be the first and last time.

"What do you say to coming for a drive with me tomorrow in my motor? I'll show you some of the lovely countryside around here, and then we'll have lunch at a country inn. You shouldn't be half-starving yourself, no matter what it is you're grieving about," he said. "And I assure you I have no ulterior motives, other than friendship."

She blinked at him, knowing he was being kind to a stranger. He was one of those rare people who summed up a situation and acted on it, and would not give her the chance to mumble and back away, which she assuredly would have done if he hadn't made it sound such a fait accompli. She bit her lip, remembering one of the silly French phrases Walter had brought back with him from France and tried to teach her.

She deliberately blocked Walter out of her mind as she answered in a husky voice.

"Well, what sort of car is it? I hope it's not that fancy dark green thing at the front of the hotel that looks as if it cost the earth!"

Luke laughed, and she could see how the little lights danced in his eyes at the simple remark.

"Kate Radcliffe, you're a sheer delight to know," he said softly and for no apparent reason at all that Kate could think about. She immediately realised what a gaff she had just made.

"It *is* the dark green one! Dear Lord, now you'll think me insulting as well as a great simpleton—"

"Why on earth should I think anything of the sort? Don't you know I'm half in love with you already?" he asked.

"Please don't say that," Kate said, tense at once. "You musn't be in love with me, not even halfway."

Thankfully, the waiters brought their food then, and the awkward moment passed. It was a while before Luke picked up the thread of the conversation again.

"I'm sorry if I embarrassed you earlier, Kate. Whatever happened between you and your husband, it's obvious that you don't want to talk about it, nor to become entangled with anyone else just yet. But you're very beautiful, and I won't be the only man to be captivated by you. You have only to look around this hotel to see how many people glance our way, and it's certainly not on my account!"

He might be complimenting her, but if her self-confidence had been battered by Walter's betrayal, Kate was just as inhibited by these remarks. She didn't want men looking at her. She didn't want another Walter. She wasn't ready to trust yet, if ever.

"I had a bad experience recently," she said quietly. "It's left me feeling very fragile, if you must know, and that's all I'm going to say."

"That's fine by me," Luke said. "But just remember I've got broad shoulders if you change your mind. Meanwhile, perhaps you'd care to give me a list of the taboo subjects, so that I don't tread on your toes too often."

She looked at him sharply, aware that he was teasing, and then she looked away, unsure how to handle such quick and easy cameraderie. She almost snapped back a reply, but it wasn't worth it. They'd never meet again after this week, and if she changed her mind about going out with him tomorrow, it would be easy enough to invent a migraine.

Apart from this delicious dinner, she didn't owe Luke Halliday a thing. And even the dinner was paid for by Walter, she remembered. She might just stay in her room tomorrow and read instead. Or watch out for the distinctive Bentley to leave

the front of the hotel, and then resume her solitary walks. She
was free to make whatever choice she liked.

Kate declined to join Luke in the bar after dinner. She had no
wish to extend this tête-à-tête any longer than necessary. She
aknowledged that he was a very attractive man and that given
other circumstances, perhaps . . . but then her insides seemed
to clench together, remembering how attractive Walter had
been, and how things had turned out.

Since coming to the Charlton Hotel she had dreamed of
Walter every night. She didn't want to, but there was no way
anybody could direct their dreams. They gave her pleasure,
even though she despised herself in the morning for wanting
the dreams to last just a little longer. She dreamed about him
holding her, caressing her, whispering her name in her ear and
against her heated flesh, and the longing for him then was still
the same.

He wasn't hers to love, and never had been, but the dreams
took no account of that. In them she was in his arms where
she ached to be, so close to him that it was as if they shared
the same skin, the same breath, the same heartbeat.

"You're the most beautiful thing in this world," he said to
her, in that husky, seductive voice that sent shivers down her
spine. "I want to spend my whole life with you, Katie, and
one day we'll be wed, I promise you."

She moved restlessly in her bed as the traitorous lies fell so
glibly from his tongue, but she didn't want to listen to her
conscience. She just wanted him to love her . . . love her . . .

"Walter, I wish we could see one another more often."

"So do I, my pet, but you know it's not possible. My job
takes me all over the country. But I always come back to you,
don't I, sweetness?"

And to her, Kate thought uncomfortably, half-awake. *You
always go back to her, the woman who rightfully wears your
ring on her finger.*

She made herself relax fully, willing the dream to return, willing herself back in Walter's arms, even though she knew she was only prolonging the agony. But dreams were all she had now, and she realised she wasn't yet prepared to let them go completely. Even another man finding her attractive had stirred up thoughts of Walter.

The dream took her over once more, and she was lying on Walter's tartan car rug on the gentle hillside where they had so often made love. She was wrapped in the cocoon of his arms, and his fingers were tracing a line from her breasts down across her belly to where the triangle of fine golden hairs covered her modesty.

She had been so embarrassed when Walter had first wanted to see her, and touch her . . . and then to do even more intimate things to her with his mouth and his tongue. In her innocence it was something she had never dreamed happened between a man and a woman, but when it had, she experienced the most glorious sensations of all, and felt closer to him in body and spirit than she had believed possible.

Without knowing that it did so, her hand strayed down to where the heat of her body pulsed between her legs. She didn't touch herself beneath her nightgown, but her eyes were damp, knowing how beautiful love between a man and woman could be, especially when you believed it was a love that was going to last for ever.

"You are going to marry me, aren't you, Walter? One day?" she had whispered to him more than once, the way she now did in the dream.

"One day, sweetness, when you're older. I doubt that your father would give his permission yet, and Donal's aggressively protective of you as well. We have to take things slowly, lass, and you know how good it can be to take things slowly," he said, suggestively, turning the conversation to his advantage as his fingers began to probe her inner softness, taking her breath away, and sending sensual spasms of love rippling through her.

46

It was only later that she had realised why Donal was so aggressively protective of her when Walter was around. Donal would have seen him in action with the French mam'selles and wanted to keep his sister out of his seductive clutches – until Donal, like the rest of them, had been lulled by the persuasive art of the master-seducer.

Kate stirred restlessly again, as the real circumstances mingled with the sweet dreams she wanted to keep close to her. She was so hot, and her mouth was so dry. She got up, and poured herself a glass of water from the en suite bathroom that she still found such a luxurious novelty. Then she stood by the French windows looking out at the night for a few minutes, willing her turbulent thoughts to calm down. She hadn't drawn her curtains, and the night was still and beautiful, studded with a million stars.

A small sound made her tense, and she caught the glow of a cigarette from the balcony next door. She could see the shadowy shape of Luke Halliday leaning over his railing, taking the night air, and she dodged back quickly, even though he wouldn't be able to see her.

It was such an intimately charged situation, to be so close to another person who was a stranger – and a stranger who had made it perfectly obvious that he didn't intend to remain that way if she gave him the slightest encouragement. Kate resolved once again that she would invent a headache tomorrow morning.

Chapter Four

She was ready and waiting for him at the appointed time. Breakfast at the Charlton Hotel was taken between eight and ten o'clock, and Kate was thankful to see that she and Luke had obviously missed one another at the first meal of the day. She didn't want it to appear that they had become fast friends too soon, or that this week had been some sort of pre-arranged meeting.

After she had got back into bed last night, smoothing down her tangled sheets, she had slept reasonably well, with no more dreams, and she felt tolerably refreshed.

A guilty thought had begun to run around her head. Luke Halliday had pursued her, not the other way around, but after her initial resistance, she knew she had put up very little more. The thought that disturbed her was whether she was just using him as some kind of therapy for her bruised feelings. It sounded so brutally callous. But even if that was the case, did it really matter? She just wasn't sophisticated enough to know. Maybe smart London girls would have no qualms about a brief fling with a man in an hotel, but Kate Sullivan wasn't a smart London girl, nor ever could be.

She was still vaguely uneasy about taking a drive in a motor car with a man she barely knew. Her mother certainly wouldn't like it, and her vitriolic father would roar that she was going the way of street women and should know better. As for Donal . . . she had seen the suffering in Donal's eyes after the way Walter had treated her, and he'd be less than happy about her going off with a stranger. She acknowledged the fact that he *was* over-protective of her, but she had always found it more endearing than stifling. But the thought of her father and brother both ganging up on her to condemn her for being flighty was enough to make her squirm. So maybe this wasn't such a good idea after all, and she could still back out.

As she half-rose from the sofa in the hotel lounge she heard Luke's voice beside her.

"So you came. I wondered if you'd take fright after all."

Kate forced a small laugh, though her heart had begun to pound. She had left the means of escape far too late.

"Why on earth should you think that?" she said, as coolly as she could.

"Because, my dear Mrs Radcliffe, you sometimes remind me of a frightened bird with those huge eyes of yours. They're very lovely, but a little bewildered too, as if you don't quite know what you're doing here."

Kate forced another laugh. "Maybe that's because I don't," she retorted, knowing it was far nearer the truth than Luke could possibly imagine.

What on earth *was* she doing here? She had asked herself the same question a hundred times already and there was no clear answer. The only sure thing was that soon she had to go back. Her parents, and Donal in particular, would be waiting and wondering just how their jilted girl was going to be when she returned home, and if her heart was truly broken. She would need watching, and they would watch her constantly to see if she was about to break.

The breath caught in her throat, and she turned away, not wanting Luke to see the sheer panic in her face. She couldn't bear the thought of facing everyone again, but there was nowhere else to go. Wherever you went, you always had to go back, and that was the truth of it. It was what her mother called facing your personal dragon.

As she rose from the plush depths of the sofa, Luke offered

her his arm. After the merest hesitation she took it, and couldn't resist the pleasant feeling that this was like being real gentry as they walked out of the foyer, and into the morning sunlight.

"I though we'd take a drive along the coast to Poole," Luke said. "And since it's such a lovely day, instead of taking an indoor lunch I persuaded the hotel to pack us some sandwiches and a flask of lemonade for a picnic."

Kate looked at him in astonishment. That anyone dared to ask the hotel establishment to supply anything other than their ritual menus, was impressive indeed. But she sensed that Luke Halliday was a man who would dare anything, and she realised anew how insular was her own small world if she could be amazed by such a thing. She would never have his kind of sophistication, nor that of the other guests here. The longer she stayed there, the more Kate knew it. She had been brought up in a modest home, and told never to try to be something she was not. Walter had made her feel glamorous and special, but the feeling had vanished like a light being turned off when he had walked out on her. But for a brief, heady while she had been something other than ordinary Kate Sullivan. She had been Somebody, because somebody else had made her so, and she would dearly like to get the feeling back, but without all the additional traumas of forbidden love, thank you very much, she thought.

"Why so pensive all of a sudden? Doesn't the idea of a picnic please you?" Luke said, when she didn't comment.

She spoke in a rush. "Oh, yes it does! It's a wonderful idea. I just wondered how you ever managed to arrange it with those hotel people. They seem so stuffy."

"They're only people, Kate. If you find it difficult to remember that, try to imagine them in their underwear – or is that too risqué a suggestion?"

"It's too risqué for you to be saying it to me when I hardly know you!" she said smartly.

51

But the laughter bubbled up inside her, unable to resist imaging the impeccable maître d' marching across the dining-room, penguin-stiff in red flannel underwear.

"Thank God. A genuine laugh at last," Luke said lightly. "It's good to see that you're human after all."

"Did you think I wasn't?"

"I think something has hurt you very badly to put such a barrier between yourself and the rest of the world. And I can feel the icy blast coming at me again now that I've tried to penetrate it."

She couldn't find a ready answer. He didn't know the true circumstances of her life, but he saw too much, and she didn't want anyone intruding on her private grief. She was calm on the surface – most of the time – but there were still moments when Walter's betrayal tore her apart. He had promised her everything, and it had all been lies, every word of it. How could she forget all of that in a few short days?

Luke said nothing for a while, and then, "Look ahead of you," he said.

Kate caught her breath. She had been gazing unseeingly at nothing in particular for the last few minutes, and now she saw the broad expanse of a bay that sparkled blue and silver in the sunlight. Small fishing boats bobbed up and down on its surface, and a few sleeker yachts and motor boats belonging to the rich were moored in the harbour.

Living on the coastal fringes of the Bristol Channel as she did, Kate was used to the sight of water and boats, but this was a different kind of water, vast and beautiful.

"You can get across to France in some of the bigger crafts," Luke said, as casually as if this was some everyday happening.

Kate stared out to sea, wondering how it must feel to have so much power beneath you, and having enough money to even own such a boat as these.

"But you have to have passports and things for that, don't

you?" she said, trying to sound knowledgeable about something that was quite outside her experience.

"Oh yes. And I wasn't suggesting we go there today. We'll just take a short cruise along the coast," he said, as casually as you like.

Kate felt as if she turned her head in slow motion. She had simply agreed to take a drive with him, and now he was talking about a cruise and a picnic. It all sounded far too intimate for comfort. Before she could get her confused thoughts into order, Luke stopped the car near a sleek blue and white motor boat. It wasn't as ostentatious as some of the other boats moored nearby, but to Kate it was all part of a different world where she didn't belong.

She recalled how she had been told that Luke was a frequent guest at the Charlton Hotel. This was obviously the reason why. He had money. And she did not. She knew she was in danger of becoming prickly again, the way people of her class did when faced with something above their station. She hated the feeling, but recognised it only too well. And she hated the thought that that word *class* had entered her mind at all. But it had. And it stuck there like a burr beneath the skin.

"You're going to tell me that thing belongs to you now, I suppose?" she said, with heavy and unwarranted sarcasm.

"I'm afraid so," Luke said coolly. "I thought we'd have our picnic on board. You needn't worry, Mrs Radcliffe. I've never lost a passenger yet."

Once she was out there, she would be at his mercy . . .

She didn't want these base feelings, but she couldn't help them. It was Walter's legacy to her that she was suspicious of the slightest overture from a man. She wasn't smart or polished, and she knew only too well how a persuasive man could seduce a girl into thinking she was his one and only, and that this was the "Real Thing".

She felt Luke put his hand over hers for a brief moment.

"You'll be quite safe, Kate. In every way."

She heard the sincerity in his voice, and knew she had to trust it. She was a fool to be scared at the thought of taking a simple boat ride. He was being kind, that was all. Taking pity on a lonely woman in a hotel. A sliver of her old pride and bravado made her tilt her chin high.

"I never thought anything else," she lied.

He held her hand as she stepped gingerly on board the boat, feeling it rock beneath her. She had never been on a boat in her life before, but she remembered how some of the local boys, including her brother Donal, home from France and full of their wartime exploits, had described the motion vividly enough to make all the listeners feel seasick.

Luke placed the basket of food and drink on the deck and fiddled with the engine for some minutes before anything happened. He was in love with his boat, Kate thought, or at least, with the mechanics of it. She could sense it by the way he handled everything about it, with as much care as if it were a woman.

She watched his strong, capable hands and felt herself blush at the sudden question bursting into her mind. How would it feel to have those same competent hands caressing her?

He glanced her way, his hair more ruffled than usual, and his hands messy with grease.

"A penny for them," he said.

"They're private, and anyway, you wouldn't want to know," she said smartly.

"I think I would, but that's another story. Hold tight now, I think we're going to make it this time."

He pulled on a length of wire that seemed to be the sole means of starting the engine and, after a few abortive splutters, it roared into life, and a blast of smoke and steam enveloped them for a few seconds, together with the pungent smells of oil and fuel.

"We'll be under way in a moment," Luke shouted. "Then she'll settle down and we'll be in a different world."

It echoed her own thoughts . . . She clung to her seat, terrified at the rocking motion, as he steered the boat broadsides into the swell and the wind, and after a short while they headed out to sea, drifting smoothly along to the chug-chugging rhythm of the engine.

"Are you a good sailor?" Luke asked.

"I hope so, for both our sakes," Kate said grimly.

She was starting to feel more relaxed now, and oddly reckless. She had left her hat and cotton gloves in the car, and long before they were cruising steadily along the coast, her golden hair was blowing free, whipping against her face and stirring up her colour still more. The tang of salt was strong in her nostrils, clean and invigorating, and Kate felt a sense of adventure such as she had never known before. It was such a small adventure, compared with some, but an adventure all the same.

She pushed up the sleeves of her frock and lifted her face to the sun, feeling its warmth on her face as Luke cut the engine to a purr and they drifted slowly along. Her eyes were soothed by the heat of the sun as it caressed her closed lids. She could be on some other planet, she thought dreamily, without a care in the world.

"You're very beautiful, Mrs Radcliffe," she heard Luke Halliday say softly.

Kate's eyes flew open. He wasn't close to her, or touching her, except with his eyes and his mind and his senses . . . and at that moment she knew as surely as she breathed that he wanted her. She didn't want to read in his eyes what his words didn't say. She didn't want this. She couldn't think of a single thing to say that wouldn't add to the suddenly charged atmosphere between them, so she said the first thing that came into her mind.

"Please don't keep calling me Mrs Radcliffe. I'm uncomfortable with the name."

Aghast, she immediately wished she could have taken back those damning words. But in some strange way, she was certain that he already knew – or guessed – that she wasn't all she professed to be.

He answered easily. "All right. Sometimes it just seems like the right thing to do when you're so intent on keeping everyone at a distance."

She ignored that. "Just call me Kate – please. And don't ask for any more explanations yet."

She realised she was implying that a time may come when she would be ready to tell him more, and she hadn't meant that at all. And with his keen mind, he would almost certainly have registered the fact too.

"Let's eat," he said, more briskly. "The best panacea for too much emotion is to get some food inside you."

Kate laughed. It was high-pitched and a little reckless, but it was a laugh all the same.

"Have I said something funny?" Luke said, smiling back.

"Probably. But I don't even know the meaning of pan – panc – whatever it was you said!"

"It doesn't matter. Who cares about big words, anyway? Eat, woman!"

Kate took one of the hotel's salmon and cucumber sandwiches that he offered, and was amazed to find how hungry she was. The sea air was everything it was reputed to be, she thought, revitalising ragged nerves. It was a marvellous picnic, the best she'd ever known.

Later, when she had eaten her fill, she leaned over the boat's rail, watching the sea birds wheel and dip and dive for fish, and thought she had never seen anything lovelier.

Luke had other thoughts on the loveliness of this day. Somehow he had managed to stop himself from asking the question that had been simmering in his brain all day long – and even before that. He realised that the idea had been there from the first moment he had seen this enchanting woman. And eventually, he had to ask her.

"Have you ever been to London?" he said abruptly.

56

They had left the boat and Luke was opening the door of
the posh green motor car for her with a flourish. Just for a
second she knew how the regal Queen Mary must feel when
she was ushered into her limousine. And the thought made
her giggle. Fancy Kate Sullivan imagining herself having the
slightest thing in common with Queen Mary!

"What a daft question!" Kate said with a grin.

"Why is it daft? Wouldn't you like to see something of your
own capital city?"

She realised he was serious, and she stared at him as he started
to drive away from Poole harbour. In profile he had a very
strong face. He was very good-looking, but it was more than
that. It was a reliable, trustworthy face. Kate heard warning
bells in her head at the thought, and reminded herself that
she wasn't going to trust any man again for a very long time,
if ever. Alarmed at her own thoughts, she spoke curtly and
without emotion.

"Girls like me don't travel. We work in sweatshops making
garments for rich folk to wear and we live in cottages, not
swanky mews places, whatever they are. And if you think I'm
asking for sympathy I'm not. I'm just telling you this, so you
don't get any wrong ideas about me."

"Why the devil are you being so defensive? I only asked
a civil question. And if you don't travel, then what are you
doing in Bournemouth?"

He sounded half-amused, half-impatient, but Kate stared
at him dumbly. For one wild second she wondered how he'd
react if she blurted out the whole truth, here and now. But she
knew she couldn't. Her pride wouldn't let her. And besides, he
was too nice to have his lovely day tainted with the likes of
Kate Sullivan's problems. He'd think her a fool for believing
in the slick promises of a travelling man. Then there was the
other shameful business. How would a respectable man like
Luke Halliday react if he knew that she had lain with a man
many times, become pregnant, and practically forced him into

marriage without ever telling him that she'd lost the child? And who was the worst sinner after all – herself or Walter? she asked herself bitterly.

"I'm on holiday," she said thickly.

"Oh, I see," he grinned, but keeping his gaze on the road ahead. "So girls who work in sweatshops can dress in beautiful clothes and have enough money and time off to take holidays in posh hotels, do they? Pull the other one, Kate."

He doesn't believe me! she thought in amazement.

"I don't know what you mean," she said, starting to feel decidedly hot and bothered now. "Unless you're implying that I'm some sort of good-time girl."

His hand was swift to cover hers, reassuring and warm.

"Good God, I would never think that in a million years. I think you're a lady, and I'd never demean you by thinking or acting otherwise. Does that answer a few of the questions I've seen lurking behind those tortured blue eyes?"

She looked down at her hands fidgeting in her lap. Whatever he saw in her eyes, she was filled with sudden shame. Whatever he saw in her, *she* knew she was living a lie.

"I told you before – I'm getting over a shock," she said finally. "Can we please leave it at that?"

"For now," Luke said. "But I hope that when we know each other better, you'll trust me enough to confide in me, Kate."

"It's hardly likely that will happen. I'm only here for a week, and then—" she stopped, seeing the bleak future ahead.

"Then what? Back to the cottage and the sweatshop?"

He obviously still wouldn't accept that she came from such a mundane background. To Kate it was quite bizarre that she should have created such a false image of herself so unwittingly. But just for a moment she tried to see herself as Luke apparently saw her.

Sophisticated – well, maybe she'd just about pass since she was staying at the Charlton alone, and she had always held herself well. A mystery woman – so it would seem. If she stood back and looked at herself through different eyes, Kate supposed she could seem a rather interesting person. Her lips twitched with mirth at the thought.

"God, what a relief," Luke said. "I thought we were in for another fit of the glooms."

"Do you know how much you blaspheme?" she said primly, for want of something to say.

"Because I refer to God a lot? It's not blaspheming. It's just an expression. I'm damned sure He doesn't mind, so why should you?"

In a second, they were almost hostile again, and Kate knew she had provoked it. She was behaving like a schoolgirl, and the brief preening at her supposed sophistication vanished.

"I'm sorry. I didn't mean to be rude. It's just that I was brought up not to do it, that's all."

Though she had done it far more often of late, she thought guiltily. Her father and brother never took a blind bit of notice of her mother's house-rules.

"So was I. But we don't always do what our parents tell us, do we? Or turn out in the way they expect."

He couldn't possibly mean her to take this personally, but it struck home to Kate all the same. Her mother hadn't been all that keen on Walter, but her father had obviously seen him as a good catch for his daughter and envisaged this fine wedding and honeymoon for his girl which was going to make all the neighbours envious.

Kate had learned a bitter lesson, and she had hated the pain she had brought to her mother. She had no intention of being sweet-talked by Luke Halliday or anyone else. From now on, only Kate Sullivan was going to be in charge of Kate Sullivan's life.

"Anyway, why don't you think about coming to London?"

Kate looked at him sharply.

"I hadn't realised it was an invitation!"

"Well, it is, but not in the way you're probably thinking.

I'm not suggesting you move in with me, delightful though I find the thought. I can find you decent lodgings, and you can come and work for me while you look for the kind of job you want. But my motives are also selfish. Ever since we met I've wanted to take some studio portraits of you. I'm keen to go into magazine work, and your face and style are exactly what I've been looking for. What do you say, Kate?"

She couldn't say anything at first. None of this was in the least what she had expected to hear. None of it was within her experience at all. To live in London, away from her parents and everything she knew, and to be independent. To work for a photographer, whom she knew by now had ambitions, and with the possibility of seeing her own face on the cover of a magazine. She began to feel dizzy and out of her depth.

"I couldn't possibly!"

"Of course you could. You can do anything you want to do. You don't have a husband tying you down, unless you've been deceiving me all this time. And you have a decisive mind. Use it well, Kate. And I promise you that whatever happened in your past, you'll be quite safe with me."

Her eyes stung as she looked away from him.

"And do you always keep your promises?" she said.

"I don't recall ever breaking one yet," he said, his voice suddenly rough.

If Kate could have read his mind then, she would have seen how badly he wanted to keep this lovely girl in his life. But Luke sensed the need to go slowly, for she was as fragile as a bird with a damaged wing, terribly afraid to fly again.

She wished he hadn't given her this new problem to think about. Because it was tempting, so very tempting to get right away from all the people who would know by now that she had been jilted – but it was impossible. Nobody from her background just picked up sticks and went off to London, unless it was for dark and dubious reasons.

She could just imagine her father's reaction. In his view, his girl would be going to the devil, courtesy of Luke Halliday instead of Walter Radcliffe. Her father would consider them one and the same, when they were so different.

They'd spent a lot of time together during the rest of her week in Bournemouth, and she could vouch for Luke being the perfect gentleman. He had never tried to kiss her. He'd kept his distance and been a good friend. Sometimes she had wondered how she would react if he *had* tried it on. She had a warm and loving nature, which had contributed to her downfall with Walter . . . and there had been moments when she had *wanted* Luke to kiss her. She shivered, knowing that moving to London would definitely not be a good idea, and choosing not to analyse exactly why.

On their last evening together, Luke asked her the question again over dinner.

"Have you made up your mind yet?"

She didn't need to ask what he meant. "Of course not. How could I decide on anything so quickly, and without consulting my parents? They'd never forgive me."

"I thought you were nearly twenty-one, and an old married lady – if that's not a total contradiction to your stunning appearance tonight, Kate. You're perfectly capable of taking control of your own life."

He seemed to be doing his best to manipulate her, but she knew he was right, at least about taking control. Until now, and ever since Walter, when everything had fallen apart, she had felt as if she was simply drifting through the days with no purpose or direction. Until she'd met Luke, she had been in danger of sinking deeper into depression, and she knew she had him to thank for lifting her out of it.

"Look, I'm not trying to rush you into anything."

Her eyes were wide, as shimmering as sapphires tonight,

and she heard him catch his breath at their luminous quality in the soft, sensual atmosphere of the candlelit dining room. He was never more sure that those eyes held secrets, which made her even more of an intriguing woman.

"But you *are*! You don't give me time to think!"

Involuntarily, he reached across the table to cover one of her hands with his own, but as he felt her tense, he released her at once. If he didn't tread carefully, Luke was well aware that he was in danger of letting her lovely elusive spirit slip out of his life for ever. And that was the very last thing he wanted.

"Believe me, it's not my intention to do so, Kate. But I don't want to lose you. If I've been too forward and too fast, then I apologise."

She bit her lip. She was so naive. Such a country bumpkin, ridiculously gauche and indecisive – hardly the way a married lady was supposed to behave.

"You haven't been too forward. But I've always consulted my parents on important matters, and they've supported me at a time when I needed them most."

"And your concern for their feelings does you credit," Luke said. "So all I want is for you to go home and think about it. Go home and remember all that I've said. You'll easily find work in London, and naturally, I'd pay you for sitting for me."

"Would you?" This had never occurred to her. People went to photographers – those who could afford it – to have a record made of their family as it grew, they were the ones who paid for the privilege.

Luke laughed. "What did you think? I wasn't trying to lure you into a life of white slavery, sweet Kate."

"Now you're laughing at me," she accused him, feeling the prickly defensiveness again.

"Not at you, only with you, so stop being so touchy, and

believe that you can be paid handsomely for just sitting still and looking beautiful."

His words only served to underline what a narrow life she had led; not to realise that for someone to have their picture in a magazine meant that the sitter had been paid a fee. If she had ever thought about it, she would have assumed it was an honour to be portrayed that way – or that people paid for it themselves!

Surely he couldn't be serious about it happening to her! Not Kate Sullivan's picture splashed all around the country for all to see! The idea was quite frightening, and she wasn't sure she would care for it at all. Strangers would ogle her, or criticise her; she would be as vulnerable as if she lived in a goldfish bowl.

"What gremlins are bothering you now?" Luke asked, as she sipped her coffee without tasting it.

"None. Except that I'm not sure I'd want my picture all over the cover of a magazine."

"Then we'll forget it," he said.

She hardly dared look at him, knowing she had just thrown his dreams back in his face. But he didn't need her. There were other girls who would do just as well . . . she wasn't going to let that thought depress her, either!

"At least let me write to you, Kate. I'd like to keep in touch in case you have second thoughts."

"That wouldn't be a good idea," she said quickly.

Because, of course, any letters he wrote would come addressed to Mrs Kate Radcliffe. Her innocent deceit was becoming more compounded by the minute.

"Then I hope you'll write to me if ever you feel so inclined. You have my card, don't you?"

"Yes. And Luke – I do appreciate your kindness to me all this week. It's just—"

"I know. Your parents need to be consulted. Do you have a committee meeting every time you go to the bathroom?"

He was coarser than usual, because he knew that despite her fragile air, she was made of steel inside, and there was nothing he could do to make her change her mind until she chose to do it herself.

Kate stared at him wordlessly, not because of the unexpected crudity of the question, but because the Sullivans didn't have a bathroom. Somehow this simple fact emphasised the difference between their two worlds.

"I'm sorry. That was impertinent and insensitive," he said. "We'll talk about something else. Do you think you'll come to Bournemouth again, Kate?"

"I doubt it very much."

"That's a pity. We might have met up at the Charlton. How did you come to choose it for your holiday?"

It was no good. He thought he was changing the subject, but somehow everything led Kate back to the trauma of what had happened.

"It was supposed to be my honeymoon."

The words were stark. She hadn't meant to say them, but once said, there was no taking them back. She saw the shock in Luke's eyes, and knew she had merely opened the way for more questions. Was she actually married or not? Why had she come here alone? And more importantly, where was the husband?

"*Please* don't ask me anything else, Luke," she said, her voice brittle. "I don't want to spoil our last evening. I want to dance tonight, and be bright and happy and not to dwell on ghosts. And if you ask me one more thing about my past I won't answer, and I swear I'll shut myself in my room and you'll never see me again!"

He lifted his hands, palms towards her, as if to ward off the tirade.

"It was only an innocent remark, my dear girl, and I certainly didn't mean to upset you."

"You didn't," she lied. "So let's forget it. And if you can

bear to dance with me again later, I'll do my best not to step on your feet too much."

"You can step all over me if it will bring a smile back to your face," he said dryly.

Chapter Five

She had drunk too much wine by the time they went dancing, but at least it dulled her senses. She didn't want to think of anything, except being in the company of a good and decent man, when she had thought there were none left in the world except in her own family. She wanted to feel nothing but the pleasure of swaying in Luke's arms to the lilting dance music in the hotel lounge, and trying to manage the steps of the latest dance crazes that had everyone laughing and, finally, to drop senseless into bed and sleep until dawn.

She was vaguely aware that the music had ended and the members of the band were putting away their instruments. The seductive strains of the last waltz had faded away, but couples still lingered on the dance floor, and she was still held tightly in Luke Halliday's arms. In fact, if they hadn't been holding her up, she had the odd sensation that she might slither quietly to the floor as if all her bones had pleasantly dissolved.

"It's time you went to bed, my love," she heard Luke say.

"I will if I can find it," she replied, her voice heavily muffled against his shoulder.

Her head was floating somewhere above the rest of her. It was a spectacularly pleasant feeling, and not at all like some of the lurid descriptions she had heard.

Not that she was drunk, or anything so unladylike. She was merely happy, as she had strived to be on this last night of her holiday. Or was it halliday? No, that was Luke . . . she felt the urge to giggle at her own inane joke, and then his arm was very firmly around her waist as he guided her out of the lounge and towards the lift.

The sensation of going up in the lift was anything but pleasant, though. Kate felt as though she'd left her stomach on the ground floor while the rest of her was moving rapidly towards the third. She gulped very quickly to keep down the feeling of nausea, terrified that she was going to disgrace herself all over the splendid hotel carpet.

"Where's your room key, Kate?" the voice beside her asked.

She fumbled in her bag and handed it to him. He leaned her against the wall until he had opened the door and helped her inside, kicking the door shut behind him. She fell across the bed, and he felt contrite for allowing her to drink so much. But she had insisted, as if to blot out everything but sharing this last night of their time together, and she had been more assertive than at any other time.

Luke hesitated, knowing he couldn't leave her like this. Her dinner gown was soft and flimsy, but even in summer the coastal nights were cold. Somehow he eased the eiderdown from beneath her and rolled her onto her back, intending to cover her with it.

As if instinctively afraid of falling, Kate suddenly clung to him. He lost his balance and fell across her lovely lithe body. Her face was right beneath his, her breath warm on his cheek. And dear God, but it was more than he could do to resist kissing that relaxed mobile mouth that parted a little beneath his touch.

Even as the unbidden surge of desire assaulted him, Luke heard her murmuring against his mouth. But it wasn't his name that she spoke.

"Walter, don't leave me. Tell me it was all a mistake . . ."

The words trailed away into a meaningless jumble, and Luke's desire left him as rapidly as it had arisen. Even though his hand had unerringly found its way to the soft swell of her breasts and felt their swift, involuntary response, he knew it wasn't for him that Kate's eyes sometimes darkened with longing. It was this faceless Walter, who was presumably the missing husband. And no matter what had happened between them, it seemed obvious to Luke that Kate still loved him.

He rose from the bed, covered and left her. At the last moment, he slid the "Do not Disturb" card over her door handle, knowing she was going to have a hell of a hangover in the morning.

He smothered his feelings with anger. It was damnable luck to fall for a woman who was clearly still besotted with another man. He no longer bothered to deny to himself that he had fallen for her. And while he could fight for a woman on equal terms with a man, providing the other man had lost his right to her affections, he didn't know how the hell you could fight a ghost.

Back in his own room, he was tempted to drown his sorrows in a half-finished bottle of brandy, but that would be a bad mistake. He was due to leave early in the morning and needed to get on the road with a clear head, since some titled clients had an afternoon appointment at the studio. He'd do far better to think about business, than to let himself be so artlessly entranced by the loveliest woman he had ever known.

Kate awoke slowly. The curtains were still closed, but the morning sun shone through the gaps, and it was strong enough to make piercing shafts of pain dance about in her head. She turned, too quickly, to peer at her bedside clock, not sure whether it was herself or the room that spun alarmingly as she did so. The eiderdown slipped off, and she gaped as she looked down at herself. She still wore the gown she had been dancing in last night. She hadn't even undressed or got beneath the bedclothes properly. She couldn't even remember getting here. Luke must have helped her . . . her fingers touched her mouth and then strayed briefly to her breasts, as a hazy memory struggled to get through.

But nothing untoward could have happened, she thought raggedly. She was fully clothed, and Luke was a gentleman. In a way, that made her disgraceful behaviour even worse.

"I'll never be able to face him," she muttered aloud. "He'll think I'm nothing but a tease. He must hate me now."

She sat up very carefully, as details of last night began to seep into her mind. They had danced, and she had felt comfortable and safe in his arms. Apart from the wildness of the Charleston and the Black Bottom, the music had been sweet and lazy and she had wanted it to go on for ever . . . but she had to catch the midday train back to Bristol where Father Mulheeny had arranged to meet her.

Kate was suddenly properly awake. It was already nine-thirty, and breakfast ended at ten o'clock. She slid out of bed, her knees buckled for a moment, but she ignored them as best she could. After a cursory splash of water to her face and armpits, she struggled into a day frock and rushed downstairs, reaching the dining room just before ten.

"Am I too late for breakfast?" she stammered.

"Not at all, madam," the waiter said smoothly. "Though I'm afraid the poached haddock's all gone. We have bacon and eggs, or boiled eggs and toast."

Kate felt herself blanch at the very mention of food, and wondered why she had bothered to come down for breakfast at all. But it wasn't just for breakfast that she was here.

"Just marmalade and toast and a pot of tea, please," she murmured. "And I wonder if you could find out if Mr Halliday is anywhere about?"

She didn't care what the waiter made of that. She couldn't bear to leave without thanking Luke properly for his kindness during this past week. She couldn't bear the thought that she might have missed him.

After a few minutes the waiter reappeared with her food and an envelope.

"Mr Halliday left early this morning, madam. He left this note for you at the desk."

"Thank you," Kate said, rigid and expressionless. It was the second time that a man had left her with only a note. Fate shouldn't be so cruel ... Walter had had his own despicable reasons, but she had never expected Luke to leave Bournemouth without even saying goodbye.

She waited until she got back to her room before slitting open the envelope, hardly knowing what to expect inside. There was a single piece of paper.

My dear Mrs Radcliffe,

I address you so formally, because I fear I would give my feelings away if I called you my dear Kate. In so little time you've become just that to me, you see.

I regret that I can't say a proper goodbye, but I've important clients to see this afternoon and I must get back to London as soon as possible. But please remember that if ever you're in need of a friend, you know where to find me.

Luke.

Kate stared at the words for a long time. And then she screwed up the note and threw it into the waste basket. Seconds later she retrieved it, smoothed it out, and placed it carefully in her handbag.

It wasn't until she was safely on the train and speeding away from Bournemouth in a compartment to herself, that the tears finally came. Such a short while ago she had fully expected to be a wife. Then, while she was still getting over the first shock of being jilted, she had met a man she thought she could trust, a man who had done the Lord knew what to her last night, and then run out on her. She knew she was over-

71

reacting. The saner part of her brain told her Luke had done nothing disrespectful when he had put her to bed. She knew it in her soul, and she knew too, guiltily, that had she been fully aware, that whatever he had wanted to do, she wouldn't have rebuffed him.

By the time she reached the village it was late afternoon, and the sea mist had already curled in, coating fields and hedgerows and spangling the branches with diamond dampness and turning the countryside into a silvery fairyland. Summer was slow in reaching the Somerset coastal areas that year.

She viewed their little cottage with a feeling of dread, knowing how awkward everyone was going to be at her return.

"It's good to see you back, Kate," her father said, his voice gruff when Father Mulheeny had deposited her at the cottage and stayed for tea and her mother's fruit cake. "You look rested."

She supposed there was no correct way to greet someone who was getting over a jilting. They weren't a kissing family, and her mother covered the moment by producing her favourite cherry pie and custard. Kate thought how shocked they would be if she said what was in her heart.

I've had a truly wonderful week. I've been cavorting with an eligible young man. I've danced until the early hours, and been put to bed by the same man, whom I hardly know. I should look bloody well rested.

She bit her lip as the swear word entered her mind, since it was not a word she ever said aloud in this house, though it seemed to fit her mood more and more often lately.

"I'm fine, Dada," she said, using her childhood name for him. "And no longer grieving, if that's what's worrying you."

It was meant to reassure him, but she saw his eyebrows draw together in a heavy frown.

"If you truly loved the man, then your grief should take more time to heal than this, girl. And if you didn't, then

72

you had no business agreeing to marry him in the first place."

"I did love him, Father, but I'm facing facts."

It certainly wasn't a lie. She had loved Walter madly, in a wild, abandoned way that had shocked and elated her, and opened her eyes to the sensuality of which she hadn't known she was capable. But that was hardly something she was going to tell her father! Especially with the eagle-eyed priest watching her covertly as well.

"Time will heal everything, girl," Father Mulheeny said. "In the meantime, you know where to come when you need a friend. The church's door is always open."

"I know it is, and thank you."

It was the second time she'd been offered friendship that day. Luke's had come in the form of a short note that was tucked in her handbag. She kept remembering something he'd said to her last evening.

"You can do anything you want to, Kate. You have a mind of your own, so use it well."

But she could just imagine the reaction here if she dared mention, however casually, that she'd met a gentleman who was keen to photograph her . . . her father, in particular:

"No girl of mine's going to be posing like some tart," he would roar. "I've heard of these arty buggers, luring young females into their so-called studios, and then having their wicked way with 'em."

And Donal, as outspoken as his father, adding his piece:

"Oh aye. It would be all innocent at first, our Kate. All tasteful poses and that. Then before you knew it, he'd have you taking off your clothes for a picture and calling it art, while he ogled your body. And God knows where it would lead after that!"

As the imaginary tirade filled her head, Kate felt a shiver of excitement run through her. She rarely looked at herself unclothed, and the only man to have seen her naked body had been Walter. But even if she had no more love for him, she remembered how it had felt to be wanted and desired so badly, and to be told that she was beautiful. She remembered the hoarseness in his voice as his fingers had traced the contours of her breasts, and then sought her more itimate places with such skilful seduction. She remembered opening up to him, and giving herself so willingly, because he'd said it would hurt him so much if she refused him and that this would prove her love for him.

She breathed heavily as the memories assaulted her. They shamed her, but even though she now wished Walter Radcliffe to Kingdom Come, at least he had proved something to her. She was a woman, with all a woman's needs and longings.

She was thankful when the priest left, and her young sisters arrived home with Donal, each with the important question as to whether they had to give back their bridesmaids' frocks. Alice hushed them, but Kate answered steadily.

"Of course you don't. You can wear them for Sunday best, and whenever else you like."

Privately, she wished she could tear them to ribbons, including the wedding gown, but that still belonged to her mother, not to her.

"Help me put the food on the table for the evening meal now, Kate," Alice said shortly, just as if she had never been away. "There's nothing like keeping the hands occupied to take away the worry in the brain."

It was ironic that everyone would think she was still pining over Walter, when she wasn't, thought Kate. It struck her that they were the ones who were going to keep his image alive, not her. All she wanted was to forget; but in their various ways, they would keep reminding her of him.

Alice dumped a huge dish of boiled potatoes in the middle of the table, and began shovelling them onto plates, signalling her disapproval of the whole affair.

"I don't have any worry in the brain, Mother," Kate felt obliged to say. "I'm perfectly well, and if you'd seen me in Bournemouth, you'd have seen how I held my head up high like the rest of the swells."

Alice paused in her potato shovelling, her eyes angry.

"That's no way to be talking, either. We all have our place in this world, and we should be content with it."

"But Kate's right, Mother," Donal said, putting in his piece while the small girls fell silent. "You can't go to a posh place without acting a bit posh, or you'd soon be put upon by the gentry."

Kate flashed him a look of gratitude, but her mother wasn't done with her yet.

"Nobody's better than the next person, and you'd all do well to remember it. The good Lord gave us our places, and we should stay in them, otherwise we go against His wishes. Isn't that right, Brogan?" she glared at her so-called God-fearing husband.

"Oh aye, missus," he said hastily, his mind wandering as always when the argument didn't centre on him.

"Well, I'm sorry, but I don't agree with that," Kate heard herself say.

Alice slapped a piece of bacon on her plate, and her eyes were as cold as charity. After all the whispering she'd had to face in the village, and now this. Kate had changed out of all recognition in one short week.

"And what gives you the right to question God's will, miss? I'm thinking Father Mulheeny might call it blasphemy to hear you talk so."

It was ludicrous, thought Kate. Her mother only ever reverted to the piousness of Father Mulheeny's teachings when it suited her. She could see her father grinning broadly and she could guess at the way his thoughts were going – Life had been duller without his Katie around to give it some spice, and a good rip-roaring argument was what had been missing in the house of late, with them all pussy-footing around and not knowing what to say to one another. And it always tickled him to death to hear his no-nonsense wife being suddenly so supportive of the priest's teachings. It wouldn't last, of course.

"I'm not being blasphemous, Mother," Kate said hotly. "All I'm saying is that we all have a right to make the best of ourselves. We don't always have to settle for what we're given if we're offered the chance of something different."

She knew she was beginning to flounder, and if she wasn't careful, her mother would suspect there was something behind all this. But Donal took the heat out of it all.

"Stop getting in a stew over nothing, the pair of you. It's Kate's first night home, for pity's sake, and just because she's seen a bit of life in Bournemouth, it don't mean she's planning to move down there, does it, our Kate?"

"Of course not. I never meant any such thing, and nor did I mean to upset anybody."

But somebody had told her she had a mind and a will of her own, and it was a waste of God's gifts not to use them. Anyway, it wasn't the thought of moving to Bournemouth that Luke Halliday had dangled so enticingly towards her.

"What was it like being on a train, our Kate?" Aileen said suddenly, unable to keep quiet a minute longer.

She turned to the child with relief.

"It was a great monster of a thing, sweetheart, with an engine pulling a long line of carriages behind it. The engine blew great gusts of smoke and steam into the air, then it sparked and hissed so much before it started moving that you thought it was about to explode!"

"I'm never going on a train then," the more timid Maura said with a shiver.

"Well, I am," Aileen said importantly. "Our Maura's always too scared to try anything new, but I bet it was exciting. Our Kate always has all the fun."

All the adults avoided Kate's eyes as the child prattled

innocently on. Kate felt sorry for them all, because their embarrassment wasn't necessary. Once she'd recovered from her hurt pride and begun to play the part of the mystery woman, she hadn't even cared that Walter wasn't in Bournemouth with her. She took a deep breath, and spoke quickly to cover the uneasy silence.

"I'd be glad if you'd stop treating me as if I'm made of glass. I've faced up to everything that happened and put it behind me," she said, mentally crossing her fingers in the hope that it was really true. "Walter made a bad mistake in courting me, but he'd have made a worse one if he'd married me, so let's all be thankful for that."

Donal's face had darkened as she spoke, and she saw how his hands clenched.

"Well, I'm buggered if I know how you can be so bloody saintly about it, Kate. If I ever get my hands on Radcliffe, I'll throttle him. I blame myself for ever knowing the bastard, and I don't intend to forget what he did to you!"

"Donal, *please*! I won't have such language in this house," Alice said, outraged at such talk at the dinner table, the small girls all agog. But brother and sister ignored her as they glared at one another.

"If I want to forget it ever happened – and I *do*," Kate said passionately, "I wish you would all do the same. It was my life he almost ruined, and I'm the one who has to pick up the pieces and start again. We can't pretend it never happened, but it will do nobody any good if you constantly go on about throttling him either!"

"It would do me some bloody good," Donal muttered.

Brogan added his piece, having been silent for too long. "What your brother means, me darlin', is that no self-respecting Irishman would let the scum get away with it if he had the chance to retaliate, no matter how much your mother wants us to turn the other cheek."

"Donal's no more Irish than I am," Kate snapped. "And

since you left the place as fast as you could, Dada, I don't know why you go on harping about its glories."

"That's enough of that talk, girl. Ireland's still me home, and she's still in me heart, so she is."

"Leave it, Kate," Alice said, knowing that when her man got that certain glint in his eyes he'd be going on for ever more about the old country and its virtues.

Kate stabbed her fork into a potato, and found herself wishing for one moment that she was sticking it into Walter Radcliffe's black heart.

There was no real difference between herself and her brother when it came to dark deeds, she thought. And they were all Brogan's children, with the same passions and weaknesses. Even to becoming seduced by the drink on occasions.

"Are you going to play the fiddle for us later, Dada, as a welcome home?" she asked, trying to lighten the atmosphere.

"I might. If you're sure it's not beneath you to listen to such a humble instrument after all your fine hotel entertainments."

"I wouldn't have asked you if I'd thought that," she said, not taking the bait.

Returning to Granby's Garments sweatshop on Monday was her next ordeal. The news was obviously hot on everybody's mind. Some of the girls avoided her altogether as if she had leprosy, and the rest were avidly curious and wanting to know about it all. Above the clatter of the machines, Kate found her nerves being stretched again as the most persistent of them wouldn't leave the subject alone.

"You did right to take the bastard's money, Kate," Vi snapped. "Take him for all you can get."

"I really don't want to talk about it, Vi."

"Well, you won't stop the gossip, my duck. And what the blue blazes did you do in Bournemouth all on your own? My old fellow saw your dad down at the pub, so we knew that's what you'd done. Was it awful?"

"No," Kate said, poker-faced, with a sudden vivid image of swaying in Luke Halliday's arms to a seductive waltz tune.

"Oh well, I can see by your face that it was," Vi said, a touch of irritation mixed with the sympathy. "Never mind. I daresay you'll tell us when you're ready. And remember, Kate, there's plenty more fish in the sea. Just because you got one rotter don't mean they're all bastards."

"I know," Kate said, wondering how long this was going to go on. The thread in her sewing machine snapped, and she rethreaded her spool with vicious movements, stabbing her finger with the needle in the process.

"Oh, come on, Kate, tell us," one of the other girls said. "We heard rumours that he was already wed and got cold feet at the last minute. Is that the truth of it?"

"If it is, then bloody good riddance to him," another girl said. "You don't want no truck with bigamists, Kate, and you can just be thankful he didn't put you in the family way."

Her heart leapt sickly for a minute, but she heard Vi coming to her rescue. Vi, who knew all about the miscarriage . . .

"Kate's not that kind of a girl, Aggie Pond, so you just leave her alone and get on with your work before old Jenkins catches you idling."

The girl flounced off, and Kate mouthed a silent "thank you" at Vi. But before their machines began their whirring once more, the supervisor called for her, She went into his little cubby-hole-cum-office apprehensively, wondering what she had done wrong now.

She wiped her clammy hands on her work overall and heard the others whispering behind her. They would all have been playing guessing games this past week as the stories about her got wilder and wilder, and old Jenkins would have heard them too. She didn't like him, and never had. He was all too familiar with his favourites, and down on the rest of them like a ton of manure.

"Now then, Kate," he said, when he'd told her to close the door. "How are you bearing up to your troubles?"

"I'm perfectly all right, thank you."

"Good. Good." His narrow little eyes seemed to pierce their way right through her clothes, and she shifted her feet uncomfortably.

"I understand the wedding didn't take place after all."

"That's right."

"But you still took the week's holiday."

"I was entitled. You know I was."

"Did I say you weren't? And I heard you went to Bournemouth to stay in some fancy hotel. Quite an adventure for a girl like you, Kate. But I always suspected you'd be an adventurous girl, given the chance."

His voice had become thicker and he moved around the front of his desk and sat on the edge and assessed her more thoroughly. His gaze moved slowly over her taut body, and in her nervousness Kate knew her nipples were sticking out in a way that she hated. Jenkins knew it too, and ran his tongue around his fleshy lips.

"How would you like to earn a few extra shillings, Kate? I could put some evening work your way if you've a mind to stay behind now and then. You'd find me very generous to an adventurous girl like yourself."

Kate's heart thudded in her chest as the implications became all too obvious. Jenkins clearly saw her as a bit of a flighty piece more than ready to jump into a new affair while she recovered from the old one. She burned with humiliation.

"I say no!" she snapped. "I don't want any evening work, thank you."

He was very agile for a portly man. Somehow he had pinned her against the door, and she could feel the hardness of his erection inside his trousers as he gently squirmed against her. It sickened her.

"Don't decide too hastily, sweet thing. I'm sure your family could do with the extra money. Let's say you've got a week to think about it. After that – well, we must review the situation. You're a good worker, but there's been some fabrics missing lately, and a girl who was preparing for her wedding would have found good use for them . . ."

"I was given the offcuts!" Kate gasped. "You know I was!"

"But maybe it wasn't only offcuts. Who's to argue if I say differently?" he said smoothly. "And I couldn't keep a thief in my employ, now could I?"

His smile was oily, and Kate felt sickened by what she saw in his face. This was sexual blackmail, and from past rumours about other girls who had suddenly been fired, she knew he'd do exactly as he said. He was a bastard of the first order.

"Anyway, you go away and think about it, girlie. I'm very good to those who please me."

He slid his arm around her back and squeezed her buttocks. Somehow she wrenched open the door and fled back to her machine.

"What did he want?" said Vi suspiciously.

"What he's not going to get," she snapped, too shaken and humiliated to say anything more, and refusing to speak to anybody for the rest of the day.

She wasn't going to last out the week, not with Jenkins ogling her every time he went through the sweatshop. By the following Monday he'd expect her answer, and he was ruthless enough to spread the dirt about her the minute she refused. She would be disgraced in the village and her family would be disgraced too.

And apart from all that, she couldn't stand the varying reactions on her non-married state from her family and her workmates any longer. She wished she could get away from everybody, but young women in her class didn't set up establishments on their own, nor could they afford to do so.

Most of the men she knew, even in this small village, were already alarmed that the war had given women too much independence. Young as she had been, she had observed enough to see the emergence of timid women into strong ones, coping with things unheared of in peacetime, while their men were away fighting at the Front.

There was one place she could go, of course. In the short time since her week in Bournemouth, Luke's image hadn't dimmed in her mind, nor had the sound of his voice, nor the warm, unspoken sympathy she had seen in his eyes, for his mystery lady.

Excitement and danger were always mingled whenever she thought of him, but there was also a strange inevitability to it all. Otherwise, why would she have gone to Bournemouth alone when her heart should have been breaking? Why that particular week, when he too, was taking a brief holiday? Why should their paths have met at all, in what she was beginning to see as a crossroads in her life.

As the idea grew on her, the only thing she balked about was telling her parents and Donal. She knew that the thought of her going to London would horrify them. London was the wicked city, where a vulnerable young woman could fall prey to any number of vices.

Maybe she should leave a letter explaining everything, and then they couldn't stop her. The irony of leaving a letter wasn't lost on her, but the more she thought about it, the more she knew it was the only solution.

It took some time to compose a letter in a way that wouldn't alarm them any more than was necessary.

Please understand, all of you, I feel the shame of what happened more as each day passes. I can't forget it while I'm here, where everyone knows about it, and I have to get right away, for a while at least.

I met a very respectable person in Bournemouth who will

help me to get work and proper lodgings in London. Please don't worry about me, or think badly of me for leaving in this way. I'll write to you the minute I'm settled.

Your loving daughter, Kate.

Once her father had gone to work on Saturday morning and her mother had left to collect some of her endless dirty washing, and Donal had taken the girls fishing, it was easy enough to leave the house with a large bag filled with her clothes. She left the note on her pillow where her mother would be sure to find it sometime later in the day, and then she took the bus to Temple Meads railway station.

Once there, she bought a one-way ticket to London. And since there was an hour to wait before the next train was due to leave, she asked if there was a telephone she could use.

She heard herself, sounding so grand, and asking to use a telephone, but her enforced confidence seemed to be working, and she was shown to the Station Master's office and told she could make her call from there. She wilted for a minute as she took Luke's card from her pocket, then took a deep breath, and gave the operator his number.

Would he even remember her, she wondered, as the endless seconds ticked by before she was connected. Or had she been no more than a diversion? Then at last she heard his voice, as close as if he were standing beside her.

"Luke Halliday," it said, efficient and professional.

And Kate's voice simply stuck in her throat, so that she couldn't speak at all.

Chapter Six

"Who is this?" he said impatiently as the empty seconds ticked by.

"Luke," Kate finally managed to croak. "It's me. Kate. Kate – Radcliffe," she added just in time.

"Good God, Kate!" The voice changed tone, becoming as rich and warm as she remembered it, but with more than a hint of surprise in it. "How marvellous to hear your voice. Where are you calling from?"

"I'm at the railway station in Bristol, and I've bought a ticket to London on the one o'clock train."

She stopped abruptly, struck with awful doubts. She sounded so idiotic, speaking in such a rush and in such a high-pitched voice. Supposing he didn't want her? Supposing he had meant none of the things he'd said? There might even be another girl in London . . . and supposing she was just making an almighty fool of herself, and the biggest mistake since Walter?

"I'll meet the train, Kate, so don't worry about a thing. I can't tell you how pleased I am to hear your voice."

"You don't know when I'll be arriving," she said weakly, since naturally she hadn't thought to do anything so clever as to enquire the time of the train's arrival.

"That's no problem. I'll call Paddington Station and find out. All you have to do is get on the train, Katie, and you can leave the rest to me. I assume you'll be wanting somewhere to stay for the time being?"

"Oh – yes – a small hotel, perhaps, until I get properly settled,"

85

she said with a gulp, knowing she was truly burning her boats, and wondering frantically how long her small amount of money was going to last out in such surroundings.

"I can do much better than that – and it's not what you may be thinking, so get that anxious look off your face."

She stared into the phone, wondering how he knew.

"I wasn't thinking anything."

"Yes, you were, but I assure you everything will be above board, Kate. Just get here and leave the rest to me."

She was shaking as she clung to the telephone cord, because everyone knew that nice girls didn't call men who were practically strangers and tell them they were coming to London on a whim. Nice girls had families who would see to it that everything was above board, and that proper arrangements for a visit were made well in advance. God, why hadn't she stopped to think how it would look?

"You don't think I'm being forward, then?" she mumbled into the phone, aware that the Station Master was hovering on the other side of his office.

"I can't wait to see you. Does that answer your question? Now, find your platform and then go and sit in the Ladies' Only waiting room until the train arrives. And don't get cold feet and change your mind, you hear?"

He had hung up before she could say another word, and she put the receiver down shakily as the Station Master came near.

"Is everything all right, miss?" he asked suspiciously. "You look rather pale, if I might say so."

"I'm quite all right, thank you. I was just anxious to know that my – my cousin would be able to meet me in London," she said, wondering how she could possibly look pale when she felt as if her cheeks were on fire with all the lies she was forced to keep inventing.

But she did as Luke suggested and went to the Ladies' Only room on her platform, glad to be away from any interested male eyes, and thankful for his sensible direction. The room was hot and stuffy, and she had an interminable wait until the train arrived. When it did, she found an empty compartment and placed her bag on the rack.

Then she sank into her seat and closed her eyes. She kept them closed until she heard the guard's whistle, and felt the lurch of the train beneath her as it started to move. And she kept a tight hold on the nerves that threatened to shake her insides out, knowing there could be no turning back now.

Hours later, the train rattled and steamed and hissed into Paddington Station, and Kate gaped at the sheer size and magnificence of it, though she thought it didn't quite outdo the Gothic façade of Brunel's Temple Meads masterpiece.

During the journey, people had come and gone from her compartment, until there was only herself and an elderly and uncommunicative couple. They were met by a young man and girl and escorted away quickly, while Kate alighted from the train, stiff and bewildered, feeling terribly alone.

The entire railway station seemed to be one mass of rushing humanity, and she stood uncertainly, jostled on all sides by impatient folk who all seemed to know where they were going. She had never felt so isolated in her life, and she was more than ready to burst into tears. She longed for her mother's calm, or even her father's blustering arrogance, but right now, she seemed to have inherited none of it.

"Kate. *Kate!*"

She heard her name being called, and her heart leapt. At last she saw Luke's tall figure weaving in and out of the other travellers. Then he was right beside her, and the tears wouldn't stop, but thankfully, ever since the war years, nobody thought it in the least odd for a tearful girl to be clasped in a man's arms at a railway station, and she leaned against the roughness of Luke Halliday's tweed jacket and sobbed her heart out.

The feeling only lasted a few minutes. Then she pulled

away from him, mortified at her own feebleness, showing herself up like that. Very aware that her puritan-minded mother would have been shocked at this show of emotion in a public place.

But Luke was smiling with obvious pleasure at the sight of her, and seemingly not in the least put out by her sudden and unexpected arrival. He wiped away the traces of tears from her cheek with one finger, and drew out a folded handkerchief from his jacket pocket.

"Here. Use this. It's perfectly clean," he said practically.

Kate dabbed her eyes, beginning to feel very foolish. "You must think me a real country bumpkin," she muttered.

"Of course I don't. I think you're perfectly delightful, and leaving home is a big step for anyone to cope with. But I suggest we get away from here as quickly as possible now and have something to eat. You must be starving."

The thought of food hadn't entered Kate's head. Now that it did, she realised how long it had been since she had eaten anything, and her stomach was gnawing. No wonder she was acting so limply, she thought, with a spurt of anger at her own stupidity. Why on earth hadn't she put some sandwiches in her bag for the long journey, like any sensible person would?

"Laying ghosts?" Luke said, tucking her hand in his arm as he led her out of the station to where the familiar dark green Bentley stood waiting for them.

"Not really. Just feeling a little out of my depth," she said honestly, "and very tired."

Lord, now he'd think she was making some kind of suggestive hint. If she had said such a thing to Walter, he would immediately have seen the double meaning in it, and made some sniggering remark about organising their sleeping arrangements as soon as she said the word . . . only they wouldn't be doing much sleeping.

"We'll have a bite at a small café not far from here, and then

I'll take you straight to Mrs Wood's," Luke said, taking control. "There'll be time enough for you to come and see the studio in the morning when you've had a good night's sleep."

"Who is Mrs Wood?" Kate asked, to cover the sudden awkwardness she felt in the company of a man fitting so easily into his environment.

"She's your landlady, and she's a large, respectable woman with a lodging house of selected guests, so there's no need for you to be alarmed. You'll find a gas ring in your room so you can cook whatever meals you wish, but Mrs Wood happily provides evening meals for those who like real home cooking – and I recommend it."

"You seem to know a lot about it," Kate said as she slid into the car beside him, feeling a fraction more reassured by the homely sound of the woman.

"I should do. Mrs Wood was an old friend of my great-aunt's, and she always took a motherly interest in me when I first came to London. She'll take good care of you, Kate."

And how about you? Will you take good care of me too? She wished she dared ask. Here in his city surroundings, Luke seemed even more dashing than he had in Bournemouth, or perhaps that was merely because he was the one familiar person she knew in a place full of strangers.

What exactly was she doing here? she wondered anew, just as she had done at Bournemouth. There were moments when she didn't seem to belong anywhere any more, as if she was somehow suspended in time until fate decided what to do with her, and she didn't like the feeling one bit.

Luke stopped the car outside a café advertising freshly-cooked meals and sandwiches. When they entered, the succulent smells wafting through from the kitchens at the rear made Kate's mouth water. A neatly-dressed waitress with a white cap perched jauntily at the front of her head showed them to a table, and Kate didn't miss the way the girl smiled into Luke's eyes, obviously approving of this real hunk of a gent.

"We'll have scrambled eggs and bacon with fried potatoes, and a pot of tea, please, and make it as quick as
you can."

"That sounds more like breakfast. Do they cook breakfasts
in the early evening in London?" Kate said, her mouth watering
at the thought. It sounded exactly like the breakfasts at the
Charlton Hotel and she wondered if Luke had ordered it
deliberately.

"They cook anything you ask for at any time in this sort of
place," he said. "But I'll take you to a really swish restaurant
one night, where you can have steak and mushrooms, and as
many strawberries as you can eat."

Kate was just as happy here, though after the way she'd
carried off her acting performance at the Charlton, she could
probably manage a meal in a swish London restaurant, she
thought with bravado. She'd have to, now that she was
here. Once she found work and settled into her lodgings,
she'd probably turn into a real city girl . . . and, without
any warning, the thought filled her with a sudden vibrant
excitement.

"Thank God," Luke said.

She stared at him across the red-checked tablecloth as the
waitress brought their pot of tea and the obligatory bottle of
tomato sauce for their meal.

"For what?" Kate asked.

"For the fact that you've decided to relax. You really are
the most stunning girl, Kate, but all your anxieties show in
your face. Do you know that?"

"I think someone may have mentioned it before," she murmured, not sure that she liked to be analysed so shrewdly.

He put his hand over hers as it rested on the table, and his
touch was warm and comforting.

"You also show your pleasure and your excitement without
any inhibitions, and that's very refreshing to me. You have no
idea how many times I've had to coax a reaction from some of

90

the people who come to be photographed. With you, I sense that it will be spontaneous."

"So all this approval is on account of how I'll respond to your photographer's instructions, is it?"

She smiled at him, half-amused at the sudden enthusiasm that made him almost boyish, and half-disappointed that he wasn't seeing her for herself alone.

She reminded herself that he was a businessman, no matter how bohemian and glamorous his business sounded to a country girl, and he would be looking for the most commercial face for his promotional purposes. She would be a fool to start fantasising that inborn kindness and a few compliments meant anything else.

"And now you've gone cold on me again," he said shrewdly. "Don't let whatever hurt you in the past embitter you and destroy that natural innocence in you, Kate."

She froze at once, knowing he saw far too much. Perhaps it was part of his trade to analyse folks' expressions to get the best out of them, but it made her very uncomfortable. Thankfully the arrival of their meal prevented the necessity of an answer.

He already knew she had expected to be married before she went to Bournemouth, but he didn't know the reasons why she wasn't. He didn't know she had been jilted on her wedding morning. Nor about the baby that had never been, or her deception of Walter because of it. They were shameful secrets which she wasn't prepared to divulge to anyone. Not even someone who may or may not come to mean something special in her life.

Kate concentrated on the meal in front of her, before she was consumed with more guilt at how she was deceiving this generous man. He thought her so sweet and innocent, and she was anything but that. By the time they reached the tall lodging house in south London she had at last begun to relax a little.

She noted its iron railings surrounding the miniscule front yard and the steps leading to a front door with its black paint flaking off, much like every other house in the endless street. Far from disappointing her, she was mightily relieved to see that it wasn't a posh place. That suited her fine, because she wasn't posh, either.

Mrs Wood greeted her warmly, inviting her into a living room that was bright and homely. Pictures of the seaside took away some of the impact of the garish, rose-patterned wallpaper, and a bobble-fringed chenille cloth covered the large dining table in the centre. Seeing the familiar trappings, so like those at home, Kate's initial awkwardness disappeared, and she felt instantly at ease with the buxom landlady.

"Now then, my duck, I'll make us all a nice cup of tea – and I'll bet you'll be wanting something to eat after your long journey," she said at once.

"Oh, no food, thank you," Kate said, recognising the motherly need to provide food. "I was so hungry that Luke took me straight to a café, but I'd really love a cup of tea."

She wondered if this refusal of food was going to offend Mrs Wood, but apparently not. Without warning, she suddenly felt desperately tired, and she stifled a yawn with difficulty. Mrs Wood tutted sympathetically.

"Then I'll put the kettle on and show you your room, and I suggest that you get an early night, and this young man can call on us again in the morning," she said, taking charge.

Luke laughed. "You see how she bosses me about, Kate? But she's right, and you must be exhausted, so you catch up on your beauty sleep, and I'll be back at around eleven o'clock tomorrow morning."

"She don't need no beauty sleep," Mrs Wood said, openly admiring Kate's looks. "And I can see now just how you've been smitten, Lukey."

Kate hid a smile. Lukey! She couldn't imagine anyone calling this elegant man Lukey, except someone who had known him since childhood, as this woman evidently had. It would be interesting to ask her something about those days sometime – if she ever had the nerve.

"Goodnight then, Kate," Luke said with a smile. "I won't stop for any tea, and I think I'll get out of here before my old darling says something else to ruin your image of me."

He hugged Mrs Wood and planted a brief kiss on her cheek. There was obviously a genuine affection between them. He didn't attempt to kiss Kate; nor should he, she thought since their acquaintance was so short.

She had read somewhere that it took no time at all to fall in love. No time at all for a special someone to be constantly edging into another person's thoughts and for love to grow, even when you didn't want it to and certainly hadn't bargained for it. The thought alarmed her, and she dismissed it quickly from her mind.

Once Luke had gone, she accepted the cup of tea and biscuits the landlady brought in on a little tin tray which had the patriotic likenesses of the king and queen on either side of the Union Jack on its scratched surface.

Kate thought she had better make some sensible conversation if she was not to be thought a complete dummy. London folk all spoke with a fast, confident air, and she was very aware of her slower voice with the comfortably rounded vowel sounds. But that was her. It was part of who she was, and she wasn't going to plum up her accent for anybody, not even toffs. Hardly knowing why she was on the defensive, she lifted her chin as she spoke to the landlady.

"Do you have many lodgers, Mrs Wood? I've never been away from home before, so I don't know what to expect."

"There's only three besides yourself, duck, two girls and an elderly gent who keeps himself to himself. You'll meet them all soon enough, though you must have a lie-in after all your travelling. I'll make your breakfast tomorrow, and you can come down and have it whenever you feel like it."

93

"Oh, but I don't want to put you to any trouble, Mrs Wood, and of course, I'll pay for any extras."

"It's all taken care of, my duck. Lukey paid me a month in advance for your room and board, so until you get yourself settled, you needn't worry about a thing. Now then, when you've finished your tea, I'll show you your room."

Kate swallowed the strong brew quickly, then followed her up the steep, winding staircase until they reached the third floor. It was a narrow-fronted building, and the rooms were long and narrow too, but of a reasonable size.

She had been shocked at Mrs Wood's words, and her calm acceptance of the situation. The thought of what her father would say if he knew she was in lodgings paid for by a man, and a virtual stranger at that, didn't bear thinking about. But she was too exhausted from travelling to worry about it tonight. The bed was the most inviting thing in the room, and after a cursory unpacking, hanging her things in the old-fashioned wardrobe and giving her face and hands a token wash in the washstand bowl, Kate slid her old nightgown over her head and fell into bed.

But despite her tiredness, the night sounds were so different in the city that she wondered if she would ever get to sleep at all. The bed felt strange, and the traffic noises which constantly filtered into the room were fifty times louder than the country noises at home. There were no bird songs, and no plaintive creaks from the timbers of the old cottage, nor the drunken lurchings of the village men going home from the pub.

But as the thought entered her head, she drifted into sleep.

Brilliant daylight was filling the room when she opened her eyes again. She had slept the clock round, and no one had woken her. And to her horror, she saw that it was already well after ten o'clock, and Luke was coming for her at eleven . . .

She leapt up and threw back the thin curtains, looking down on a street scene that was entirely unfamiliar. A surge of optimism filled her veins at the thought that this was home now. She had burned her boats in coming to London. This was her new life. And if the dingy streets weren't exactly paved with gold, she told herself, they were now her streets.

She washed and dressed quickly and hurried downstairs, following the scent of cooking, to the large kitchen where two girls a bit older than herself were laughing over a newspaper account. They looked infinitely more sophisticated than Kate, with their chic, boyishly bobbed haircuts, and they looked at her curiously as she nervously entered the room.

"Now then, you two," Kate heard Mrs Wood say, appearing red-faced from the blackened stove in the corner of the kitchen-cum-dining-room. "This here's Kate Radcliffe, and she might look younger than yourselves, but she's already a married lady, and why she's here is no business of yours or mine, so you just mind and behave yourselves."

The colour flooded Kate's face, and the words made her feel as old as Methuselah. Luke had obviously told Mrs Wood exactly the tale she had told him. But the girls were smiling at her in friendly fashion, holding out slim hands tipped with red-varnished fingernails in greeting. Kate shook each one briefly, very much aware of her own fingers pricked from her sewing.

"Please call me Kate," she said quickly.

"Pleased to meet you, Kate," the darker of the girls said with a pronounced Irish accent that reminded her immediately of her father. "I'm Doris and this is Faye. Sorry the old fellow's not here to make your acquaintance right now, but you'll meet him later."

They fell about giggling again, and Mrs Wood tut-tutted at the pair of them. They obviously shared some private joke, but Kate didn't care. Doris was no more a Londoner than she was, and when Faye spoke to her it was with a strong north-country accent which reminded her uncomfortably of Walter for a moment, but then reassured her.

They were all strangers here. London was a hotch-potch of

people, just as her father had always said. Only when he'd said it, it wasn't with any sense of magnanimity, but with dark, scathing undertones that said you never knew who you were mixing with next.

"What are you doing here then, Kate?" Faye said.

"Getting a job, I hope."

"She's going to sit for my Luke first of all," Mrs Wood said proudly. "And if the two of them make their fortunes, she won't need to do no other work at all."

The girls convulsed, and Doris's eyes sparkled.

"You just be careful posing for pictures, Katie. You never know where it might end up."

"That's enough of that kind of talk," Mrs Wood said sharply. "Kate's a respectable married lady, like I told you, and my Luke knows how to treat ladies."

"So where's your husband then?" Faye asked. "If I had a man looking after me, I'd never have come down to the smoke looking for work. But there's not much pleasure in slogging your guts out in the mills all day long."

As Mrs Wood slapped a great big meal on the table in front of Kate, she managed to answer coolly, "I'm a working girl, same as you, and as for my husband, the less said about him the better, if you know what I mean."

They didn't, but her apparently worldly attitude stopped any more questions. It was amazing, Kate thought, just as she'd done in Bournemouth. You acted a part and, providing you did it convincingly, everybody believed it.

It was easy to see the admiring, knowing glances between the two girls now, clearly assuming that Kate's husband had been a rotter, and she'd run out on him. And good for her. It was a strange way to win people over, but it had obviously worked with these two.

Luke called for her promptly at eleven o'clock. Doris and Faye made no attempt to get out of the house until they'd caught sight of him, flashing their heavily made-up eyes at him and flirting outrageously.

"Mrs Wood calls them harmless butterflies still finding their city wings," he told Kate, when they'd left the house to go to his studio. "You don't have to worry about their antics. They just like to shock, that's all."

"I wasn't worried!" she said, wondering if he thought she was actually jealous because they seemed to find it so easy to flirt, while she found it so difficult.

"Good. Because, as I've told you before, nobody could hold a candle to you, Kate."

"I wasn't fishing for compliments, either."

"You don't need to. But you're always going to get them, wherever you go. You must know that."

She didn't know it. She didn't count Walter's compliments, since she knew now that they were as false as Walter himself. Until she had met Walter, she hadn't paid much attention to her hair and her looks and her clothes, but making her trousseau and dreaming about being married had changed all that. She'd had someone she wanted to look pretty for, and now she had Luke, who told her she was beautiful.

"You've gone into your silent world again. Come out of it, Kate. Nothing's ever as bad as it seems."

"Isn't it?" And what would he know, she thought resentfully, with his inheritance and his Bentley, and his studio, and his up-and-coming business.

He put his hand over hers as he steered the car carefully along the empty Sunday streets. Presumably everyone had either gone to church or were still in bed, she thought.

"Whatever happened in the past, it's over, Kate. You've taken a great step forward in coming here, so don't make the mistake of stepping backwards. You're far more likely to fall over if you do."

He spoke lightly and in riddles, but somehow the riddles

made sense, and she let her hand remain in his until he had to put it back on the steering wheel again.

They stopped outside the windows of a large showroom, in which there were framed portraits of wedding groups and families. The name Luke Halliday was emblazoned in gilt letters over the doorway and again at the top of each double-fronted window.

Kate's heart lurched, and her mouth dropped open in dumb surprise. Whatever she had expected, it had been nothing like this. All she knew of photographers was a little tin-pot place in the nearby town that wasn't for the likes of her, anyway. But this . . . the façade alone was so splendid, and it made her embarrassed that she had dared to telephone this important man to come and fetch her from Paddington Station, and expected him to take care of her.

"Impressed?" came Luke's smiling voice.

"Why didn't you tell me?" she said angrily. "I had no idea it would be this grand!"

But of course she should have done. The Bentley and the boat in Poole harbour, and the Charlton Hotel in Bournemouth where he was such a regular client, should have told her without the need for words.

"Does it matter? We're all the same underneath the trappings, Kate."

He recognised her feeling of inverted snobbery, and the instinct to sneer at something beyond her experience. But he didn't know everything about her. She lifted her head and remembered the actress inside her.

"I doubt that. I'm hardly the same as Doris and Faye."

"Thank God. Well, are we going to sit here all day, or are you going to come inside?"

"Said the spider to the fly," Kate murmured, voicing the thought that had sprung to her mind that first evening when she'd accepted his invitation to dine with her at the Charlton. She made herself laugh.

"Of course I'm coming inside. It's what I came here for, isn't it?"

Luke grinned and squeezed her hand. Sometimes she seemed as sweetly open as a summer rose, and at others she was as deep and secretive as the ocean, and he still couldn't make her out at all. But he was working on it, and he had no intention of letting her out of his life now that she'd come so delightfully into it.

He almost surprised himself at the depth of his feeling for her. She was so fragile in appearance and yet inwardly so strong, he was sure of it. Something had hurt her very badly in the past, but she had survived, and he admired that.

He unlocked the door of his showroom with his usual surge of pleasure. Although it has been bought courtesy of his great-aunt's money, the fact that it had flourished beyond his wildest dreams was due to himself, to hard work and an eye to the future. In business, it didn't pay to sit back and rest on your laurels. You had to sense what the future trends were likely to be, and it had worked out marvellously for him so far. If there was an even better future to come, he wanted Kate Radcliffe to be a part of it.

Kate was even more impressed by the plush interior of the showroom. The floors were carpeted in soft green and there were matching velvet-covered chairs and sofas where the clients could sit and wait and take tea, or browse among the sample books of photographs demonstrating single or group poses. The whole ambience was of restful elegance, and designed to make nervous clients feel at ease.

"I had an assistant for a short time," Luke said casually, "but she was more interested in trying to get me to take photographs of her for her boyfriend than dealing with clients, and she was a bit short on finesse as well, so I had to let her go. If you want to attract a better class of customer, then you have to give them class. Don't you agree?"

Kate said she did, while being none too sure what finesse was. Nor was she quite sure whether or not he was hinting at the offer of a job for her in the studio. Probably not.

What did she know about photography, anyway? On the other hand, from what he said, would she need to do anything other than to take down a client's name and offer them tea? Any fool could do that. She felt a flicker of interest at the thought. It hadn't been what she intended when she came here, and her pride wouldn't let her push him to do any more for her than he was doing already. A job that she knew, stitching and machining in a sweat-shop, just like the one at home, was all that she'd had in mind.

But it occurred to her that she wanted more. She wanted to move on, just as she'd moved on in coming here in the first place.

"Come through to the back and I'll show you my working area, and then the darkroom. Have you ever been in a photographic studio before, Kate?"

"Never," she said, "and what's a darkroom?"

"It's where I take innocent young ladies to see what develops," he said without expression.

At her startled look, he laughed out loud.

"I'm sorry, Kate, but I couldn't resist it. It's the standard joke about darkrooms, and not a very good one. It's simply the special room where the developing and printing is done, and if you've never seen a photograph come to life, you'll think it's truly magical to see how the images gradually appear on the white paper."

She couldn't work up the same kind of enthusiasm for something of which she had no knowledge, but she couldn't doubt the enthusiasm in Luke's voice. He spoke of the process as lovingly as if he spoke of a sweetheart, and

she knew well enough that it took that kind of commitment to make a business a success. Luke had all that, and
more. She was filled with a new and burgeoning admiration
for him.

Chapter Seven

The studio itself was full of equipment. Several large cameras stood on tripods, and there were various angled lamps to light or shade the sitter. There was a floor-to-ceiling backcloth of palest green baize behind several chairs and couches where the clients presumably posed. There was also an entire range of props and accessories, including a small box of children's toys. The sight of it touched Kate. Here was a man who obviously paid great attention to detail and wanted to get the best out of his clients, for himself, and for them.

In one corner of the studio she was surprised to see a large phonograph machine with a stack of records in their paper sleeves on a shelf alongside. At Kate's enquiring look, Luke said it often helped to relax his clients if soft music was playing in the background. The more she heard him talk, the more she could tell he knew exactly how to put people at their ease; he had a great knack for it, as she had already discovered.

"The lucky chaps who came back unscathed from the war were keen to be photographed in their uniforms for their wives and sweethearts, Kate. Then, when their children came along they came back for family photos, and quite often the smaller ones were understandably nervous, especially when the flash bulbs went off. But I've already told you that, haven't I? I don't want to bore you with it again."

"You never bore me," Kate said quickly. "Anyway, I love to hear it, it's a lovely story, and it's good to hear about that kind of continuity. There were so many who didn't come back at all, and others who probably made the most of their time in France in other ways."

"That didn't apply to all of us," Luke said shortly.

She knew he had been in an Infantry unit in France during the war, and had thankfully come home unscathed. It was where he had been shown so many photographs of loved ones, tucked inside soldiers' wallets and pocket-books.

He must have seen horrors as well, and Kate was ashamed of her unthinking words. She wondered what on earth had made her say such a thing. By the bitterness in her voice, she had almost betrayed the strong suspicion that Walter had been one of those main-chance philanderers.

"What I mean is," she went on carefully, "not everyone had a bad war, did they?"

"Most of them did, and there's nothing about a war that's good, Kate. All the medals and all the honour and glory in the world count for nothing when a man's life is cut short and a family is left behind to grieve for him."

She felt chastened at once, and she was aware of a small tension between them. It wasn't helped by the knowledge that she had been unwittingly reminded of Walter, when she was trying so hard to put that part of her life behind her for ever. But perhaps it was burying her head in the sand to think she could forget so easily. Walter had been everything to her, as she believed she had been to him, and the hurt of his betrayal flared up when she least expected it.

"Come on, cheer up," she heard Luke say. "You can't take the sorrows of the world on your shoulders, Kate. And I didn't mean to upset you."

"You haven't. It's just that I once knew someone . . ."

"And he didn't come back?"

"Something like that," she mumbled. Walter hadn't come back to her, though not quite in the way Luke was thinking.

"You must have been very young at the time, though in my opinion people often underestimate how deeply the feelings of children can be hurt," he said. "But we all have a past, Kate. The trick is in knowing how to keep it in its proper place."

"Yes, sir," she said solemnly, glad of his misunderstanding, and his chuckle broke into the tense atmosphere.

"I'm sorry. That sounded pompous and schoolmasterish, didn't it? Come on, let me show you my darkroom, and then we'll go for a drive around the city. All the tourists want to see Buckingham Palace, and I can't imagine that you'll be very different."

Kate's eyes sparkled, even though such a thing had never even occurred to her. The thought of actually seeing the palace where the king and queen lived was enough to take her breath away. Even more so to think she was now living in the same city as these remote and important folk.

Luke drew in his breath at the sudden sparkle in those fabulous blue eyes, and he couldn't resist trailing a finger down her cheek in a light caress. Kate felt a ripple of pleasure at his touch. It was uncomplicated and non-sexual, and nothing like as predatory as Walter's, nor as calculating as the odious Jenkins.

"When I photograph you, Kate, I want you to think of whatever it is that's exciting you right now," he said.

"Why?" she asked, dismissing Walter from her mind again. She was fishing for compliments, and she didn't care, because it seemed that they were hearing the same music once more.

"Because I want to capture that mixture of innocence and sensuality and expectation in your face," he said.

Kate felt her skin tingle. It was the professional speaking now, she reminded herself, but she would have been a fool to think it was only that. She could see something more in his eyes, she could hear it in the timbre of his voice, and she could sense it in everything about him. The ripples of pleasure in her body turned to mild alarm, knowing she was alone with him, and very much on his territory.

"There's nothing to be afraid of here, Kate," he said gently, as if reading her mind. "And nor should you flinch from being told how you appear to other people. Most women would pay a king's ransom to have what you've got."

"Stop it, please!" she protested. "You'd better hurry up and show me this darkroom and get me out of here, because I'm starting to feel very hot and embarrassed."

Luke laughed. He tucked her hand in his arm as he led her through a bamboo curtain to another part of the building. She saw a door prominently labelled DARKROOM – DO NOT ENTER WHILE RED LIGHT IS ON. There was a large lamp fixed to the wall, and as Luke opened the door and turned on the light switch, Kate saw the outer lamp light up before he closed the door behind them.

She was immediately enveloped in a dull red glow that barely lit the room and the strong smell of chemicals filled her nostrils. But any apprehension she felt was dispelled by curiosity about the contents of this room, which was unlike any other she had ever been in. A long workbench and a double sink unit took up all one wall, and bottles of chemicals and packs of photographic paper of all sizes were ranged along the shelves above. There were hanging racks of negatives and plates, and a large magnifying glass at the end of the workbench.

"Are you impressed?" Luke said, smiling.

"Amazed, more like!" Kate said. "I had no idea what it involved. What's the magnifying glass for?"

"I take a number of photos of my subjects, and the best way to see any flaws before printing them is through the magnifier. Everybody wants to look their best in a photo. And quite frankly, I can't wait to work with you and see your lovely face in an elegant frame. It will be my centrepiece in the showroom window."

"Now just hold on a minute, Luke," she protested with an uneasy laugh at the prospect. "How do you know I'm going to be at ease in front of a camera? I might turn out to be completely useless and you'll have wasted your time on me."

She was thankful that the subdued rosy glow in the dark room hid her face as she turned away from him, knowing the words sounded all too provocative. But they had been said, and once said, words were there for all eternity.

Luke's arms went round her, and he turned her very gently towards him.

"The time I spend with you has already become the most important in my life. Don't you know it by now?"

He bent his head towards her, and before she could protest, she felt the touch of his lips on hers. It was no more than an innocent kiss, but here in this confined space, in the intimate glow of the darkroom light, it took on a very different meaning for Kate, and she struggled to get away from him.

"Don't – please," she gasped. "It's not what I came here for, and if I've given you the wrong impression—"

The agonising thought had surged into her head that it had been so short a time since they had left Bournemouth, and here she was, running after him. Or at least, that was how it might appear – that she had seen him as a well-heeled young man, and decided she could do very well out of their acquaintance. Why hadn't she stopped to think?

"For God's sake, calm down!" Luke said quickly. "What sort of a man do you think I am? I've no intention of molesting you, my dear girl, and my reputation would soon be shot if word got about that I lured young girls to my studio to seduce them."

He let her go and backed slightly away from her, as if fearful that she was about to call "rape" to whoever might be in the vicinity. Kate suddenly saw the foolishness of her action in treating a gentleman as if he came out of the same mould as that snake Jenkins.

"I'm sorry," she whispered. "I know I reacted in a very stupid way. But it was far too impulsive of me to take you at your word and rush off to London without even contacting you properly beforehand. I've probably given you quite the wrong impression of me, Luke. I'm not fast, and I'm not ready for – for – well, I can't—"

"You don't have to apologise, or say anything by way of explanation until or unless you feel ready to do so. I just hope that when that time comes, I'll be the one you confide in. As for taking me at my word, it was exactly what I wanted you to do. I never say anything I don't mean."

She felt quite unable to answer. Apart from her family, the men of her acquaintance hadn't been so understanding of her emotions. Walter had only been thinking about himself as always, and Jenkins had been just as bad in seeing what he could get out of the heartbreak of a vulnerable girl. Luke deserved more than that. He deserved better than her.

She went down in the doldrums so quickly it almost left her reeling. What was wrong with her, for pity's sake? If Walter had gone through with the marriage, she would have had to face a horrific future, and at least she had been saved from that. And this good and kind man was obviously fond of her, and she had really enjoyed his company at the Charlton Hotel. Yet the first time he had made the mildest sort of pass at her, she had felt herself freeze. Vi had had a word for that, sniggering at a woman at work who'd had such a problem. Frigid, Vi called it. It happened to some women who had had a bad experience with a man, putting them off the good things in life for good and all. Kate knew that what Vi meant was being intimate with a man. But being frigid wasn't going to happen to her! It couldn't. She had a loving nature, and it had so nearly been her downfall. She had loved too wantonly and too well, and she had responded to her lover with all the passion he could ever have desired. She had never considered that Walter's actions might have left her incapable of responding to another man. And she didn't want to think of it now.

"I think we should go out and get some fresh air," she heard Luke saying now. "A walk in the park sounds favourite. What do you say, Kate? There's plenty of time.

Mrs Wood's promised us a splendid Sunday dinner at two o'clock."

"Sounds good to me," she mumbled, even if Sunday dinner at two o'clock in the afternoon seemed a very rakish time to be eating. But nothing here was as she had expected it to be, so maybe nothing should surprise her any more.

Once outside the darkroom she felt even more exposed. At least in there she had been comparatively hidden by the very low lighting. She felt as if every foolish thought in her head was etched on her face.

"You must think me very naive, Luke," she muttered.

"I think you're very young, and very charming. And if that's being naive, then I hope you never lose that quality." He made his voice lighter, seeing that her face was still showing signs of distress. "Anyway, you wouldn't really want to be as hard-bitten as Doris and Faye, would you?"

For a moment, she couldn't think who he meant, and then recalled the two girls at Mrs Wood's boarding house.

"They seemed very nice," she protested.

"Oh yes, so they are, but anybody with half an eye can see that they're on the prowl for husbands, and that's enough to put any man off."

"Well, at least you know that doesn't apply to me."

She remembered what one of the girls had said about not having to work again if she had a man to look after her, and knew that Luke's words were probably true. It didn't alter her opinion that the girls were a refreshing change after some of the toffee-nosed women guests she'd seen at the Charlton Hotel.

"I do know it, so now let's forget it and go and take the air like real Sunday morning people, shall we?" he said with a grin.

But if he thought she was labouring the point, at least he now knew where he stood, thought Kate. It wasn't that she didn't like him, or sensed that liking could easily turn to something more, it was simply that she was afraid to let her feelings show any more. It had been her downfall once already. Besides, it was too soon. It was much too soon even to think about the intimacies of love with someone else, or to wonder if she was capable of it any more. And right now, she was too afraid and still too vulnerable to find out.

They drove to the park in Luke's car, and when they merged into the crowds of elegant folk strolling about, Kate's spirits began to soar. It was a different world to her country life, but there were similarities in the earthy scents of foliage and the sweetness of full-blown summer flowers. There was a glitter of sunlight on the expanse of water Luke told her was called the Serpentine because of its shape. On it stately swans glided, and ducks swam trailing their busy little families behind them. It was all as heady and familiar to a country girl as the warm summer air.

"It's far more beautiful than I had expected," she exclaimed, her gauchness evaporating in her delight. "I thought it would be all blackened buildings with no air between them and no sight of the sky."

She gazed upwards as she spoke to where a drift of fluffy white clouds was the only thing to mar the blueness of the heavens. She was far more beautiful than Luke had remembered, with a tug of desire in his loins that wouldn't be denied, no matter how much he tried. But it was obvious that something or someone had hurt her very badly. He knew human nature well enough to know that if he tried to reveal his feelings for her too fast, he would frighten her away for good. As it was, he could hardly believe that she had actually come to London when he'd never expected to see her again, and he blessed the luck that had kept him safe all through the war, and was still on his side now. For all that she had called herself a country hick, she could fit in anywhere, he thought, in admiration. She held herself so tall and straight, and that shimmering golden hair which she wore long and loose caught the sunlight as if it were made out of spun gold. It wasn't a fashionable style, but on Kate it looked stunning.

The glances of people passing-by told him that plenty of others were appreciating her too, even if she was quite oblivious of their glances. It wouldn't surprise him if some of them were wondering whether she was an actress or a member of some European royalty.

"You're staring at me," she said, breaking into his musing. "Do I have a smudge on my nose or something?"

"You do not." He laughed. "I was just wondering if you knew how much attention you were attracting."

"Why?" she said in a fright.

"Because, my dear Mrs Radcliffe," he spoke formally once more as he tucked her hand inside the crook of his arm more tightly, "you light up this old park with your beauty, and I'm not saying that with any ulterior motive, but simply because it's true."

"Stop it, Luke. I've seen so many beautiful ladies in the park this morning that I know you're just teasing."

"I assure you I'm not. See those two gentlemen on that park bench over there. They were deep in discussion until you came near, and now they can't take their eyes off you."

She looked, and as she did so, the two gentlemen rose to their feet and tipped their hats to her. Without thinking, Kate inclined her head towards them with a small smile and then continued walking with her eyes straight ahead.

"And from the way you handled that little scene, you're either a consummate actress, or you were born to it. Are you sure you're all that you seem, Mrs Radcliffe?" Luke said, with barely concealed mirth.

Her preening vanished at once. "Of course I am! I'm exactly what you see. And I've asked you before not to call me by that name."

"Why not, if it's your rightful name? It's the one you signed on the register at the Charlton Hotel," he said, with more curiosity than censure.

"It's the name of the man I expected to marry," Kate said

111

in a rush. She knew she couldn't go on deceiving him for ever, providing she only gave him enough information to satisfy him.

Luke decided not to examine this startling comment further, but he couldn't leave it entirely.

"So why do you hold on to it? You're free of him now, presumably, so am I allowed to know your real name?"

"It's Kate Sullivan," she said abruptly.

"Maybe you should revert to it then, unless you feel a loyalty to the Radcliffe name. Kate Sullivan would look very well on your portraits and on any commissions we get together."

It all sounded so grand and important. Somehow he made things so easy for her, putting everything into perspective. He didn't know whether Walter was alive or dead, but his innocent use of that one word "loyalty" had made her see that she didn't owe Walter a thing.

"You're right," she said. "So I'll be Kate Sullivan again, and gladly so."

And one day, Luke thought silently, if I have my way, you'll be Kate Halliday.

Her thoughts were winging ahead, and she went on speaking quickly. "But just for the moment, Luke, for Mrs Wood's benefit, I'll keep the Radcliffe name, since that's how she knows me – and the other lodgers too. It would cause too much curiosity if I suddenly reverted to my old name on such short acquaintance. But for business purposes I'll be Kate Sullivan. Is that all right?"

"Of course it is."

After they had admired the riders in Rotten Row, and strolled among the morning walkers, they left the park, and Luke took her to see Buckingham Palace as he'd promised. Kate stared at it silently, with a huge sense of disappointment in its sombre appearance.

"I don't know what I expected, really. But I suppose it

was something more like the palaces in Maura and Aileen's picture-books, all romantic fairy-tale spires and turrets," she said, half-seriously, and feeling rather foolish.

Luke laughed. "Not in smoky old London, I'm afraid, although the Tower is a little more like you've described. If you want to see turrets, and a building with a beautiful façade, then you'll like the Tower."

"Will I? Isn't that where they imprisoned the little Princes?" she said, dredging up her village school history lessons, so that she didn't seem like a complete dummy. "It doesn't sound like a very romantic place to me!"

"Well, maybe one of these days I'll take you to France and show you what a real château looks like. That will certainly satisfy your romantic little heart."

"You'd better explain what that is," she said at once.

"A château is just the French word for a castle. Some of them were used as army barracks during the war, though I was never lucky enough to be housed in such a splendid place, and had to make the best of it in a disused monastery for much of my time there."

He carried on talking normally, turning the conversation away from the pleasurable thought of taking this delightful girl to France. It would be a perfect place for a honeymoon, and Luke found it difficult for a few minutes to get the erotic connotations out of his mind. But he knew that the thought of a honeymoon would be the least desirable thing on Kate's agenda.

If he could have read her thoughts, he'd have been surprised. She was thinking bitterly that Walter obviously hadn't been billeted in a château in France either, or she would undoubtedly have heard him boasting about it to anyone who would listen. He had always been a bragger, she thought now, she'd just never seen it.

"Shall we go back to Mrs Wood's yet, or do you want to see anything more?" he asked.

"Since I don't know what else there is to see, I'll have to leave it up to you," she said.

"Well, just as they say that Rome wasn't built in a day, you can't see London in a day, either, so we'll leave any more sightseeing for another time. And you still have to meet Thomas Lord Tannersley."

Hearing the name, Kate took fright at once as they waked back to the car.

"Who's this Lord person when he's at home?" she said, once Luke had started up the Bentley, using one of Vi's favourite expressions. "I know I won't be any good at meeting titled folk, Luke. Is he one of your clients, or what?"

"Calm down, you goose. Lord is supposedly the old rogue's middle name, that's all, though I'm quite sure he bestowed it on himself to make himself seem more respectable."

"Well, isn't he?"

Luke laughed. "He's what's known as one of nature's gentlemen, despite the way he looks. He has what he grandly calls an antiques stall in Portobello Road, though it's what most people would call a bric-a-brac and junk stall. But he's a real character, Kate, and you'll like him, I promise you."

And that was just the kind of remark guaranteed to make you think exactly the opposite, Kate thought.

"When do I have to meet him, then? I'm not sure I can cope with all these new experiences at once!"

Luke laughed again. "You can hardly avoid it, since you're living in the same house."

The penny dropped. "He's the other lodger, then?" she exclaimed. "The one the girls were giggling about? I thought there must be something odd about him. Has he got two heads or something?"

"No, but you'll find him a little outrageous to say the least. He once fancied himself as a thespian, and puts all his energies into promoting the theatrical image. It helps to bring the crowds to his stall, and he doesn't do too badly on it, either, despite some of the rubbish he sells."

"And you admire him," Kate said, stating the obvious.

"Why not? He's an entrepreneur, the same as me."

"And what's that?" she said, not bothering to disguise the fact that she didn't understand the word.

The thought flitted through her mind that she was no longer defensive about admitting it. Not with Luke, anyway. She didn't have his education, or his polished way of speaking, but it didn't seem to matter. And if he didn't bother about such things, why should she? And that was a lesson you didn't learn at school.

"You could describe it as somebody who seizes opportunities when they arise, and acts on them. Just like you did, Kate, in coming to London."

She began to laugh. "I hardly think you could call me an entre – whatever you said! I think I took the easy way out of a difficult situation."

She clamped her lips together, knowing she was on the verge of saying too much.

But Luke interpreted it in his own way. "It's never easy facing the world again after a bad experience. That's why so many people have to get right away and make a fresh start. The past is the past."

"But if you don't face up to it, there's always a danger that the past will come back to haunt you," she said slowly, reminded of some of her recurring dreams about Walter, and it was as though a shadow of premonition threatened to cloud this lovely day. "You can't escape what is past, Luke. It's part of what you are."

"What a little philosopher you've become all of a sudden," he teased.

"I have, haven't I?" she said, pushing the unpleasant thoughts away, and rather liking the sound of this. Kate Sullivan, philosopher indeed! It sounded far too grand for

115

the likes of her ... but just like the flamboyant-sounding
Thomas Lord Tannersley, she could be anything she liked,
here in the anonymity of the big city.

"I'm glad the thought of it seems to have cheered you up,
anyway. I thought those glooms were going to attack you
again."

"Never!" she said, her eyes determinedly bright. "I refuse
to let them."

"Good."

Luke brought the car to a smooth halt outside the door of
84, Jubilee Terrace. "Then let's see what Mrs Wood has got
cooking for us."

The house seemed full to bursting as they entered the parlour.
Doris and Faye were listening to the outpourings of a very large
man who dominated the room. He wore a yellow waistcoat over
a green shirt and green-checked trousers. His shoes were of
brown and white patent leather, just like the co-respondent's
shoes in the picture shows, Kate thought daringly, with a wild
urge to giggle. His hair was long, and he sported a flamboyant
moustache and neat goatee beard. He wouldn't have looked
out of place at one of the visiting travelling fairs that the
countryfolk flocked to.

He turned to the newcomers at once, his face brightening
as soon as he saw Kate. He came towards her with his hands
outstretched, and she automatically placed her own in his,
while he looked her up and down approvingly.

"Ah, at last I meet my beautiful Rapunzel with the glorious
golden hair," he said in a booming voice. "And now that I
have, my heart is instantly smitten. Would that I could turn
this frog into a prince and rescue you from your captive prison
and make you mine for ever," he went on grandly, mixing his
fairy tales with grand and careless abandon.

He raised her hands to his lips, and Kate felt another wild
urge to giggle at such theatricals. It was impossible to dislike

116

him, even though she had never been in such company in her life before. The girls were giggling too, clearly anticipating her reaction and relishing it. And although Luke had already warned her, he was so much more everything than she could ever have imagined. Why hadn't Luke ever photographed him, she thought! Or maybe he had. Surely he had.

"Ah, Luke, me boy," Thomas said sorrowfully now, as he released Kate's hands. "If I had met this lovely lady first, I would have carried her off to my lair, and you would have had no chance at all with her, I promise you."

"I'm not sure I have any chance with her now," Luke said, with a grin, enjoying the whole bohemian atmosphere of the house, and especially the way he could see how Kate was relaxing more by the minute.

"What?" Thomas boomed. "Then you're not the man I thought you were, boy."

"Oh yes he is," giggled Doris, raising her finely-arched eyebrows at Luke, flirting outrageously with her eyes and her suggestive voice, and letting the scarlet-tipped nails reach out to stroke his cheek for a brief moment.

Kate felt the most ridiculous surge of jealousy at the way they all seemed to know each other so well, and were so comfortable in one another's company. Then, as if to cover her confused feelings, Mrs Wood called them all to come to the kitchen if they wanted to eat that day.

Luke held out her chair for her, and then sat opposite her at the long table. He smiled into her eyes and she felt the familiar warm glow at knowing that this kind and considerate man had taken her under his wing. It would be so easy to feel more than gratitude towards him, and warning bells were starting to ring in her head again.

Deep down, there was something more fundamental that nagged away at her conscience. She had made love with Walter so many times; she had had his child growing inside her, and even though the miscarriage had saved her from a terrible disgrace, there were still moments when she grieved for the child that had never had a chance of life. She knew another man would be able to tell that she was no longer a virgin.

At present, Luke simply thought something had happened to prevent the honeymoon trip to Bournemouth taking place, and most likely he assumed that Walter had died shortly before the wedding, and that she was still grieving for him, and loving him. But if she ever allowed herself to fall in love with Luke Halliday, and that love was reciprocated to the point of marriage, how could she bear to see the disgust and censure in his eyes when he discovered she was not the innocent victim of circumstance he obviously believed her to be?

"Eat up, Kate. Don't you like roast beef and potatoes? I thought you country girls were supposed to have hearty appetites," she heard Mrs Wood say. "Don't be shy, my duck. There's plenty more where that came from."

"Oh, I love roast beef, and this is simply wonderful, Mrs Wood," she said hastily.

"And she makes gravy just like mother used to make, doesn't she, Kate?" Faye said with a grin. "Thick enough to stand a spoon up in it."

"Don't you be cheeky, my girl, and who's this she? The cat's mother?" Mrs Wood said with a grin, taking no offence. "You just get on with your dinner as well and pass those Brussels round the table before Kate starts to think she's come to live in a madhouse."

Kate caught sight of Luke's smiling face and smiled back. She didn't think she'd come to a madhouse at all. It was all so homely, just like a big family mealtime at home before they all got too strained to know how to talk to one another.

Chapter Eight

Being an essentially private person herself, Alice Sullivan had always respected another person's right to privacy so when her daughter Kate didn't turn up for the midday meal on that particular Saturday, she didn't think too much of it. Kate often felt the need to be on her own lately and, when she wasn't working at Granby's Garments, she spent more and more time tramping about the countryside by herself, trying to get her thoughts in order.

Alice understood that need, even if her menfolk didn't. The younger girls certainly didn't, and were always complaining that Kate didn't play with them any more. But Alice knew her girl had to find her own way of recovering from the humiliation of what Walter Radcliffe had done to her.

Alice's lips tightened whenever she thought about him. She wasn't a woman for cursing, but if she had been, she would have cursed the day Donal brought him into the house, so brash and breezy with his fast-talking ways, just the type to turn a gullible young girl's head. Her heart ached, thinking of the way Kate had looked on that terrible morning when she had read Walter's letter. Her face had frozen, as if all the life had been taken out of her in a single swoop.

It wasn't in the Church's teachings to hate, but Alice had never been as enamoured of the Church as her man professed to be. She always thought it was more of a clinging to the old ways rather than devotion that made him declare that a Catholic was always a Catholic, no matter what happened in this wicked world. But Alice hated Walter Radcliffe with a passion that surprised her.

It was Maura and Aileen who came running downstairs with an envelope clutched in their hands during the late afternoon, and at the sight of it, Alice's heart turned over. Surely Kate hadn't left the hateful thing around for the girls to read? It should have been destroyed long ago.

"This was on our Kate's pillow, Mammie," Maura said importantly.

"And what were the two of you doing in Kate's room?" she scolded them, to give herself a moment to think. "Haven't you been told enough times to respect other folks' belongings?"

"We were only looking for the book she was reading to us last night," Aileen said, scowling. "Anyway, this has got your name on it, and Dada's too, so we brought it down for you."

A premonition, as keen as a blade, shot through Alice's gut. She took the envelope, holding it by its corner as if it were red hot.

Seeing the girls' curious faces, she shooed them out of her kitchen and sent them down to the village on a quickly invented errand.

Alice had always considered herself a courageous woman. Even facing the fact that Donal might not come back from the Front had stiffened her resolve to be the strong one in the family, should it be needed. But she didn't feel strong now. She stared at the names written on the envelope, and felt as if her bones were turning to jelly and she resisted opening it for as long as possible.

"Don't be spineless, woman. Take a hold of yourself," she muttered to herself. "Our Kate wouldn't have done anything foolish and wicked."

But she couldn't deny the horrific vision of her lovely daughter lying face down in one of the Somerset rhines that criss-crossed and drained the moors, her lovely golden hair bedraggled and filthy in one of the near-stagnant ditches. She swayed for a moment, and leant against the scrubbed kitchen table for support, then ripped open the envelope.

It was difficult to focus on the words Kate had written. All Alice felt at first was an overwhelming sense of relief that her girl hadn't been so browbeaten to have done away with herself, and committed the worst sin against the Church. The relief swiftly changed to something like anger as she wished the intrusion of the Church didn't keep coming into her mind, when it mattered far less to her than the need to keep her family together. And Kate, of all people, had torn it apart.

The menfolk came into the cottage a short while later, rubbing their hands together at the thought of a hearty evening meal of rabbit pie and vegetables, sniffing the air as if to relish the cooking smells.

"What's all this, then, missus?" Brogan said jovially, when he saw his wife staring unseeingly out of the kitchen window with no evident sign of food being prepared. "Is it day-dreaming that you've descended to now, then? I thought you'd gone past all that sort of caper at your age, and left it to the young 'uns."

"What's wrong, Mother?" Donal said sharply, quicker to take note of her pinched face and shadowed eyes than his father. "Has something happened to one of the girls?"

She looked at him mutely, the words of explanation sticking in her throat. He was such a fiercely protective young fellow, caring for his family, and the females in particular, like a mother hen. And having had to do so on many occasions when his father was too roaring drunk to do anything other than be put to bed to sleep off his night's revelries.

"Not the little ones," Alice muttered.

"Kate, then. Is it Kate?" Donal said. "Where is she? Why isn't she here?"

Brogan seemed to have lost the power of speech for the moment, as if for once, he had the gift of sight of the Little

People, and knew what was to come, and was totally unable to know how to deal with it.

"You'd better read this, since it's addressed to us both," Alice said chokingly, turning to Brogan, angry that for all his shenanigans he rarely seemed capable of taking command when it was really needed.

He took the letter and scanned Kate's words quickly. Donal read them over his shoulder, and in seconds the silence in the cottage was shattered.

"What's all this!" Brogan roared. "Has the girl taken leave of her senses? Going to London, indeed. And what kind of so-called respectable person lures a young girl away from a decent home? If I get my hands on the woman . . ."

If it was a woman, Alice thought. That was one thought that she dare not speak, not when her man was looking purple-faced and near to apoplexy now.

Donal exploded next, his hands clenched so tightly together that the veins stood out like ropes behind his knuckles. "What can she possibly want with going to London?"

"Going to the devil, more like," Brogan bellowed. "I never thought I'd see the day when a daughter of mine sank into a den of sin—"

"For pity's sake, Brogan, calm yourself or you'll be having a seizure," Alice snapped at him, seeing the beads of sweat on his forehead. "And have a bit of trust in your daughter, can't you? Our Kate was brought up to be a sensible girl, and she'd not have had her head turned by some scheming person."

"Oh no? What about the Radcliffe scum, then? She didn't have such scruples about having her head turned by him, did she, woman?"

"Look, we're getting nowhere by standing here and shouting at one another," Donal said. "We've got to think what to do about this. And Mother's right. If Kate says the person was respectable, then I'm sure that she was."

"So what do you plan to do about it, my clever young feller?"

122

Brogan said sarcastically. "Go chasing up to London to bring her back?"

"If I have to. She's not twenty-one yet, remember."

"Of course I remember, you young bugger."

Brogan was roaring again, blustering as usual when somebody had an idea he should have thought of himself. "And how do you suppose we do that? London ain't exactly a village, by all accounts. She could be anywhere."

"Give me time to think, can't you?" Donal retorted. He snapped his fingers. "First we'll go to the priest."

"Oh aye, and what's he going to do, dumb-bell? Say a few Hail Marys and have her miraculously restored to us?" Brogan sneered, his erratic faith rapidly disappearing.

"No," Donal snapped. "But I'm sure he'll let us use his telephone to find the number of that hotel where she stayed in Bournemouth. And then we'll ask the people there for the name and address of the person who befriended our Kate."

Alice let out the breath she seemed to have been holding for hours. While Brogan panicked, Donal could be relied on to find the solution to everything. She gripped his arm.

"That's good, Donal. You two go off and do what you can, and I'll – I'll –" she finished lamely, never having felt so helpless and disorientated before.

"And you'll prepare some food, woman, for there's no sense in all of us starving on account of the girl's thoughtless behaviour," Brogan growled.

"Dada's right," Donal said. "Keep yourself busy, Mother, and we'll be back with news as fast as we can. And try not to worry," he added, knowing it was a useless piece of advice.

They struck out across the fields towards the priest's house, each of them reluctant to bother the man with their private problems, but knowing there was no other solution to finding out quickly where Kate had gone. And the sooner they got her back, the better.

"So what do you propose we do with the information when we have it?" Brogan snarled, when the silence had lengthened between them.

"We go to London and demand that she comes home, of course. The woman can't keep her there if you threaten her with getting the law on her for abduction."'

Brogan eyed him uneasily. "It was hardly that, if she went of her own free will, was it?"

Donal scowled too, knowing he was skating on thin ice, but helpless to know what else to do. "We'll think about that when the time comes," he said. "Just as long as we make her see sense, and that her place is here with us."

Father Mulheeny admitted them with a sigh. The Sullivan men never came to his house unless there was trouble, and he thought he'd already dealt with that. Kate had had a bad experience, but she had to put it all behind her now, and be thankful that no real harm had come from her involvement with the Radcliffe man. Privately, he didn't quite know how he would have dealt with the situation if he'd gone ahead and married the pair of them. Nor how much guilt he himself would have borne for sanctifying the marriage of a bigamist in his church, however innocently. One of the crosses he had to bear was that he could be as vain as the next man in guarding his position in the community. And despite the pious front he put on for his flock, he had his own livelihood to consider. The consequences of how the marriage of a young village girl to a bigamous man might have affected him didn't bear thinking about.

"And to what do I owe the pleasure of this unexpected visit?" he greeted the Sullivan men, distantly polite.

Donal spoke at once. "We've come to ask if you have a book of telephone numbers, Father Mulheeny."

The priest stared at him. Whatever he had momentarily expected to hear, it had been nothing like this.

"Now why on earth would you want such a thing, Donal?"

"To find the number of the hotel in Bournemouth where our Kate stayed for the week," Brogan put in, unable to keep quiet any longer. "It seems she met a person from London there, and the woman's evidently turned her head, and now she's gone off to London herself and we mean to find her and bring her back."

The priest crossed himself quickly as the rush of words sank in to his brain. Sweet Mother of God, but this could mean any number of things, and remembering his own shameful aknowledgement of the sensual young woman Kate Sullivan had become, he spoke sharply, saying the first thing that came into his head.

"You're quite sure it was a woman, are you?"

Without really being aware of what he was doing, Brogan Sullivan lunged forward and grabbed the priest by the throat.

"Dada, for pity's sake, control yourself!" Donal shouted, wrestling to try and pull him off the older man as they both staggered back against the wall.

"Can't you see what the ould bugger's implying?" Brogan shrieked. "He's thinking our Kate's nothing but a whore."

Despite the fact that it was the way his own mind had worked, Brogan was having no truck with somebody outside the family putting such thoughts into words. Not even this sanctimonious old bugger. As he saw Father Mulheeny's eyes begin to bulge in his crimson face, he realised what he was saying and doing, and he let go of the priest's neck with a feeling of horror.

" 'Tis begging your forgiveness I am, Father," he croaked. "Sure and I don't know what came over me, and 'twas only fear for my lovely daughter that made me lose my senses for a moment. If I've committed a mortal sin against you and the Church for such a despicable attack on your holy person, I can only ask for your complete forgiveness, if you can find it in your heart to be so generous to a sinner—"

"Be quiet, man!" Father Mulheeny rubbed his sore throat

tenderly as the babbling tirade went on. Brogan Sullivan, humble, was as much of an embarrassment as Brogan Sullivan, ranting and raving in his cups.

"You'll know he meant nothing by it, Father," Donal said swiftly, glowering at his father. "'Tis anxiety for Kate's welfare that's turned his brain, which is why we've come to ask if you can help us with the telephone number we need."

But the thought had also been put in Donal's mind now, that the person who had befriended Kate hadn't been a woman. But that was something he didn't want to think about yet.

Father Mulheeny was still looking resentfully at the abject Brogan, and thinking that God had surely tested him with the likes of this one. Offering an eye for an eye wasn't really in his nature, and he would dearly have loved to throttle the man himself . . . he sent up a few silent Hail Marys for his own salvation from wicked thoughts, and forced himself to pat Brogan's arm.

"I'll overlook your lapse in the circumstances, Brogan, so let's hear no more about it. A visit to the church for confession might not come amiss, though," he added, remembering his priestly duty.

"Oh, I'll do that, Father," Brogan said, wishing the old fool would get on with what they'd come here for.

"The telephone number, Father," Donal prompted. "We have the name of the hotel."

"I'll have to call the operator to ask for it," he said importantly. He was one of the few people in the vicinity to have a telephone and preened himself on it.

"And then Donal will be able to speak to them?"

Father Mulheeny looked at him coldly. "Of course. But perhaps it would be best if I were to do the speaking for you, since my position will add some weight to the enquiry. Give me all the details, please."

It wasn't strictly church business, but he supposed that since

Kate Sullivan was one of his flock, it could be construed as such. And the men agreed thankfully.

Once he had been given the name of the Charlton Hotel, he told them to sit down while he spoke to the operator and was put through to the hotel. They fidgeted, not looking at one another, each more troubled than they cared to admit by this new idea the priest had put in their minds.

"Hello, yes. Is that the Charlton Hotel?" they heard him say loudly a short while later. "My name is Father Mulheeny, and I'm enquiring about a guest who was staying there recently. Her name is Miss Kate Sullivan."

After a wait he frowned and gave a heavy sigh as he glanced at the silent Sullivan men.

"Then did you have a Mrs Kate Radcliffe staying there?"

Donal clenched his hands as he heard the name, but when he saw the priest nod at them, he swallowed his fury and listened intently to the one-sided coversation.

"I'm anxious about the young woman's welfare," the priest went on smoothly. "I understand she became friendly with someone while she was there, and it's very important that I contact this person. Can you help, please?"

There was a pause, then the priest spoke more sharply.

"I assure you, young man, that as a priest I understand all about confidentiality, but this young woman could be in danger, and I would prefer not to inform the constables that you have withheld information."

Donal knew he could never have handled things so coolly, and that Brogan would have bellowed into the telephone and got nowhere – or simply frozen with fear at having to speak into the instrument.

"I see. Thank you. You have been very helpful," Father Mulheeny said a little while later, after scribbling down the information he was given on a writing pad. "I'm sure the matter can be easily cleared up now. Goodbye."

He put the telephone back on its receiver and looked at the

two men carefully. He kept his distance from Brogan, not relishing another attack with what he had to report to them.

"Well?" Brogan snapped. "What did they tell you, man?"

Father Mulheeny reverted to his best saintly manner. "It seems that Kate spent much of her week's holiday in the company of a gentleman by the name of Luke Halliday—"

"*What!*" Brogan roared, until Donal restrained him.

"If you want to know what happened, be quiet and listen, Dada," he snapped.

"I'm told that Mr Halliday is a much-respected guest at the Charlton Hotel," the priest went on. "He is a photographer by profession, and he lives in London. He and Kate spent much of their time together, so if you're convinced that London is where she's gone, it would seem likely that this is the person she has gone to see."

He was painfully tactful, though he privately thought it highly unlikely that Kate's flight to London to be with this man could be an innocent one. It was a thought that was clearly echoed in the faces of the two men sitting so tensely on his sofa now.

"Give us the address, man," Brogan snarled again.

Father Mulheeny did so with a heavy heart.

As he watched them leave and go marching back across the fields to report to Alice, he knew that if Kate had been his daughter, he would have felt exactly as these two were doing now, and raised heaven and earth to get her back home where she belonged.

"I don't believe it!" Alice, normally so unemotional, was almost beside herself at the news. "Our Kate's not a bad girl, and she would never go chasing after a man she hardly knew!"

"By all accounts she got to know him pretty well while she was in Bournemouth," Donal said grimly.

He still couldn't rid himself of the thought that if he hadn't brought Radcliffe here and opened his sister's eyes to the romantic world the bastard had evidently shown her, then she wouldn't have sought so desperately to prove to herself that she was still attractive, and perhaps found solace in the arms of this other man. Donal cursed his wild imagination which took him off into realms where he never wanted to be.

"What are you going to do about it?" Alice said, white-faced. "You'll not bring the police into it and shame us all, will you?"

"No, we won't do that, woman. It would shame our Kate as well, and until we see what's what, we'll give her the benefit of the doubt," Donal said, ignoring the way his mother flinched at the implications. "We'll go to London to find this man and see what he wants with our Kate."

"Both of you?"

"Aye, both of us," Brogan growled. "Now, for God's sake, let's have some food. All this arguing has given me a pain in me belly fit to rot me guts. And then we'd best check on the pot money to make sure there's enough for the train fares and a night or two's lodging. And you make sure there's some clean underwear for us, missus."

They all knew that the grumbling and gabbling was his way of covering an emotional situation none of them wanted to think about too deeply, but which was the only thing on all of their minds.

Maura and Aileen were canny enough to know that something was wrong. But it had been decided they would simply be told that Kate had gone away to stay with some distant relatives for a while, and that the men were going to see that all was well, but they left the telling to Alice. Neither Brogan nor Donal had the stomach for it, nor for the wailing they knew would come from the girls.

Donal paid a second visit to the priest late that afternoon, and got him to telephone for the times of the trains to London at the end of the week. A few days' solid casual work was needed to put sufficient money in their pockets for their needs, and Father Mulheeny grudgingly agreed to take them to Temple Meads for the morning train on Friday.

"You'd best go and see that Vi Parsons that Kate works with, to tell her Kate won't be coming in for the week," Brogan told his son. He was becoming more resentful by the minute at the situation she'd left behind for them to sort out, easily overlooking the fact that Donal was doing most of it and refusing absolutely to think there would be any problem in bringing Kate home.

"And will I tell Vi where she's gone?"

"No. Give her the same story, that she's gone to stay with relatives for the time being. The less folk who know our business, the better."

"They'll not keep her job open for her indefinitely."

"It don't sound as though she wants it, does it? Nor any of us no more," he added bitterly. "I always thought that by going to Bournemouth alone she was getting above herself, and this is the outcome."

"Just be thankful she didn't go with Walter Radcliffe," Donal retorted. "I'll go and see this Vi woman tomorrow. I've had enough for one day."

On Sunday morning Vi opened her cottage door and was surprised to see Donal Sullivan standing there. Kate's tall brother was quite a catch as far as looks and brawn went, and if Vi didn't already have a man of her own ... Thankfully, her Bert was out trapping rabbits, so she asked Donal into her untidy parlour and wished she'd thought about cleaning up.

But it was too late for that now. She cleared a space on a chair by booting a squealing cat out of the way, so he could sit down. He remained standing anyway, his arms folded uncomfortably, as he tried not to breathe in the stale smell of last night's supper.

"Is summat up with Kate?" she said at once, knowing there couldn't be any other reason that brought him here.

"Nothing's up with her, but she won't be coming to work on Monday," he said abruptly.

"It's that bastard, Jenkins, ain't it?" Vi said without thinking. "I knew he'd had a go at her. His sort always goes for the shaky ones."

"What do you mean?" Donal said sharply.

Vi kept her eyes guarded. It was a sure bet that none of Kate's family knew about Kate being put in the pudding club by her fancy travelling man, nor that she'd lost the baby. Only Vi knew that. Common she might be, but women's secrets weren't for the telling. Though she could tell a thing or two about oily Jenkins if she had the mind to do so, but she decided to play it cautiously. After all, she needed the work, and the bastard knew better than to try anything on with her.

"Well, we all know Kate's nerves were on edge and – this is only guesswork, mind you – but old Jenkins was probably offering her extra evening work and a bit of comfort besides, if you get my meaning. But Kate would never have agreed to any of his smutty nonsense, so good luck to her for keeping away from his wandering hands for a while."

"She's keeping out of his way for good," Donal snapped. "You can tell him she won't be coming back to Granby's, ever."

Vi's eyes widened, but before she could ask anything more, Donal had turned on his heel, wrenching open the door of the cottage and breathing fresh air again as he strode back across the fields.

It got worse, he thought savagely. Just when you thought you knew all there was to know, something else cropped up. Being harrassed by that bastard of a supervisor at the sweatshop was probably just enough to tip Kate over the edge.

He was tempted to go and find him and tear him limb from limb, but much good that would do. He'd end up in the cells for a couple of nights, and he needed his wits about him for the journey to London. He'd had the dubious experience of travelling in France during the war to sharpen his knowledge of wider horizons than a small Somerset village, but he knew his father would be getting more apprehensive by the minute.

London was as far out of Brogan Sullivan's environment as the moon, and when he was nervy he hid it with aggression. It didn't bode well for the confrontation with Kate and this Halliday chap. Donal prayed that he could quieten his father down a little before all hell broke loose.

"What do you say to coming to the studio for a few days next week and letting me take some preliminary shots?" Luke asked, far more casually than he felt. His fingers were just itching to click the shutter on his camera and capture that lovely smile for all eternity.

They had finished eating Mrs Wood's gargantuan Sunday meal and were recovering in the sitting room with cups of steaming tea. Mrs Wood was doing the washing-up, refusing to let anyone enter her kitchen while she did so. Doris and Faye had gone man-hunting as usual, and Thomas Lord Tannersley was sleeping it off upstairs. Even from here, they could hear him snoring, loud enough to waken the dead.

"I can't," Kate said flatly.

"Why can't you? What's stopping you?"

"The need to find work is stopping me," Kate said. "I haven't come to London to be a sponger, Luke, and I'm already embarrassed that you've settled my account with Mrs Wood for a month. I want to pay you back as soon as I can."

He put his fingers over her mouth for a moment.

"It doesn't embarrass me in the least, and believe me, it's a drop in the ocean."

"Well, it's not to me," she said crossly, pushing his hand away. "And I don't intend to be beholden to anyone, thank you very much."

132

"What an old-fashioned sweetheart you are," Luke said. "I can't imagine Doris or Faye turning down the chance of free lodgings for a month."

"Well, I'm not Doris or Faye, am I!"

She wasn't smart or glamorous, and she didn't know city ways, but she knew enough not to let a man take advantage of her – not for a second time, anyway.

"The jobs won't disappear in the next couple of days, Kate. But you should give yourself a little time to get acclimatised to London first, and I really would like you to sit for me. I'm offering you a job, if you'll only see it and, of course, I'll pay you."

As she opened her mouth to speak again, he went on, "Or we can just take your fee from what you owe me for the rent here. We'll draw up a proper contract, and I'll pay you the going rate for a week's work. You can even offer my booked clients a cup of tea if it eases your irritating conscience, and be my temporary assistant for the week. How does that sound?"

"Is there a going rate?" Kate asked, oblivious to anything else he said.

"Of course," he said, inventing figures in his head.

"All right. I'll do it." Kate felt her heart beat faster, and thought she must truly be a country hick to feel that this job was so daring. Sometimes she wondered why he bothered about her at all, when he could have his pick of so many glamorous and sophisticated women.

Luke suggested she brought a selection of garments with her to the studio, especially the stunningly shimmery frock he had first seen her in. He couldn't forget his first sight of her when she had entered the dining room of the Charlton Hotel like a beautiful, golden vision. She had looked so anxious, as if she was ready to take flight if anyone so much as looked at her. Luke Halliday had looked and fallen in love. He no longer bothered to deny it to himself. He was simply mad about the girl. Whatever had become of the errant Radcliffe husband, he was the loser.

Kate was still uneasy. "You know I'm new to this, Luke, and I'll be stiff and awkward."

"No, you won't, because you'll be with me, and I'll lead you all the way," Luke said with admirable restraint, when what he really longed to do was to pull her into his arms and hold her close and chase all the fears away.

Dear God, he was getting far too sentimental for his own good, he thought in alarm.

"And you won't want me to do any sort of –" she paused, unable to say the words

"Nude posing?" Luke said brutally. "Is that what you're afraid of, Kate?"

She flinched. "I don't know. I've heard of such things. Vi – the woman I used to work with – said her husband had a magazine with some very – well – rude – poses in them. I couldn't do anything like that, Luke."

"I could say that you're insulting me for thinking I'd suggest such a thing, but I can see you're really disturbed about it, so let me assure you that nothing of the kind has ever occurred in my studio, nor ever will. Satisfied?"

She looked into his honest eyes and was ashamed of her suspicions. She nodded.

Luke thought that there was nothing he would like more than to hold her naked body, not for the camera's benefit, but for himself, for the need to possess her for ever. He smothered his healthy male urges and held her gently, pressing his lips to her cheek in a chaste kiss.

Chapter Nine

Luke was prepared to take things slowly. He had a number of clients booked for sittings in the middle of the week, but Monday was free and the end of the week was also clear. What he wanted was to get Kate immersed in the ambience of the studio, be introduced to the clients and help him put them at their ease, and then to share in the excitement of seeing the finished photographs come to life in the darkroom.

More than anything, he wanted Kate to be a part of his life, and to forget all about this idea of working in a sweatshop. He still wasn't convinced that it was her real background. In many ways she remained his mystery woman, and while the thought was an intriguing one, his greatest desire was to solve the mystery, and chase away the occasional clouded look that shadowed her lovely eyes.

"You're staring at me," Kate murmured on Monday morning.

He had collected her from Jubilee Terrace and driven her to the studio. Now she was seated on the pale green sofa surrounded by photographic equipment. She felt frankly terrified of looking into the soulless eye of the camera.

"I'm trying to decide how to sit you," he said, putting on his professional voice.

"I thought I was already sitting," Kate said pertly, to cover the fact that she didn't know what to do with her hands.

To tell the truth, she felt pretty daft to be what Vi would call tarted up on a Monday morning, even though she wasn't wearing her best frock yet, since Luke wisely suggested she kept that for the end of the week when she was more used to posing. He had every intention of making those the most spectacular photographs.

"Kate, relax," he said softly. "Lean back against the sofa, drop your shoulders and let your hands rest together on your lap. Doesn't that feel better already?"

She had to admit that it did, and whatever confidence she had, came from knowing that she looked good. The frock she wore was a pale beige colour, low-waisted and loosely pleated over her bust. It wasn't her favourite, but it was one that she felt comfortable in. She wore several long strings of amber beads and a plain bangle on her arm, since she didn't want to look too ostentatious.

Last night she had washed her hair and it hung straight and gleaming under the lights. She had applied the merest touch of carmine to her lips, and her cheeks were flushed enough with nerves not to need any artificial help.

Kate could see how important all this was to Luke. He wasn't doing this entirely just out of the goodness of his heart. He saw her now, not as a person, but as an aid to his professional abilities, and she wouldn't let him down. Her chin lifted and, as it did so, the fall of her golden hair caressed her shoulders. Without being aware of the subtle change in her attitude, she visibly relaxed, and her eyes become warm and lustrous instead of being strained and anxious.

"That's perfect," Luke said softly. "Hold that thought, sweetheart, whatever it is."

Her mouth parted in a small smile, and she blinked as the flashbulb went off. For a few moments all she could see were bright circles of light wherever she looked.

But as long as she forgot the glassy eye of the camera and thought of something pleasant as Luke suggested, it wasn't so bad. Luke instructed her to look slightly above or at the side of the lens occasionally and then the flash wasn't directly in her eyes.

It wasn't always easy to stay relaxed, though. Luke knew what he wanted from her, and as he took photograph after photograph, sometimes tension got the better of her, then she felt the irritating little nervous twitch at the corner of her mouth. But finally he decided they had done enough for one day, and Kate's relief was mingled with a growing excitement knowing she was about to see herself portrayed in celluloid for the very first time.

Some hours later she stared silently down at the woman in the photographs. A softly beautiful woman who looked sometimes remote, sometimes sensual and provocative, especially when those brilliant eyes looked directly into the camera. She had seen herself in a mirror many times in her life, but this was the first time she was seeing herself as others must see her, and it was an embarrassment as well as stirring an undeniable feeling of pleasure inside her.

"I don't really look like this, do I?" she asked.

"Of course you do. The camera never lies," said Luke.

"But I'm so – so—"

"Beautiful?" he finished for her.

Kate felt herself flush. "I would never say that about myself! It's far too vain!"

"Then let me say it for you. You're very beautiful, Miss Sullivan."

She drew in her breath, for there was no disguising the look in his eyes now. It was a look she had seen before, in Walter Radcliffe's eyes. It had scared her then as much as it did now, or perhaps even more, having once responded to it with all the warm sexuality she hadn't even known was in her nature.

"Kate, whatever life did to you in the past, we all have to go on," she heard Luke say quietly now. "Don't waste your future by looking back on what can't be changed."

"You're right," she said in a muffled voice. And oh, it

was so tempting at that moment to tell him everything, but he was too decent a man to hear the sordid details of her encounter with Walter Radcliffe, and she couldn't bear to see the derision in his eyes. Besides which, there were some things she could never tell anyone. So the moment passed.

Since Kate was now officially hired by Luke for the week, she alternated in sitting for him, and having her first taste of acting as his receptionist for the elegant clients or the homely family groups who came to the studio. She preferred the latter, but people were all the same beneath the trappings, as she remembered Luke once telling her.

She was amazed to find how easily it all came to her and she was able to carry off this new role with admirable efficiency. There was no doubt that the clients, especially the more nervous and less wealthy ones, were reassured by her soft Somerset accent and manner.

"Kate, you're the best asset ever to have come my way," Luke declared on Thursday afternoon when the last clients of the week had gone. "My last receptionist was a bit of a dragon, and she frightened half the clients away before they even stepped into the studio. But you have the opposite effect, and I'd be a fool to lose you."

"So what are you saying?" she asked, not too sure.

"I'm offering you the job, my sweet girl, and whatever aspirations you had in other directions, I'd be honoured and happy if you would accept."

Kate gulped. "You mean you want me to always work here, giving customers cups of tea and chatting to them, and then I'd be able to watch the pictures coming to life in the darkroom – and all that?"

"And all that," Luke said with a smile. "So what do you say? Your photographs in the showroom window would attract plenty of takers, and when they came in with their enquiries and saw this vision of loveliness inside, actually in the flesh, so to speak, we'd be well set up."

"For pity's sake, Luke, stop it!" Kate said, scarlet-faced. "You're embarrassing me now."

But she could also see that for all his flattery, he was being very much the astute businessman and that he considered she was going to do his business nothing but good. It reassured her, yet in a funny way it disappointed her too. She quickly turned her thoughts away from that, as he seized hold of her hands.

"So do we have a deal, babe?" he said, speaking in the pseudo-American twang he'd picked up from his army days, which always made her laugh.

"I'll have to think about it," she said slowly.

But although she hedged, her spirits were lifting by the second. He was setting her free in more ways than one. She wouldn't have to work in another sweatshop under the gimlet eyes of some other supervisor in Jenkins' mould. Skilled as she was with her needle, she could buy her own fabrics and sew her own garments to her heart's content and in her own time. It was a heady feeling, and she owed it all to Luke, and the look of pleasure and gratitude she gave him then was enough to make his heart turn over.

"Come on, we've had enough for one day," he said briskly. "It's time I took you home."

Her spirits lifted even more. Home was Jubilee Terrace now, and she was beginning to feel like a real city girl at last. As yet she hadn't written to her family, but now that she was settled in a home and a job, she felt she could hold her head high as she did so.

Something else had been simmering in her mind for the last day or so. To be a real city girl, she really should have her hair cut, even though the thought of it made her quail a little. But Doris and Faye's smart city bobs were so sophisticated, and as she wanted to be like them, just a little, Kate yearned to have the same look. She mentioned it in the car on the way back to Mrs Wood's.

"I can understand it," Luke said. "Though if ever a woman's hair was her crowning glory, yours is, Kate. Don't be too hasty in having it cropped. But why not compromise and pin it up for some shots tomorrow, and see how you like it?"

"That's a wonderful idea," she said, glowing. And Luke wished he could always make her glow like that, and not just for having had a sensible idea.

On Friday Kate carefully arranged folds of tissue paper over the lovely chiffon frock with the chic handkerchief points at the hem, then placed it in a carrying bag. She adored its shimmering hues of cream and gold, and she planned to wear it exactly as she had done on that first night in Bournemouth, with a gold bangle on her arm, and a wisp of chiffon tucked inside it.

Her heartbeats quickened, realising that she no longer thought about the special reason for making that frock, but only that it had made her special in Luke Halliday's eyes. It had turned out not to be a honeymoon frock, but one that marked a turning point in her life, if only because it had given her the confidence she had so badly needed at that time. But she knew she was only fooling herself in thinking that was the only reason she loved it.

She had spent the morning absorbing the atmosphere in the busy local streets and enjoying the freedom, while Luke had been developing and printing some of the week's work at the studio. As she slid inside his Bentley that afternoon, she wondered where all the honesty that she had valued so much in her life, had really gone. She gave an involuntary shiver, and Luke glanced at her.

"Let me guess. You're having second thoughts about having your hair cropped in a new style. It's not compulsory, Kate, and in many ways it would be a crying shame to cut off that

140

lovely hair. Have you practised pinning it up to see the effect as I suggested?"

She stared at him blankly, her thoughts a million miles away from his at that moment. Then she shook her head.

"I'll pin it up when the time comes. But I'd like to see a picture or two with it both ways, if that makes any sense," she finished.

"I'll take as many shots as you like," he said with a smile. "Don't you know by now that you're my favourite model?"

The word sounded glamorous and slightly risqué, but she had complete faith in his professionalism. She was more relaxed in the poses he suggested for her, none of which could be construed as in the least suggestive.

"Put one hand behind your head, holding your hair away from your neck, Kate," he instructed a while later. She did as she was bid, while he looked approvingly at the swan-like sweep of her throat that the gesture revealed.

He took several shots, and was re-adjusting his camera filters when they heard the persistent ring of the showroom doorbell. Luke uttered a small curse at being interrupted, but before Kate could move, he told her to hold the pose while he told the callers he was closed for the afternoon.

Kate shut her eyes, leaning back against the softness of the sofa for a moment, her hand still holding up her hair provocatively. For this particular pose, she was half-reclining on the sofa, and there was soft music playing in the background on the phonograph. If Luke took any time at all in turning away the callers, she thought she could quite easily have fallen asleep.

The next second she was suddenly, blisteringly awake, as the familiar sound of her father's voice came roaring into the peaceful atmosphere of the studio. Her heart raced, but before she could move a muscle, Brogan had come storming through the bead curtains, followed by Donal, both of them glowering down at her, puce in the face.

"So this is what you've come to, is it, my girl?" her father bellowed. "Showing yourself off half-dressed for all and sundry to ogle you. As if it wasn't enough to let yourself be taken in by that bastard Radcliffe—"

"Dada, *please*," Kate said faintly, seeing the shock and fury on Luke's face. He tried to remonstrate with her father, but was rudely brushed aside in a loutish manner. In seconds, Kate was utterly humiliated, all her fragile confidence gone.

Whatever must Luke think of her and her family now? Displaying such boorish behaviour in this select part of town, with the two men looking so countrified and out of place in the city, in their ill-fitting clothes and boots. Kate was ashamed of herself for thinking that way, yet half of her shame was in their defence, knowing that their actions stemmed from misplaced love.

"Get yourself dressed decently, girl," Brogan continued to roar. "You're coming home with us this minute."

"Do as he says, Kate," Donal snapped. "We've not come all this way for nothing."

Kate felt her hackles rise. Luke stood silently by with his arms folded tightly across his chest. She could see that he was seething, and she knew from the whiteness of his clenched hands that he'd dearly like to punch the pair of them. And so would she. Her temper flared.

"That's exactly what you have done, then," she snapped back. "I'm not coming back with you, not today and maybe not ever. I've made my choice and I'm staying here."

"You young whippersnapper," her father yelled. "Do you dare to defy me? Do you know what heartache you've caused your mother this past week? Get off that sofa and get yourself properly dressed, and do it now!"

Kate stood up swiftly, as tense as a spring. Whatever coolness she still possessed, simply vanished.

"Don't try to blackmail me with worrying about my mother, Dada! She's a woman, and she'll understand my need to get away better than you ever will," she screamed. "Don't you dare talk to *me* about heartache! You should know how much of that I suffered when I discovered Walter already had a wife when he'd promised to marry me!"

The minute she had spoken, she clapped her hands over her mouth, and almost at once felt the sting of tears. She had ruined everything now. Luke would be aware of all her shame and the reason she had been at the Charlton Hotel, posing as a widow or however the genteel clientele there had seen her. And here she was, shouting like a fishwife at these two oafs who couldn't help meddling in her business.

She felt someone's arms around her, and she knew it wasn't either of her menfolk. Dear Lord, but this would only be making things worse, she thought frantically, as she felt herself pressed against Luke's comforting chest. Now they would surely believe she had come here to be this man's lover.

"I think it's time we all sat down and talked things over calmly," Luke said, his educated voice taking command, and momentarily stopping the Sullivan men in their tracks.

"We ain't come all this way to sit and talk over the teacups." Brogan growled.

"I wasn't actually offering tea, although if my receptionist and assistant would care to make us all some, I'm sure it would be very welcome," Luke went on pointedly.

Kate nodded, moving out of his arms to go silently towards the tiny kitchen at the rear of the studio. She couldn't bear to look at Luke as she went, but she was aware of the astonished faces of her father and brother, and knew they could never have expected to hear their Kate referred to in such terms.

She put the kettle on the gas with shaking hands and prepared the tray, praying that her father wouldn't be tempted to stick out his little finger alongside the narrow porcelain teacup handle, or even worse, to slurp from the saucer.

She realised with a small shock that in so short a time she

had moved on and moved away from them. It was sad and yet inevitable after Walter's betrayal.

When the kettle boiled, she poured the water into the teapot with her hands still shaking, spilling it over her fingers and hardly noticing it. She could hear the raised voices from the studio more clearly now.

"The girl's been brought up to be respectable," Brogan was shouting. "I'll not have a daughter of mine wandering the streets of London and doing God knows what—"

"She's hardly wandering the streets, man," Luke snapped. "She has respectable lodgings with an old friend of my family, and a job here for as long as she wants it. If you doubt my credentials, I'll introduce you to Mrs Wood at Jubilee Terrace, which is where Kate lodges, or I can get a reference for you from the Charlton Hotel in Bournemouth, or from one of my titled clients, if you wish."

There was no doubting the sarcasm in his voice now, and there was a brief silence from the Sullivans as this information sunk in. As if a man of Luke Halliday's stature would need references for the likes of these two . . . but at the inference, Kate's fierce family loyalty surged to the surface. She pushed through the bead curtain with the tea tray. They looked at her in some relief as she put the tray on a side table, not knowing how to deal with this situation.

"Can you all please stop arguing for the moment and drink your tea?" Kate said in a high-pitched voice. She looked directly at Luke. "I'll change my clothes and then perhaps we can all go back to Mrs Wood's. I'd like Dada – my father – and Donal to meet her."

She glared at Brogan now, and for once he seemed uneasily subdued as this newly confident young woman poured out three cups of tea and handed them to the men. Then she swept out of the studio to the elegant changing room kept especially for Luke's clientele. She avoided looking at herself in the mirror after the first glimpse of her white face and tortured eyes. Five minutes later, wearing her day frock, she folded the shimmering chiffon and put it away.

Mrs Wood was spending the afternoon baking. Her hands were immersed in flour up to the elbows as she joyously pummelled the dough. All her lodgers had their own keys, so she didn't bother to look up as she heard the front door open and shut. But then the kitchen door opened, and Kate Sullivan's pale face peered around it.

"Mercy me, but you gave me a fright, my duck. I thought you'd be gone for the rest of the day."

She registered the pallor of Kate's face properly and paused in her pummelling. "Has my Lukey been working you too hard already?"

"Mrs Wood, my father and brother are here to meet you," Kate said in a strangled voice. "Luke's here too, and if you could come into the sitting room for a minute or two—"

Normally, Mrs Wood would have told her the visitors could wait but the baking couldn't, but this was different. This looked serious. She nodded and wiped her floury hands and arms on a cloth before joining the foursome in the sitting room. And what a motley foursome they were, she thought.

There was Luke, decidedly grimmer than usual; Kate looking as if she was about to burst into tears at any minute; and two rough-looking men, as out of place as a plate of jellied eels at the Lord Mayor's banquet.

"So these are your folks, are they, Kate?" said Mrs Wood, as nobody seemed inclined to speak first. "It's nice to meet you both, I'm sure."

Brogan growled beneath his breath, while Donal muttered a short greeting, and Kate could see that they had never expected something like this. The atmosphere was so homely, with the warm smells of baking tantalising their nostrils, and Mrs Wood like anybody's mother. If they had half expected Kate to be living in a den of vice, this certainly wasn't it.

Luke's mouth curved into a semblance of a smile, seeing their discomfiture. He spoke boldly now.

"Kate's folks were afraid she'd got herself into bad company in London, so we're just assuring them that she hasn't, and that she's very comfortable here."

Mrs Wood laughed in astonishment. "Well, for pity's sake, I should think she is. I pride myself on my establishment, and I don't allow no ruffians here. Then, of course, I've got my Lukey's patronage, which counts for a lot – almost as good as royalty."

"Don't overdo it, my old dear," he said cheekily. "But I'm sure you'd allow Kate to show her folks her room."

It would give him time to talk with Mrs Wood, and try to come to terms with the revelations he'd heard all too briefly. Kate would have to tell him about the bigamist now – if she could bear to. His heart ached with love for her, imagining what she had gone through, but this wasn't the time for speculation, and he saw her turn to the other men.

"Come upstairs with me, Dada and Donal."

She almost fled out of the sitting room, glad for the first time to be away from Luke's curious eyes. She could no longer hide the fact of her jilting from him now. She would have to tell him, and the shame would come surging back again, just when she thought she had been dealing with it reasonably well.

She led the way upstairs, and stood silently while the men slowly looked around the room.

"Well? Does it pass?" she said stiffly. "Whatever you may have thought, I haven't gone to the devil, Dada, and if it hadn't been for Luke I doubt that I would survived as well as I have. Mrs Wood's been like a mother hen to me ever since I've been here."

She was suddenly choked, thinking of the kindness she had received in London.

Donal spoke roughly, "You've got to understand how we felt, our Kate, finding a note like that and thinking the worst.

146

We didn't know what kind of person you'd got mixed up with, did we?"

"Well, now you do know. Luke's the kindest, most gentlemanly person in the world, and he's done nothing wrong," she said flatly. "And whatever you say, I intend to stay."

Brogan flared up at once. "Now, we'll have our say on that, Katherine!"

"No you won't. I'm going to stay in London and make a new life for myself."

It was the first time she'd ever really stood up to him and, although she was shaking inside, she stared him out. His face reddened angrily.

"You'll do as you're told, girl. You're still a child—"

"No she's not, Dada," Donal said slowly. "She's gone through more painful experiences than many young women her age, but she's been brought up to be sensible. If she's set on staying here, maybe we should let her, for a while, anyway."

Kate looked at him with grateful eyes. He had no idea of just how painful were the experiences Walter Radcliffe had inflicted on her. The traumatic memory of the miscarriage would never be forgotten.

She thanked God nobody knew about that but Vi, and she would never tell. If her family had known, and the whole story had come out now, she couldn't have borne the shame of seeing Luke's reaction.

"Just for a while, then." Brogan gave in, tired of all the fuss now. "But you'll write regularly to your mother, telling her of your doings, miss."

"I'll write to her tonight," Kate said, guiltily aware she had been remiss in not doing so before. "And you can take the letter home." She paused. "When are you going back?"

"Tomorrow morning, we don't plan on staying any longer," Donal said. "We'll find somewhere to sleep tonight."

"Mrs Wood can probably let you have a room for one night,"

Kate said. "And I know she'll give you a good breakfast to see you on your way."

It was persuasive enough, and although Kate wondered how they would take to Doris and Faye and Thomas Lord Tannersley, at least they would know she was in safe hands in Jubilee Terrace. And it would put off the moment when she would have to tell Luke everything – or nearly everything.

By the time Luke arrived in his Bentley to take the Sullivans to Paddington Station the next morning, they had become more comfortable in Jubilee Terrace. Doris and Faye were clearly taken with Donal's good looks and his country accent. And Brogan was relieved to see that for all their chic appearance they too were out-of-towners, as Mrs Wood called them, and unlikely to lead their girl into bad ways.

"You didn't have to offer to take them to the station. They would have taken a taxi-cab," Kate murmured when she was sitting beside him, and the men were silent in the back, overawed at the magnificence of the vehicle.

"I thought you'd like to see them off on the train," he said. "And if I wasn't there, you might even have got on it and I'd never see you again."

Would you even want to see me again, now that you know how many lies I've told? she asked him silently. But at least now you know I did work in a sweatshop. I didn't lie about that, and I'm not grand at all.

She was very nervous when the train finally steamed out of Paddington. In his pocket, her father had the carefully written letter she had penned to her mother, explaining everything in detail and telling her not to worry. And that if, and when, she became rich and famous, she'd be sending money home. She almost scratched that bit out, wondering if it was too flippant, but in the end she decided to leave it in.

"So now we'll go to the studio and you can tell me everything," she heard Luke say as they got back into the car, and drove out of the station approaches and into the Praed Steet traffic. "They say confession's good for the soul, and I suspect you've been keeping too many things to yourself for far too long, Katie. And I've got pretty broad shoulders."

"Don't," she said tightly.

"Don't what?" he said, glancing at her.

"Please don't be kind to me. I can't bear it."

"What do you want me to do, then? Tell you what a little fool you must have been to believe the lies that a rogue like this Radcliffe fellow turned out to be?"

"If you like."

"I don't like," Luke said shortly. "I remember the haunted look in your eyes when I first saw you in Bournemouth, which told me you loved him, no matter what he did. Am I right?"

Kate looked down at her hands lying loosely in her lap. Her ringless hands now, since she had discarded the shameful sight of a wedding ring she wasn't entitled to wear.

"I loved him once – or thought I did," she said carefully. "But this is hardly the place to discuss such things, is it?"

"All right, it can wait," Luke said. "But I think I'm entitled to know the truth now, Kate, don't you? I'd like to think I'm your friend, and friends confide in one another, don't they?"

She swallowed. He was the best friend she'd ever had, and she nodded mutely, turning away from him as if afraid that he could see the guilt and shame of her wanton relationship with Walter etched on her face.

They drove the rest of the way to Dundry Mews in silence, and Kate felt as if she had aged years since the last time she'd been there. She expected them to talk in the seclusion of the studio, but Luke led her up some stairs at the back of it into his living quarters, if such a term could be applied to such luxurious surroundings.

She hadn't been invited there before, and she was immediately tongue-tied at the quality of the elegant furniture and the deep-piled carpets in his spacious sitting room. There were

149

framed paintings on the walls, and on a side table there was a tray of glasses and decanters of spirits. As she sat down gingerly on the edge of a pale blue velvet chair, Luke poured them each a glass of brandy.

"For medicinal purposes," he said with a half-smile as he anticipated her protest.

"I'm not ill!"

"You're very tense, and that's almost as bad. Drink it, Kate, and then we'll talk," he ordered.

She did as she was told, feeling like a leaf in the wind, and wondered how on earth she was going to tell this honourable, decent man, anything at all about her association with a rat like Walter Radcliffe.

Chapter Ten

"So where do we begin?" Luke said quietly.

And where will it end? he asked himself silently. If she was still holding a torch for this Radcliffe fellow, he might as well kiss goodbye to any romantic notions he had about Kate Sullivan. The hell of it was, he knew it was much too late for that, she was already embedded too deeply in his heart.

She spread her hands helplessly, and Luke didn't miss the way they shook, or the pain in her lovely eyes. She must have *really* loved him, Luke thought savagely, knowing he was subconsciously turning the knife in his gut, but unable to stop it.

"Are you really my friend, Luke?" Kate asked, taking him by surprise with the quietly voiced question.

Without thinking, he knelt by the side of her chair, just managing to resist the temptation to draw her into his arms.

"Always," he said sincerely, and then more teasingly, "No matter what heinous crime you've committed, you can be sure I'll always stand by you, Kate."

She gave a faint smile. "Even if I turned out to be the biggest fool in creation for believing everything I heard?"

"Even so. But why wouldn't you believe what you were told? We all have to take people on trust. So I understand that Radcliffe promised you marriage when he was in no position to do so?" he prompted, since she seemed so reticent to put it into words.

"We were to be married on the day I went to Bournemouth,"

she said. Her lips were dry. She had to tell him about that dreadful morning, swiftly, before her nerve failed completely. "I was dressed in my mother's wedding gown, and my little sisters were rushing about in their bridesmaids' finery. And then Donal came tearing up to my room with a letter and, for a split second before he started raving about him, I thought it was going to be some sweet note from Walter."

"Go on," Luke said. He was already anticipating what the bastard had done, but the best therapy was for Kate to say it all, however painful. He'd seen enough of that kind of letter arriving at the Front to know the agony it caused. Some poor devils had gone cheerfully over the top rather than go back to an empty house and an empty life.

"It was a note all right," Kate said bitterly. "But there was nothing sweet about it. It was to tell me he already had a wife, so he couldn't go through with the marriage. If he did, he'd be risking a prison sentence."

"He did you a favour," Luke said brutally, hating to see this lovely girl so near to breaking point as she recalled the horror of that day.

"Don't you think I know that now?" Kate almost snapped. "But I couldn't see it at the time. All I could see was the shame and humiliation of it all. My mother was in a terrible state, and my father – well, you've seen my father! I hardly have to tell you what he was like. And Donal blamed himself for bringing Walter to the house in the first place."

"He was your brother's friend then?"

"They met in the army in France. Walter was – is – a Yorkshireman and a travelling salesman. He was in our part of the world on business, and he thought he'd look up his old army acquaintance, and that was how I met him."

"And being a travelling man with the gift of the gab, as they say, he swept you off your feet," Luke supplied as she gazed into space.

Kate's eyes were still heavy with pain, and she looked at him, thinking that if he only knew the half of it, he wouldn't be giving her such unspoken sympathy. If he ever dreamed how she'd let herself be seduced by that sweet-talking travelling man, and found herself pregnant, he'd be thoroughly disgusted with her. When he was photographing her in some special pose, he often referred to her angelic golden looks, but if he knew the truth, instead of thinking her such an angel, he'd think her a slut.

She shuddered, and this time Luke didn't attempt to resist his need to hold her close. And for Kate the temptation was just too great to resist leaning her head against him, feeling his warm sympathy flowing between them.

"It's over, Kate, and you have to forget it, or it will destroy you."

He said the words against the fragrant scent of her hair. It was as soft and sensuous as fine silk between his fingers, and it was more than he could do to resist stroking it. Despite knowing it would be a fatal mistake to rush her in any way, he felt a throb of desire in his loins that wouldn't be denied.

She had gone very still against him, and very slowly he moved his head back a fraction from hers to look into her eyes. Before he could stop himself, he was kissing her mouth and holding her tightly against him as if they shared the same skin. And for all that Kate had told herself she would never trust another man again, she ardently kissed him back, with all the wasted passion she had once spent on Walter. When she realised what she was doing, she struggled to be released from his embrace, but even though the kiss had ended, Luke still held her close.

"Kate, I won't apologise for that, because I've wanted to do it ever since we met. I can see now why you're so wary of people, but you mustn't let one bad experience colour the rest of your life. You know that, don't you?"

"Yes," she mumbled. "But I can't forget it so quickly, either. He did mean a lot to me, Luke. Otherwise, I'd never – well, I'd never have agreed to marry him, would I?"

She felt obliged to say it to justify everything, even though Walter had effectively killed any remaining love she had had for him. Perhaps it was just as well if Luke thought it meant she was still pining for him, it gave her time to adjust to this new life she was sharing with him.

"Kate, I want to show you something," he said, after a few moments of just holding her, while her rapid heartbeats begin to slow down a little.

She felt a frisson of alarm. After all, she was alone with a gentleman in his apartment, and she was in a highly vulnerable state. She knew Luke was worth twenty of Walter, but even now, she couldn't quite convince herself that all men weren't only after one thing. Luke saw her suspicious look and gave her a little shake.

"You'd better start trusting me, Kate. We're going to be spending a great deal of time together if you're going to continue working for me."

"You meant what you said to my father then? About me having a job here as long as I wanted it?" she said.

"Of course I meant it. I told you once I always mean what I say. Do you want the job or do I have to advertise for another dragon?"

She gave a small smile for the first time that day, and her facial muscles had a hard time accepting the new conditions because she had been holding them in check for so long.

"If you want me, I'm happy to accept," she said.

"I do want you," Luke said.

"So what do you have to show me?" she asked, because for all his lack of expression she knew very well he wasn't only referring to the job he offered her. He was offering her himself. She pushed away the thought; she simply wasn't ready for that yet, if ever. She didn't want any romantic entanglements. Besides, she still wasn't sure whether or not she was frigid after

what Walter had put her through, and there was only one way
to find out. The thought of Luke discovering that she wasn't
as virginal as he obviously believed was enough to make her
take fright at once.

"Come into the next room," he said now, "and you don't
have to worry, Kate, it's not my bedroom."

"I wasn't worried," she lied.

The went into a small boxroom. Pinned up around the walls
were dozens of Luke's pictures, some of them framed. Many of
the pictures were of family groups that had obviously turned
out especially well, and which he wanted to keep. And one of
the narrower walls was completely covered in pictures of Kate
Sullivan.

Her mouth dropped open as she saw the images of herself
taken during the week, including the ones from yesterday when
she was wearing the shimmery chiffon frock she adored, and
which always gave her such confidence. Until her men folk
had arrived, and spoiled it all.

Looking at the pictures, she thought faintly that Luke had
made her look as glamorous as an American movie star. All
the poses he had suggested, whether they were sweet or sensual,
were simply stunning, even to her own eyes.

"When could you possibly have done all this work?" she
gasped, the surprise of it all quickly removing all the unpleasant
reminders of Walter.

"Some of it was done during the week, but I spent most
of last night in the darkroom doing the rest. I wasn't feeling
much like sleeping, and in my experience the best way to stop
yourself from thinking too much is to keep your hands and
your brain occupied."

She didn't ask what had been keeping him awake. Instead,
she stared, wide-eyed, at the pictures he had produced. There
was no doubt, within her limited knowledge of photography,
that Luke was very accomplished indeed.

"So what do you think?" he asked.

155

"I think you're simply the best," she said sincerely.

"Why, thank you, ma'am," he said with a smile, but he was quite moved by her reaction. He'd expected her to express some pleasure in the way he'd captured her loveliness, but there was less vanity in her than he'd ever seen in a girl before, and yet this one had it all, the looks, the charm and the personality. From his observations, most girls would be admiring the images of themselves, rather than complimenting the photographer.

"But what on earth are you going to do with them all?" Kate said, starting to laugh. "You wasted a lot of film on me taking all these, Luke, but I'd like to have one or two of them to send home, if you wouldn't mind."

He burst out laughing at her artless words.

"Oh, Kate, you do me a power of good. No other girl in the world would be so damn modest as you. Can't you see what a stunner you are and that you're any photographer's dream?"

So was that all she was to him? She knew better now than to ask such leading questions, and the memory of that kiss a short while ago told her something very different.

"Well, all right, if you say so. But I still can't understand why you took so many. What are you going to do with them all?" she persisted.

"My idea is to get a portfolio together and take them to an agency that deals in magazine work," he said, at once the professional again. "If we're lucky we might get a commission. But then again, we might not, and it might all come to nothing, so don't count your chickens."

"I won't," she said. It wasn't at all important to her, anyway, but she could see that it was to Luke. And since he had helped her so much, she was quite willing to do all she could to further his ambitions.

"Anyway," he went on briskly, "now that we've sorted out your troubles, shall we go out and have a spot of lunch? Have you ever been to a Lyons Corner House?"

"I shouldn't think so, since I don't even know what it is!" she said pertly. "Is it respectable?"

He began to laugh again. "Oh Kate, you really are priceless sometimes."

"Is that good? And why are you laughing at me?"

"If I am, it's only because I think you're adorable," Luke said, with absolute truth. "Lyons Corner Houses are a national institution, and the waitresses in their uniforms are known as nippies—"

"Oh, so it's just another tearoom, is it?" she interrupted scornfully, quite used now to the street corner tearooms that seemed to be everywhere in London.

"You could say that," Luke said, the lights in his eyes dancing with good humour. He spoke with some relief, thankful that she was in good spirits again, after what had been a pretty traumatic twenty-four hours.

Long before the summer ended and the leaves in the London parks had begun to turn to red and gold, Kate's birthday had come and gone. There had been letters and cards from home, wishing her well, and she was glad her family had clearly accepted her new life. Especially since she had lived up to her promise and sent a little money now and then for their special treats.

She began to feel as if she had always been a part of Mrs Wood's bohemian establishment, and the special meal Mrs Wood had put on for her birthday had touched her immensely. Even more, she felt a real part of Luke Halliday's business world. Luke assured her she had a natural talent for the role of receptionist/assistant, and that she had exactly the right attitude for putting nervous clients at their ease.

She preened at his compliments. She was happier than she had ever been since the shock of discovering she was carrying Walter Radcliffe's baby. Perhaps she was happier than she had a right to be, she sometimes thought uneasily, for she believed that in this life there had to be a price to be paid for wrongdoing. And as yet she hadn't paid for the sin of fornication and its consequences.

"Why the sudden shadow on your face?" Luke asked her now as they relaxed with tea and cake in his apartment after a satisfactory session in the darkroom, where the splendidly posed photographs of a titled lady and gentleman had smiled out at them both.

Luke closed the studio on two afternoons during the week, and on Saturday mornings, which was when he devoted his time to producing his fine-quality pictures. Kate loved those times. It was just as Luke had said, watching the images come to life on the photographic paper was truly magical.

"I was just thinking how lucky I am," she said honestly. "Such a short time ago I thought my world had come to an end, and instead of which—"

"Yes?" he said softly as she paused.

"Instead of which, I have good friends and a new life, and if I've learned anything in the last few months, it's that nothing lasts for ever, not even the bad times."

"That's quite a lesson to have learned, Miss Sullivan," he said, more touched than he was willing to show. "But I always knew you were resilient – and if you need me to explain the word to you—"

"I don't," she said. "I know what it means. But how about you? Aren't you disappointed that none of the agencies you've approached seem interested in a country girl model for magazine pages?"

She spoke lightly, putting the onus on herself, for she knew how much store Luke had set by the magazine work. So far it had come to nothing, no matter how many agencies had seen his portfolio. She saw him shrug.

"I'm pretty resilient too," he said. "I've learned to wait for the things I want the most."

Kate avoided his eyes, although her heart began to beat

faster. Luke was her friend, and so far he had seemed content to remain that way. But she knew instinctively that he wanted to be more than that. Deep down she knew she wanted it too, but she was too afraid to let herself admit it except sometimes when she was half-asleep at night, when the memory of his kiss stirred her.

When he spoke again, it was in a brisker manner, very well aware that any hint at a deeper relationship made her uncomfortable.

"I wanted to say something special to you, Kate. I normally close the studio for a week during May and again in September. And you already know my favourite happy hunting-ground, don't you?"

She looked at him blankly for a moment, and then her face flooded with colour.

"You mean Bournemouth, I suppose," she said, her voice suddenly flat, her feelings about the place still very mixed.

"Didn't you ever hear the old proverb that facing your enemy is the best way of dealing with him?"

But her enemy was Walter Radcliffe, and what he had done to her could never be dealt with in the way Luke implied.

When she didn't answer, he went on, "Why don't we take another holiday down there, Kate? We could go out on the boat whenever we liked, and we'd enjoy ourselves from the outset, instead of fencing around one another for most of the week."

"I couldn't possibly do that!"

"Why not? You're over twenty-one now, remember. You don't have to answer to anyone any more."

Unconsciously, she fingered the delicate gold chain Luke had given her for her birthday. She had been almost too embarrassed to accept it, but she had also loved it far too much to refuse.

"How could I go back to the Charlton Hotel? The last time I was there I was registered as a married woman, in case you've forgotten."

She turned her face away from him, biting her lips, and wishing she didn't have to think of that awful day. Luke had to fight back the temptation to say she could register again as a married woman, if she would only say the word.

"We don't have to stay at the Charlton. There are other hotels," he said coolly. "You will be my cousin, recovering from a recent bout of influenza, and needing the sea air."

The irony of inventing more lies wasn't lost on Kate, but the sense of freedom he was offering her was becoming very tempting.

"Are you really serious?" she said at last.

"Of course I am. Don't you know that I—"

"Always mean what you say," she finished for him.

"Well then?"

"Well then, all right!" she said, suddenly reckless. "I'll be your cousin for a week, providing we don't have to face the same people in the Charlton Hotel."

It was a shame, though, because her memories of that hotel were certainly not all bad. Those of the latter part of that week were more than pleasurable – floating in Luke's arms on the dance floor and getting slightly tipsy and having to be taken to her room, were just a few of them. There were others . . . the warm caress of his hand on her breast, and the sweetness of his kiss on her softly parted mouth. She veered her thoughts away, knowing that she could be heading for a dangerous situation if she went away with him. What would her parents say if they knew? And Donal? And what would Mrs Wood think? All her sudden enthusiasm fizzled out.

"Luke, I can't go," she said.

"Good Lord, surely you haven't changed your mind already. Even for a woman, it must be a record. Why can't you go?"

"Because – well, *because*, that's all!"

"Would you feel happier if I said you were my fiancée? Strictly for the benefit of the hotel staff and the other guests, of course. There's nothing wrong with an engaged couple sharing a week at a respectable hotel, Kate, in separate rooms, naturally. All sorts of people were thrown together during the war, and it made people see that it could be perfectly respectable. And the upper classes have never seen anything wrong in having houseparties for both sexes."

Kate ran her tongue around her dry lips. He made everything sound so feasible. Just as Walter had. She felt Luke take one of her hands in his and hold it tightly.

"Kate, you have nothing to fear from me. I would never do anything to harm you," he said gently. "I just think it would do us both good to get away from the stuffy old city."

"You'll be the one to tell Mrs Wood then," she said, a little choked. And he knew it was her way of capitulating.

Mrs Wood wasn't in the least perturbed by the news.

"It's a lovely idea, Lukey, and you've worked this girl hard enough these last few months. She deserves a break."

Kate smiled. It hadn't seemed like work at all, and the weeks had flown by. She was honestly amazed to find just how relaxed and serene they had been, and how easily she had slipped into her new life, as if she had been born to it. Her spirits lifted at the easy way her landlady accepted the idea that she and Luke were going away together, and her heart skipped a beat as the words slid into her mind. Going away together . . . no matter what anybody said, there was a wicked ring to them, and it was exciting and daring. When Doris and Faye were told the news over supper that evening, they were frankly envious. As an old theatrical trouper, Thomas Lord Tannersley wouldn't have turned a hair either, had he been at home that evening to hear it.

"Don't go thinking the worst, and imagining any goings-on in Bournemouth, you two," Kate said to the other girls while Mrs Wood was in the kitchen making tea for them all. "You both know that Luke's a real gentleman."

"More's the pity," Doris said. "You're not telling us he's never tried it on with you, are you, Kate?"

"Of course he hasn't!"

"Oh, come off it, love. Anybody can see he's only got eyes for you," said Faye. "This might be just the time when he'll make his move. Are you sure you know what you're doing, Kate? And if not, I'll willingly change places with you," she added with a sly grin.

"I know what I'm doing, and it'll all be above board, I assure you," Kate said, in her primmest voice.

"Oh aye, bed-board, if you're not careful – or if you're lucky!" Faye said, almost convulsing as Mrs Wood came back into the room. Kate hastily shushed them both.

"What's all this, then? Can anybody share the joke, or is it a private one?" the landlady said.

"Oh, it's very private, I'd say, wouldn't you, Kate?" Doris said, smothering a laugh with difficulty.

She ignored them and turned to Mrs Wood. "Doris and Faye were just giving me the benefit of their worldly experience, about going away with a gentleman, Mrs Wood."

The landlady dumped the tray on the table and glared at the two girls, her face its usual scarlet from the cooking.

"And I can just guess what was in their minds," she said smartly. "Well, let me tell you two charmers that I've known Lukey since he was a small boy, and there ain't a kinder, more considerate and gentlemanly person on this earth."

"Well, that's just what we've been saying!" Doris said innocently. "He's a real saint and no mistake."

And if the implication was that it was no way that she or Faye would want a man to behave in a seaside hotel, Kate chose to ignore that too. But there was one thing she was sure about, she wasn't going to write and tell her family about this September holiday, and she didn't care to examine why.

* * *

The Bentley covered the miles smoothly and efficiently, and Kate began to feel as if they were real gentry as they left the London suburbs and headed south-west. She trusted Luke's driving as much as she trusted the man himself, and she had told herself to stop worrying about anything, and made up her mind to enjoy it.

"Happy?" Luke said.

He glanced at her, hearing her little sigh of pleasure as she leaned back against the luxurious upholstery.

"Very," she said. "I do appreciate all this, Luke."

"Stop it," he said.

"Stop what?"

"Stop thinking you have to thank me for every damn thing. Don't you know I'm only doing this so that I can have your undivided attention for a week instead of sharing you with half the world?"

She looked at him in astonishment, unsure whether or not he was serious, and he laughed.

"Kate, I'm sorry. I shouldn't tease you when you always take the bait so readily."

"No, I don't—"

"Yes, you do, my love, and it's one of the things that's sweet and natural about you. Don't ever change, Kate."

Sweet and natural ... Walter used to say that about her. Kate was angry that she suddenly remembered it, just when she least wanted to.

"But we don't stay the same for ever, do we? We all grow into different people, Luke. You can't tell me the war didn't change you in some ways, or that your new profession didn't give you a new angle on life."

"Quite true. And thanks to my dear old great-aunt Min, my life definitely changed for the better. Whatever the reason for your being in Bournemouth that first time – which I'm not going to mention again – if it hadn't been for the change in your circumstances, we'd never have met, would we?"

"And are you glad that we did?" Kate asked, unable to prevent the provocative question leaving her lips.

"What do you think, lady?" he said with a grin.

They were booked in to the Parkstone Manor Hotel, which was on the Poole side of Bournemouth, well away from the Charlton. Before they left the car and went inside, Luke drew out a small box from his pocket.

"You're here as my fiancée, Kate, so it's sensible for you to wear a ring on your finger. You can give it back to me when we return to London," he added, to allay any alarm she might have at the suggestion. "It was another of my great-aunt Min's legacies, so I hope it fits."

He opened the box and Kate saw a pretty Victorian-style opal ring inside. Weren't opals reputed to be unlucky? The thought flashed through her mind and out again as Luke took the ring and slid it onto the third finger of her left hand. Impulsively he raised it to his lips and smiled at her.

"Now we're official. Just for the duration, as they say."

"Just for the duration," Kate murmured.

It was a beautiful thought. But it was also so awful . . . the last time she had come to Bournemouth she had worn a wedding ring she wasn't entitled to, and now she was wearing his revered great-aunt's ring. For someone who believed in honesty, Kate knew she was going to have a hell of a lot to answer for when the great day of reckoning finally came.

"So are you ready to brave Parkstone Manor?" Luke said. "They won't eat you, Kate."

She took a deep breath. "Of course I'm ready. And I won't let you down, Luke."

She didn't quite know why she said that, but she owed Luke such a lot, and she'd play the part of his fiancée to the best of her ability. In public, at least.

And in the end, it was all very easy. The hotel was discreet and comfortable in an old-fashioned way, and their rooms were on different floors, as if to state that this was a respectable establishment that didn't cater for any funny business. But she learned that Luke had requested it anyway, and it flitted through her mind that Doris and Faye would have been mightily disappointed to know it.

The week couldn't have been more different to the ruined honeymoon, because she had someone to share it with, and she didn't spend half the time brooding and weeping.

It was a perfect Indian summer, with warm sunshine and mellow breezes. In the mornings they took invigorating walks along the beach, and in the afternoons they drove into the harbour at Poole and took out Luke's boat. And because he made no demands on her, Kate had never felt so idyllically relaxed in her life.

While they were idly drifting in the boat in the latter part of the week, she leaned back with her eyes blissfully closed, and Luke spoke quietly.

"Tell me if I'm speaking out of turn, Kate, but has the enemy finally been disposed of?"

She opened her eyes slowly, knowing he meant the spectre of Walter. And of course he had gone. The bad times had gone. Any love she had for him was gone.

But there was still something remaining that Luke didn't even know about, and never would, although, if he was to mean anything to her sometime in the future, he would have to know. She shivered at the thought of destroying the pedestal he seemed to have put her on.

"So not entirely," Luke said, answering his own question. "Then forget I asked, and I won't mention it again."

"Just give me time," Kate pleaded.

"That's just what I am doing. But how much time do you need before you realise that you're a warm, lovely woman, and some other man would love you and cherish you for the rest of his life, given the chance?"

165

She would have been an idiot not to know he was talking about himself. She could see the love in his eyes and hear it in the sudden deep vibrato in his voice. If he felt half the passion for her that she had experienced for Walter, then she knew she was turning her back on something wonderful. But only temporarily, she thought desperately, for by now she couldn't imagine her life without Luke Halliday.

"I do know it, Luke. But I was so badly hurt, and I have to get over it in my own time. But I *will* get over it, and in answer to your unspoken question, I no longer feel anything for Walter. I just can't forget what he did to me."

"You must try, Kate," he said, more seriously. "If you don't, it will fester inside you and ruin your life for good."

If you only knew the truth of that remark, she thought. In the eyes of the world, I'm already ruined.

"Anyway, let's stop talking about Walter. He's in the past, and I want to keep him that way," she said, with enforced brightness.

"I couldn't agree more." Luke started up the boat's engine once more and they cruised back to shore. Kate trailed her hands in the sun-kissed water and thought she must have been blessed after all, to have a second chance at happiness.

Chapter Eleven

They returned to London a week later, and Kate reluctantly handed back the opal ring to Luke as soon as he stopped the car in Jubilee Terrace. She had felt so happy wearing it, and any superstition surrounding the gems had been dispelled, but it wasn't hers to keep, and she wasn't entitled to wear it.

"Thank you, Kate," he said. "I'll keep it safe for when you agree to wear it permanently."

"Are you so sure of me?" she asked lightly, trying not to let her heart jump at his words.

"No. Just hopeful. But I warn you, I shan't be patient for ever," he added.

She knew she couldn't expect it. They had danced most nights at the hotel, and she was very well aware that Luke was a passionate man. But he was treating her like a frightened virgin, no less, she thought, when nothing could be further from the truth. She shivered, knowing the last thing in the world she wanted was to shatter his illusions about her.

The girls at the boarding house were eager to hear all about the week away, and were frankly disappointed when Kate didn't tell them anything in the least salacious.

"You mean nothing happened at all?" said Faye.

"Of course something happened. We didn't just sit in the hotel twiddling our thumbs. We went out in Luke's boat every day, we walked along the beach, we danced in the evenings—"

"And what then?" Doris asked, her eyes gleaming as she

167

leaned forward across the table where they were eating Mrs Wood's home-made scones and jam.

"And then we went to bed. *Separately*, you numbskulls. What do you take me for? Or Luke, come to that? He's got a reputation to think about."

"Oh phooey," Doris said rudely. "What a waste of a week. Are you sure dear Lukey's quite normal in the equipment department?"

Kate looked at her blankly for a minute, not understanding. When she did her laughter was tinged with an embarrassment she hoped they couldn't detect. It hadn't needed words to know, when she was pressed tightly against Luke, that he was perfectly normal in every respect. And very aroused by her. And wanting her.

"You're shockers, both of you," she said crisply. "And I'm not going to say another word about the holiday if you can't stop making these daft remarks. You'd better not make them in Mrs Wood's hearing, either, if you don't want to be slung out on your ears."

And, visibly disappointed, they knew it was all they were going to get out of her.

Kate reported for work on Monday, having been told she needn't come in before 11 o'clock, to recover from the long drive home. So she spent a lazy morning in Jubilee Terrace, feeling better than she had in months. It was the invigorating sea air, of course; but she knew in her heart it was more than that. You could be in the most exciting place in the world and be thoroughly miserable if you were alone, or with the wrong person. But with the right one, any place could be wonderful.

"Kate, I thought you'd never get here!"

The minute she went inside the showroom Luke grabbed hold of her and whirled her around in his arms before she could even catch her breath.

"What's happened, for goodness' sake? Have you come into a fortune or something?"

"Yes! Maybe. We both will, if things turn out the way I think they could."

His excitement was as tangible as if it were a living thing. Her heart began to beat faster as she registered the familiar ambitious gleam in Luke's eyes.

"Have you heard from one of the magazine agencies?"

It had to be that, she thought. Short of being commissioned to photograph royalty, she didn't know what else could have got him so animated on a damp Monday morning.

"Look at this," he said, releasing her from his embrace and pulling her towards the reception desk. All she could see was the usual stack of letters and accounts that she would be opening as soon as she had taken off her hat and coat. He hadn't even given her time to do that yet.

"What am I looking at?" she said.

He picked up a postcard and held it under her nose. It wasn't the usual country or seaside advertising scene with a slogan such as "Come to Weston-Super-Mare where the sun always shines". It was the picture of a provocatively smiling girl, wearing a white fur stole over a slinky satin dress.

"Do you know her?" Kate said, wondering what this was all about, and feeling a stab of jealousy at the enthusiasm he was showing for the girl now.

"Not *her*, no. But the fellow who sent the postcard from New York is an old American army buddy. Knowing how keen I am on photography, he thought I'd be interested in what he calls this pin-up photo card. He tells me they're becoming all the rage in America."

"And I suppose you can see the potential for this over here! I don't know about that. It's rather daring, isn't it?"

He seized both her hands in his, and the light in his eyes burned into hers.

"We could be on to something that's never been done before on this side of the Atlantic. At least, not in the way Rob says it's taken off over there. We already have some stunning photos of you, Kate, and we could take more. *Dozens* more, in all sorts of poses and outfits. We'd then submit them to various printing firms to see if they'd commission a set of postcards for a trial period. We could make a killing, Kate, and you'd be the nation's postcard sweetheart."

He took her breath away. He had a such a quick brain, seeing the potential in a situation in a split second. But she could see the potential in it, too, though she hardly thought these so-called pin-up photo cards could ever be as popular as the more regular landscape ones. But she wasn't sure she'd want to be so blatantly portrayed as the girl on the American card. She was a platinum blonde, and her come-hither eyes were heavily made-up. Her mouth was very full and provocative, and she gave out a message that was undeniable.

"You wouldn't make me look like that, would you, Luke?" she said uneasily.

"I couldn't make you look like that if I tried," he said, but she knew that he could. He was skilled enough to get any look he wanted from her.

"So what do you say? Are you with me, Kate?"

She couldn't help but be swept along by his enthusiasm, but she felt cautious. There had been so many disappointments over the magazine work, and Luke had been so sure it would happen. She couldn't bear it if this was destined to be another slap in the face for him.

"Kate?"

"I'll have to think about it – but you know I'll probably say yes in the end," she said in a rush, realising that if she turned down the idea out of hand he would be upset.

"That's my girl!" he said jubilantly, and before she knew what he was about, he swung her around in his arms, and held her close, planting a kiss on her lips. It began as a kiss of gratitude, but it quickly became more than that. Luke's hands moved sensuously up and down her slim back as he pulled her close to him. The kiss became more passionate. It was a lover's kiss, and Kate broke away from him with difficulty, her cheeks hot and her eyes bright.

"For pity's sake, Luke, we're in the showroom in full view of the window! What will people think to see the gentleman photographer and his assistant cavorting like that?"

He grinned. "Well, since there's nobody about, who cares? And if there were, they'd just be thinking what a damn lucky fellow he is to have a girl like that in his arms."

She wasn't *his* girl. But Kate knew that anybody who saw them together, whether it was here in London or in Bournemouth, would naturally assume that she *was* his girl. He was so attentive and protective of her, and she was becoming more and more dependent on him. It scared her.

"Well, if you don't let me get down to sorting through the rest of today's post, they'd be more likely to think what a lazy assistant you've got," she said smartly.

He let her go, his mind still buzzing with all the new possibilities for his work. Kate picked up the rest of the pile of letters and tried not to notice the way her heart was hammering in her chest.

"Just as long as you promise to keep that look on your face when I begin the new poses for the postcards," he said.

"What look?" Kate asked, turning away from his scrutiny.

"That just-kissed look."

He blew her another kiss and went through to his studio to make the preparations for his afternoon clients, whistling cheerfully. Kate put the letters down again and glanced at herself in the mirror on the showroom wall. What she saw were the glowing eyes, tinged red cheeks and dewy mouth of a woman who had definitely just been kissed, and what's more, had enjoyed it very much. She touched her fingers to her mouth for a moment. She was beginning to enjoy everything about being with Luke, far too much for comfort. Despite all her resolutions, she was falling in love with him, and there was nothing she could do about it.

The showroom bell rang then, and she turned towards it thankfully, ready to answer the first enquiry of the day, and smiling reassuringly at the small family who wanted a portrait done for a special birthday. It took her mind off the fact that falling in love with Luke was a complication she didn't want to have to think about too much.

Once Luke got an idea in his head, he acted on it as quickly as possible. It was something that had been drilled into him during his time in France. If you wasted too much time looking over your shoulder to see what your enemy was doing and weighing up all the pros and cons, it might be too late for you to do anything at all. There had been ditherers in his unit, and all of them had paid the price, they had either been killed or horribly maimed. He had seen it all. A soldier was trained to obey orders, even those that had turned out to be the most tragic and reckless ever given to men by their officers. He didn't often think about those times any more, but the urgency to act when the time was right had been instilled into his mind.

He knew in his gut that this was right. The postcard from Rob was the trigger which set his imagination working, and once he'd got the commission from a suitable printer, and his own pin-up postcards went into production, Rob would be the first person to receive one. With unfailing optimism Luke never doubted that this time he was onto a winner. But for now, they were to let nobody know of their plans.

With Kate as the nation's postcard sweetheart, how could they fail? They were in this together.

He smiled with satisfaction, knowing how sweetly insidious that sounded. With the buoyant optimism that allowed no thought of rejection in his mind, he knew the time would surely come when she accepted that they were meant for each other, and the ghost of the Radcliffe swine would be laid to rest for ever.

*   *   *

"You have a client due at two-thirty this afternoon, Luke, and I've arranged for the Dalgliesh family to come in tomorrow at the same time," he heard her say behind him.

At his vague look, she put her head on one side, as quizzical as an exotic and beautiful bird.

"Where on earth were you just then? Away with the fairies in cloud-cuckoo-land, by the look of it," she said, remembering one of her mother's favourite scoldings.

"Not exactly. But you and I were riding just as high, my sweet, and more successfully than either of us dreamed of."

She put her hand on his arm. "Luke, it's fine to dream, but there's a long way to go between dreaming of something, and making it happen."

"I know that," he said, refusing to be dampened by her hesitant words. "But we'll make it this time, Kate, I know we will. Anyway, just as long as we're in it together we can't fail. But not a word outside these four walls, remember."

"I'll remember. But you'd better come down to earth and get yourself organised now, or you'll find yourself losing the clients you've already got."

In the few months before Christmas there was always a demand for family portraits as gifts. And just as if the thought of the new venture gave added impetus to his skills, he was inundated with work, and the postcard plans had to be postponed. Old and new clients were charmed by the excellent results and the enthusiasm of the photographer who showed endless patience with nervous parents and irritating children, and just as much by the soothing words of the lovely assistant who brought them cups of tea and lemon squash while they waited in the elegant surroundings.

"That's your picture in the window, isn't it, Miss?" Mrs Dalgliesh said when she and her family came to see the proofs of their family's portraits.

"Yes, it is," Kate said, smiling.

173

"You should be on the silver screen, that's where you should be, my girl," her husband put in. "You're wasted here, and you can just tell that young feller-me-lad I said so."

Kate laughed. "I'll tell him, but I assure you I'm more than happy with the job I'm doing."

She realised again how true it was. She was happier than she had ever been in her life before, and on their very next free afternoon, Luke was going to take the first batch of specially posed photographs aimed at the postcard market.

Luke had decided that most of his original photos, however good they were, didn't do justice to the look he wanted to create. He hoped Kate wasn't going to be difficult about it. He didn't want to make her look like a vamp, but he definitely wanted the look in her eyes and the half-smile on her mouth that would appeal to men and women alike. You had to look at the commercial value of the market, and with the new Hollywood talkies all the rage now, the image of the pin-up girl had definitely come into its own.

He broached the subject to her delicately, and got the reaction he half expected.

"I'm not going to dress up like a tart for anybody," she said at once.

"Do you think I'd ask you to do that? Do you think I'd want to see your picture plastered all over the place looking like that? It wouldn't do either of us any good, would it?" he said tetchily.

"But you want me to wear figure-hugging frocks, and put a lot of make-up on my eyes, like the girl in the American postcard," she accused him. "What does that make her look like, if not a tart?"

"It makes her look what she is. A beautiful woman in an artistic pose unafraid of her own sexuality," he snapped.

She flinched at the word. Sometimes he riled her so much, and it was usually because something he said reminded her of

Walter's earthy brand of persuasion. *You're the sexiest thing on this earth, doll, and you can hardly expect any sane man to keep his hands off you when you look at him with those gorgeous come-to-bed eyes.* He hadn't been able to keep his mouth off her either, or his demanding, virile body . . . and it had been so thrilling to have this worldly man so mad about her that she would have given him everything. And she had.

"If I've offended you, I'm sorry," she heard Luke say stiffly. "But we have to move with the times, Kate. If I'd wanted you to pose like Little Miss Muffet straight up from the country, I'd have said so."

"But that's what I am, isn't it?" she flashed at him.

He took her hands in his, suddenly realising how upset she was becoming.

"You've come a long way since those days, my love, even if it ever applied to you, anyway."

"Don't tell me you never thought of me like that! I was gullible enough to fall for the wrong man, wasn't I? That was straight up from the country in the way most people mean it."

"God damn it, Kate, I didn't mean anything of the sort. Don't twist my words. And if you don't want to pose for the postcards, I'll get somebody else, so forget it."

His words hit her like a punch in the stomach.

"You wouldn't do that, would you?" she whispered.

But why wouldn't he? There were plenty of beautiful girls in London, and he could take his pick from any of the magazine agencies. With his growing reputation, she was sure any girl would jump at the chance to work with Luke Halliday, and to share in the success he expected to come from the postcards.

"I would if I had to," he retorted. "I intend to go ahead with my plans, with or without you. But that's the last thing I want. I want *you*, Kate. I've always wanted you."

The air was filled with a new tension, and she could see that his brief anger was forgotten. She couldn't doubt his meaning, and in one tingling instant she knew how badly she wanted him too. She wanted him to make love to her, the way Walter had made love to her, and the scandalous, erotically wicked thought was in her head before she could stop it.

"Luke, you don't have to look for anybody else for the photographs," she said shakily, shocked by the force of her own feelings, and desperate not to show them. "It may sound selfish of me, but I don't think I could bear to think of some other girl being part of it all instead of me."

"That's just what I hoped you'd say. So let's stop wasting time and get down to work, shall we?"

Instead of warming to her then as she had half expected, he became brisk and businesslike, and she breathed a little easier, because if he'd taken her in his arms then, there was no way she could have resisted him. And knowing so well how wanton and abandoned the passion between two lovers could be, she knew she daren't let down her guard for a moment.

At least now she was sure of one thing. She wasn't frigid. Not if the warm and sensual sensations that flooded through her every time she secretly imagined what loving Luke would be like, were anything to go by. She had imagined lying in his arms far more often than she dared to admit, even to herself. No, she thought, I'm not frigid, I'm just afraid of letting another man see just how passionate a woman I can be. She had let go of all her inhibitions once, even though she had been brought up to know it wasn't a woman's place to be as loving and passionate as a man.

As the indoctrinated thought entered her head, Kate questioned it almost angrily. Why shouldn't a woman have the same kind of needs as a man? They were both put on this earth to procreate, so what kind of a God would dictate that a man took all the pleasure and a woman get all the pain? Why shouldn't she enjoy it without feeling guilty? Kate was fully aware that it was more than possible . . . she had enjoyed Walter at the time, she couldn't deny it. It was only the stuffy convention of society that said you should just lie there like a log and let a man take his pleasure.

"I wish I could read your thoughts at this moment." Luke's voice penetrated her day-dreaming. "Wherever they are, and whoever they're with, I envy him. And you once had the nerve to tell me I was away dreaming with the fairies, or some such crazy thing!"

She felt her face burn, because whatever her thoughts, her longing had been all for him, and no one else.

"Perhaps you should thank your lucky stars you're not a thought-reader then," she said pertly.

"That sounds ominous. Did I figure so badly in them?"

"Who said I was thinking about you?" Kate countered airily, and far more coolly than she felt.

Her hands were quite tacky. Keeping her feelings to herself was going to be even more difficult from now on, now that she knew she was falling in love with him.

With another burst of suppressed anger at herself, she wondered what the devil was wrong with her to be so resistant. It was what she wanted, wasn't it? So why resist? She knew the answer only too well. Every man expected his bride to be a virgin on their wedding night. And she wasn't. You could get away with most things, but not that, she thought bitterly. It was the inescapable, physical fact that damned a woman who had already been spoiled.

"All right, so let's get going. We'll start with the evening frocks you've brought, just so you can get the feel of it all. But we'll go to the West End tomorrow and buy some ready-mades as well."

"What's wrong with my clothes? I'm a skilled needlewoman, and nobody ever accused me of wearing home-made frocks!" she said, bristling at once. "Besides, how can I possibly afford the kind of ready-mades in the West End shops? I don't have that kind of money."

"But I do."

How shocked her mother would be if she could hear such an outrageous suggestion. Her father would call Luke a low-down pimp, and Donal would probably feel like killing him.

"I'm no kept woman, Luke Halliday! I've never let a man buy my clothes yet, and I don't mean to start now."

"You can sometimes be the most irritating woman on this earth, and that's a fact. Nobody's trying to make you a kept woman," he snapped. "You don't even have to keep the ready-mades if you don't want to, or wear them ever again, as long as we produce something stunning for the sample photos we show to the printers. It's just an investment, Kate, and I'm only providing the props. I do it here every day, don't I?"

His words took the wind out of her sails for a moment, he was always so plausible. But men always were when they wanted something.

"I hope you won't be so prickly when you find yourself a husband, or the poor sap won't know what to do for the best. I presume you'll allow him to buy you something now and then?"

"That's different. And I'm not looking for a husband. I leave that to the likes of Doris and Faye."

She bit her lip, wondering how they had come to be wrangling like this. She heard the echo of Walter's hoarse, urgent voice in her head. *Frustration is a terrible affliction, Katie. It makes me mad with you when I don't mean to be, and it's only because I want you every minute of the day and night.*

Oh yes, they could be plausible all right, when it suited them. She didn't want to think that Luke's irritation lately might be due to the same kind of frustration.

"Do you want to get started or not?" she said quickly.

"I don't think I do, after all," he said to her surprise. "I think we both need to sleep on things, Kate, and I doubt that I'd get the best out of you today in the mood you're in."

He had some gall, she thought! It was his mood that was affecting *her*, not the other way around.

178

"I'll run you home and you can tell Mrs Wood I'll be in this evening for the meal she keeps nagging me to have with you all," he went on.

It wasn't Kate's place to put up any argument about that. *Lukey* would always be welcome at Jubilee Terrace, with or without an invitation. She knew that. She gritted her teeth.

"I'll see you later then. But don't bother to drive me home. I'd rather walk, thanks. I need to think."

It was a long walk from the showroom, but she didn't care. Besides, if her feet began to hurt too much, she could always catch a tram. She just couldn't bear the thought of sitting next to Luke in his motor car and feeling more tongue-tied with him than she had ever been before.

It was late in the afternoon when Kate finally reached Jubilee Terrace. She'd made a detour and sat in the park for a while, even though the air was getting decidedly chilly now that the days were getting shorter. She'd smiled at some small boys with their father throwing bread to the ducks on the pond, and watched some chatty, uniformed nannies taking home their charges in their baby carriages. And she'd felt a sudden pang at seeing how everybody seemed to have someone else to talk to, and she was the only lonely person in the world.

The minute she was enveloped again in Mrs Wood's warm, noisy household she knew how feeble she was becoming. It wasn't a family home, but they were all a kind of family. Doris and Faye were upstairs and she could hear the tinny music from their phonograph, and Thomas Lord Tannersley was practising his lines in the parlour for some third-rate show he was going to be in. And she was a silly cow for letting herself get so melancholy and so ratty.

"I'm glad you're home a bit early today, my duck," Mrs Wood said cheerfully. "My old bones tell me the weather's on the change, and once those old pea-soupers start to come down on us, you'll not want to be out and about."

At Kate's blank look, Thomas Lord Tannersley gave his loud chuckle.

"I daresay you'll not be familiar with the term, my dear young lady, coming from the outer reaches of the country. Pea-soupers are thick, choking fogs that stifle half of London and bring the city to a grinding halt quicker than any of the Kaiser's shenanigans ever did."

"Now then, Mr Tannersley, don't you go patronising Kate. I'm sure she knows what fog looks like."

"Of course I do! Even in deepest, darkest Somerset it covered the fields and moors in winter mornings, only it wasn't thick and choking. It was a feathery white mist and it spangled the trees like diamonds."

She stopped abruptly, struck by the most enormous and unexpected feeling of homesickness; seeing in her mind's eye the way it could transform the most mundane countryside into a kind of fairyland. And that must surely be the daftest kind of homesickness, she told herself severely, remembering how many times she'd walked to Granby's sweatshop through the wretched mist-damp fields, her feet soaking wet in her boots.

"It sounds pretty," Mrs Wood remarked. "Not that I ever had much desire to spend any time in the country myself. I went there once, but I didn't care for all that open space and farmyard smells."

Kate sensed that she was gathering up steam to ask more, but she didn't want to talk about home. She made a mental note that it was time she wrote to her mother again, and promised herself she would do so later that evening.

"By the way, Mrs Wood, Luke told me to say he'll be coming for supper this evening."

He didn't ask, she thought, half-hoping the landlady would object. He just assumed it would be all right . . . but one look at Mrs Wood's face and she knew the answer.

"That's the best news I've had all day," she said, beaming. "I like to have all my young people around me."

"Does that include me, dear lady?"

"You'll always be young at heart, Mr Tannersely, so I daresay it does," she told him with a smile.

Chapter Twelve

The Sullivans weren't a great letter-writing family. When Donal had been away fighting for King and Country there had been sparse little notes sent home from France, just to let them know that all was well. Unknown to the older Sullivans, the notes had been even sparser than they might have wished, simply because Donal had been careful to conceal the real wartime horrors from those at home.

Brogan Sullivan had never had much time for putting pen to paper, preferring to put his hands to more practical uses. It had been left to Alice to write to Donal, care of some obscure field address which meant nothing to her, and sending him what foodstuffs and knitted comforts they could afford.

But then there was Kate. Kate had always been more inclined towards learning and letter-writing than any of the others, Brogan mused now as his wife came into the parlour waving the large envelope with the London postmark on it. Kate was a good girl, even though he'd been hard pressed to stomach the fact that she'd gone off to London like she had. Following on so soon after what he considered her very ill-advised Bournemouth trip, it had seemed far too much like a flighty bit of panic because of the way that bastard Radcliffe had let her down.

But once he and Donal had stormed the big city, and the boarding-house woman had quelled his fears for his girl, he was reasonably satisfied that the Halliday fellow was a horse of a very different colour. He was a proper gent. He'd see his girl right, if anybody did.

"So what does Kate have to say, Mother?" he said now, as she scanned the two pages of the most recent letter. "And close that perishing door to keep the cold out." There was a decidedly wintry chill in the air as the year neared its close.

It was a month since Kate had agreed to pose for the postcard pictures. As promised, she had said nothing to anyone of Luke's new venture. But she knew her parents were always looking for news from her, and she wrote more often now.

At that moment Brogan was thanking the Almighty that his younger sprats had gone off to school, or else he'd never get to hear half of it sensibly for their clamouring. In their star-struck minds, London was the centre of the universe, and Kate had acquired the status of one of them fancy picture-palace queens. He frowned slightly, hoping to God the young 'uns weren't going to follow suit when they were old enough to leave the roost, but contenting himself with thinking they had a long way to go yet. He saw his wife nod as she read the letter.

"Our Kate's happy, and that's the main thing," she said. "She's doing a job she likes, and she says Mrs Wood sends her regards to us all, and reminds you to send her some fresh Somerset veggies like you promised."

Brogan snorted, wishing he'd never said such a rash thing, since any cabbages and carrots from their own garden would be dried up and curling yellow at the edges if they had to take days to go through the post.

"When Kate comes home for Christmas, she can take some back with her," he said instead.

Alice frowned. "She don't mention nothing about coming home for Christmas, Brogan."

"Of course she'll be coming home for Christmas, woman," he bellowed. "Families are always together for Christmas, so don't talk so daft."

Alice kept her mouth shut. It was pointless to rile him over something that was uncertain as yet. Reading between the lines, it wasn't hard to see that Kate was happier than she

184

had been in a very long time. And with a woman's intuition, Alice had a shrewd idea that much of that feeling was due to Luke Halliday.

Folk usually wanted to spend the holidays with the ones they loved, and contrary to the old ways, that didn't always mean families. She sent up a quick prayer that her girl wouldn't be let down a second time.

"What's in the other envelope?" Brogan growled, not wanting to dwell on the unpleasant thought that Kate might prefer to stay in London for the holidays rather than coming home – a notion that was unthinkable to him.

There was a second envelope inside the larger one, and when Alice took out the contents, she stared in shocked disbelief at the half-dozen photographs she spread out on the parlour table.

"Well, I don't know what to say to this, I'm sure," she said, after a few minutes of complete silence.

"Are you going to keep it all to yourself then, or am I ever going to get a look-see?"

Alice handed over the photos of a Kate she didn't know. They weren't her Kate at all. Oh, they all had Kate's face, and Kate's mouth, and Kate's hair ... but they still weren't her Kate. They were photos of a different person, looking out at her through Kate's eyes.

"Good God Almighty!" Brogan exploded, just as she had known he would. "What does the bugger think he's playing at?"

As he thumbed through the set of photos, his face grew progressively blacker and Alice tried to calm him down.

"If you mean Mr Halliday, you know very well he's a professional photographer, Brogan. You said so yourself, and artistic people see things differently from the rest of us—"

"Arty farty, my backside!" he roared. "Whatever he calls himself, he's got no call to make any girl of mine look like a floosie!"

Alice flinched. "I'll thank you not to use that language in my house," she snapped.

"*My* house, woman! And I'll say whatever I like in it!"

"Well, it's too late to stop our Kate being photographed, isn't it? It's already done, and whatever you think about it, she does look a real picture," she said defiantly. "I never saw her look so bonny before."

Only once, she amended. And that was on the morning of her wedding, when she thought she had all of life before her, before Walter Radcliffe ruined it.

But if this Halliday fellow was the means to bring back the sunshine to it, then it couldn't be such a bad thing. And being normally a woman without a romantic thought in her head, she blushed to be thinking such poetic nonsense.

"You women are all the same," Brogan snapped. "Look at you now, going all soft and red in the face over a few pictures. I tell you, if I thought there was any hanky-panky going on there, I'd have the police down on him."

"You'll do no such thing. You and Donal have already seen that all's well, and I won't have our Kate upset by any more of your suspicions. She's been brought up in a God-fearing household, and she'll not forget that. And if she wants to be photographed to make the best of herself, there's nothing wrong with it, as far as I can see."

As she asserted herself, Brogan grinned sheepishly. He was twice as big as she was – and twice as ugly, he usually added – and it wasn't often that Alice took umbrage against him. But when she did, he always backed down.

"You can be a hard woman when you want to be, Alice, me darlin', but I'll respect your wishes and trust Kate to know what's right."

"So you should," she retorted, not quite knowing how she came to be defending the photos when they'd shocked her so much in the beginning.

But Kate did look lovely in them, and why shouldn't she

want her folks to see her looking so fine? It would be different if she hadn't let them see the photos at all. She was going to write straight back and tell her so – and also to get things sorted out about coming home for Christmas, Alice added determinedly to herself.

Kate was thinking the very same thing. Part of her would have loved to invite Luke down to the cottage for the modest Sullivan festivities, but a far bigger part of her rebelled at the very idea of it. She knew she was being a snob of the worst kind, but she couldn't bear for him to see how poorly they lived. Even if he fitted in so well at Mrs Wood's boarding house, he was still a gentleman. It was probably because of that very thing that he *was* able to fit in anywhere. But Kate still couldn't risk having him look down on her family. He'd had a taste of them already.

She decided that the best thing was to broach it head on. She'd never been one for beating about the bush, anyway, and when they had a breathing space one morning, she spoke casually.

"How much time can you spare for me to visit my folks for Christmas, Luke? We won't be so busy as we are now, will we, and if you can let me have a few days . . ."

"Why are you so nervous about asking me for time off?" he said. "Don't you think I'll want some time to myself as well? Of course you can visit your family, and I'll be happy to drive you there."

"I'm not asking you to do that, Luke." Kate had anticipated this, and had her answer ready. "The roads are going to be so slippery around Christmas, and it's much easier for me to catch the train, and Father Mulheeney will always meet me for the last part of the journey. I know he'll want to be checking up on me, anyway, to see that I've not gone to the devil since living in the big city."

She finished with a laugh, but she knew she was talking too

fast and her voice was too high for comfort. It was futile to think Luke wouldn't notice it. She saw him give a small smile, and knew he could see right through her.

"Have it your way, Katie. But I presume you won't have any objection to my arranging your ticket for you and driving you to Paddington?"

"Of course not!" Kate said, remembering the last time they had met there, when she had fallen into his arms and thought of him as her salvation.

She still did, she admitted to herself, although she was still keeping him at arms' length – most of the time.

She avoided his eyes, wishing she could forget all about inverted snobbery and invite him home, the way girls were meant to invite their intendeds home to meet the family. But she couldn't. In these last months, helped by her own easy adaptation to her new life, he'd built up his own image of her. He'd changed the way she thought about herself too, giving her confidence and a poise she'd never known before. He'd shown her how to hold her head for the photographs, tilting her chin and smiling into the camera, and imagining that she smiled into the eyes of a lover. She had been a little shocked when he'd first said those words to her, but he'd told her coolly that the camera was a perfectly respectable inanimate object, and it wouldn't be at all offended by whatever she chose to do to it. She had obeyed him, and he had made her beautiful.

"Luke, you must see that I need to do this," she said hesitantly. "You're always telling me I should face my enemy, and although I certainly don't think of my family in those terms, I need to let them see that I'm well and happy. And I have to do it alone."

He pretended to back off. "Am I arguing?"

"No." But she felt oddly perverse at that moment. Why wasn't he arguing? Why didn't he insist on taking her home, and announcing to them all that he intended to sweep the irritating Kate Sullivan off her feet and marry her?

"Then stop worrying about it," he said. "And if you're wondering, I shall do what I always do, and join Mrs Wood and however many of her motley gang stay around for Christmas dinner. I daresay it will only be the old boy, but Mrs W. usually gathers in a few neighbourly folk for her knees-up."

"It sounds just like home," Kate said.

"Why shouldn't it? Christmas is Christmas, no matter where you spend it. And I shall miss you, Kate."

She looked at him dumbly, knowing she would miss him too. He went on briskly.

"But I shall have plenty to do to keep myself occupied. I intend to get the postcard portfolio ready to show to the printers directly in the new year."

"You musn't work over the holiday! You must relax."

As she heard herself, she knew she had indeed changed. The old Kate Sullivan barely had any time off from Granby's Garments, and the workers there were begrudged every moment they spent away from their machines. There had been little time for relaxing in her old life, or for strolling in the park, or window-shopping in some of the West End shops where she had finally succumbed to letting Luke purchase some ready-mades for her far more easily than she ever imagined she would. The frocks and accessories were strictly for business purposes, of course, she thought quickly, even though she knew that several of the pretty outfits would be going home with her to wear at Christmas. Not that there would be anywhere special to wear them, except for her family's benefit.

"What are you smiling at now?" Luke said.

"Nothing. Just wondering how my father would react if I wore the scarlet fringed frock on Christmas Day!"

Luke laughed. They both knew it was her favourite, and it made her look fabulous. She had worn it for one of the best shots he had taken of her, but since the photograph was black and white, it hadn't mattered that she had sent a copy to her

189

folks. If Brogan had been aware of its rich, hot colour, Kate knew just how her father would have reacted to it. Scarlet frock . . . scarlet woman!

"I think you'd be wise not to take it home," Luke agreed. "But promise me you'll wear it when I take you up West on New Year's Eve. We'll go dancing, and you won't deny me the pleasure of seeing in the New Year together, will you, Katie?"

She drew in her breath.

"It sounds wonderful, and I shall look forward to it," she said. And once Big Ben had struck the midnight hour and the New Year had begun, she would resolve firmly to put all the various traumas of this last year behind her. From now on, the best way was to forget the past, and to look forward to better times.

Once the decision about Christmas had been made, Kate wrote home and told her family she would be arriving on Wednesday, the day before Christmas Eve, and that she would telephone Father Mulheeney to meet her at Temple Meads station.

It was naturally a busy time of year for the priest, but she had no doubt he would want to make sure his wayward ewe lamb was still surviving. Luke put through the call for her two weeks before the day.

"Is it really Katie Sullivan who's calling?" the priest said, elaborating the obvious as usual. "Sure and 'tis good to hear your dulcet tones, me wee one. But you're not wanting to tell me any bad news, I trust?"

"Not at all, Father," Kate said, feeling just as awkward with him as she ever did, knowing she was hardly an asset to his flock. "I wondered if you would be able to meet me at the train station when I come home for Christmas. I know it's cheeky to ask, and if you're far too busy, I'll understand."

"Not at all, not at all! In fact, I was asking Donal when we would be seeing you again, and he didn't seem to know. But

190

I'll see to it, Katie girl, and 'twill be good to see your smiling face again, since your mammie tells me you're in much better spirits these days."

"Yes, I am. Thank you, Father."

She gave him the details quickly, and put down the telephone with a huge feeling of relief. For some reason her hands felt quite damp.

"What is it about a priest that always makes you feel such a sinner?" she said to Luke with a laugh.

"Maybe it's the fact that they invite all those confessions, whether or not you've got anything to confess," he said, just as lightly. "I can't say I know very much about it, but it's all part of the Catholic ritual, isn't it?"

"It is," Kate said.

And although she'd had plenty to confess, wild horses wouldn't have dragged her secret out of her in the confessional. And in Father Mulheeney's eyes such neglect would be a sin in itself, to add to the major one of fornication.

"You've got that lost look in your eyes that hasn't been there for quite a while, Kate," Luke said. "If the priest has such an effect on an innocent young girl, I can quite see why hardened sinners wouldn't care to risk having their secrets wormed out of them."

"Everyone has secrets, Luke, even me," she said, her eyes bright. "But they wouldn't be secrets if we shared them with everybody. And can we please change the conversation?"

Especially since she was nothing like the innocent Luke assumed that she was. But she could hardly tell him it was one of the main things that made her uncomfortable whenever she thought about Father Mulheeney.

He met her as arranged at Temple Meads station after the tediously long journey from London. She had decided to travel with as few clothes as possible for the few days she would be away, but she was weighed down with parcels for

191

the family, and with the gifts that Luke and Mrs Wood and the other lodgers had insisted she take with her to be opened on Christmas Day and not before.

It was like having a second family, and Kate had made sure she left gifts for them all as well. She could imagine them opening them on Christmas afternoon after they were all satiated with Mrs Wood's succulent roast goose and plum duff, and the bottles of stout and beer the neighbours had promised to bring in.

There would be gifts under the tree that Kate and Doris and Faye had helped to decorate, and there were so many paper trimmings around the room they almost needed the gas light on permanently to counteract the gloom. There was mistletoe, bought from a barrow in the market, instead of being gathered from the trees and hedgerows the way it would be done at home. The girls had caught Luke under it, naturally, and Thomas Lord Tannersley had kissed Kate soundly, insisting in his theatrical way that it wasn't every day an elderly gent kissed such a pretty leading lady. And Luke had kissed her . . .

"Ae you warm enough, Katie girl?" Father Mulheeney said, as they climbed into his old car outside the station. "There's a rug to cover your knees and you'd do well to use it, for it's getting to be real nose-nipping weather now."

Kate laughed, doing as he said, and pushing away the image of herself in Luke Halliday' arms, while the rest of Mrs Wood's household cheered.

"I haven't heard that expression since I left home," she said to the priest.

"I daresay London folk have their own quaint ways, but you know we're blunt enough to see things as they are."

"And this is really nose-nipping weather," she agreed, hoping he wasn't going to go into one of his pious tirades all the way home to Edgemoor. "I've told them about our morning mists down here, Father, and how pretty the fields are then, compared with the awful yellow pea-souper fogs in London. I've already had a taste of them, and it really is a taste. It gets right down your throat and into your lungs."

If she was babbling a little, he didn't seem to notice it, and she was glad to see he was more interested in concentrating on his driving until they were out of the town environs and heading towards the Somerset village.

"You'll be coming to church with your family tomorrow night, of course, Katie," he said, when the familiar roofs and spires and farmhouses began to come into view a while later.

"Of course," she said quickly.

"Good. And you'll be glad to know we've lit candles for you while you've been away."

She felt a spurt of anger. He made it sound as if she'd either been at death's door, or done something terribly wrong. She knew she'd done the latter, but he didn't know it, and she really didn't see why she should be made to feel guilty over Walter's betrayal.

"Thank you, Father, but there was really no need," she managed to murmur.

He glanced at her. "There's no mortal so perfect that they can't be thankful to have candles lit for them in God's house, girl," he said more sternly. "But 'tis clear from the look of you that you've got over your bad times, and for that we must all be thankful."

He was like a dog with a bone, Kate thought irreverently, stirring up all the memories she was trying so hard to forget. Coming home had been bound to evoke them, and she didn't need further reminding from this old man.

Away across the fields, where the cottages were dotted about like the illustrations in a child's picture book, she could see the curl of smoke from Vi Parsons' cottage. Kate had already wondered if she could bear to call on her, or if the visit would be too embarassing on both sides. Vi had been a good friend, and although she had always trusted her not to say anything about the miscarriage, deep inside Kate wanted a bit of reassurance on that score. But there was no need to make up her mind in advance, sometimes it was best to let events take care of themselves.

"Nearly there," Father Mulheeney remarked above the chugging of the car engine, as if registering the silence of the girl beside him. "I daresay it will all seem a little strange to you after all this time, Katie. It aways feels odd to come back to a place after a time away, even though it's where you belong."

If he was trying to make her feel guilty at going away, it was having the opposite effect, thought Kate. London was her home now, and this village was the alien place. It was where she had first met Walter, and away on that hillside he had seduced her. She gave a sudden shiver, as the unwanted images of herself and Walter, writhing in ecstasy on the sweet-scented grassy slopes, surged into her mind. They were images she didn't want to recall, or to remember the caress of his fingers on her skin, or his mouth seeking the inner warmth of her, and teasing her into an erotic response she hadn't even known she was capable of feeling. She didn't want to remember his hoarse words begging her to touch him and caress him. To kiss him in a way that had seemed so foreign to her at first, but which had opened the floodgates of desire in her so that she was willing to do anything he wanted . . . be anything he wanted . . .

"Kate, are you all right?" she heard the priest say sharply. "You've gone very pale, my dear girl."

She was breathing very shallowly, as if she was about to faint. She pushed down the pulsating feelings she didn't want with a great effort, and forced a smile to her lips.

"I'm quite all right, Father. I'm probably over-excited at coming home and seeing my family again."

"Then you'd do well to calm yourself, girl. An over-indulgence in excitement is not good for you."

"I'll try to remember that, Father," Kate said solemnly, but she was struck with a great desire to laugh at his words, because how could any normal person be expected to completely control excitement, any more than they could control sadness, or happiness, or pain?

As they neared the cottage, the door burst open, and two small figures came hurtling outside, prancing up and down beside the car until it stopped, chattering and squealing like a pair of magpies. Kate opened the car door and enveloped them both in her arms.

"We've been waiting for you for ages and ages, our Kate! Have you brought us any presents?" Maura shouted. "Mammie said you'd be sure to bring us some stuff from London!"

"Now then, you girls," Father Mulheeney admonished them. "You know it's a sin to be covetous."

"But it's Christmas, Father," Kate said with a laugh, her spirits upflifted by the sudden glow of being in familiar surroundings which had been oddly missing until that moment. "And you can't blame these two little sweethearts for wanting their presents, can you? Jesus had His presents on His birthday, didn't He?"

She didn't know why she said it, nor even how the words slipped out, but they obviously seemed to satisfy the priest. He nodded, as if to imply that Kate Sullivan wasn't totally a lost soul if she could speak of her scriptures so easily and naturally.

"We've collected branches and berries for the parlour, and Donal's bringing back a tree tonight. We waited for you, our Kate, to help us decorate it," Aileen shouted now.

They were so het up that Kate wondered if their voices were ever going to regain a normal pitch. She hugged them both, loving the childish excitement in their eyes, and the way that Maura seemed to have filled out and blossomed in the months she had been gone.

"Will you come in for a cup of something, Father?" she asked with a smile. "I know Mammie would wish me to ask you."

"Thank you, no, child," he said. "As you might guess, there's plenty of work to be done at this time of year, but I'll be seeing you all tomorrow night at the midnight mass. Enjoy your time together, all of you. And Kate – 'tis good to see you back in the bosom of your family again."

Once he had helped Kate unload the packages that had the girls squealing with anticipation again, he left them to their giggles as the old car backfired, smoking like a chimney as it chugged away. The Sullivan girls instantly forgot him as they hugged one another, and the smaller ones escorted their sister into the cottage, arms linked.

Alice was in the kitchen, and the warm familiar smells of crusty meat pies and baked apples met Kate's nostrils as they went into the cottage and dumped the packages on the old sofa. The smells made her nose tingle and her mouth water. It was a long time since breakfast, when she had last eaten anything.

"Mammie," she said, reverting to the old childhood name she used to use. "It's good to be home."

"Then sit you down and I'll make us both a nice cup of tea," Alice said briskly, unable to bring herself to hug and kiss this beautiful girl who was her daughter.

If they had been a kissing family, she would have found such demonstrations easy, but they weren't, and she contented herself with fussing about with tea making and putting a huge plate of scones and butter and jam on the kitchen table to tide them all over before the evening meal.

"So what have you brought us, our Kate?" Maura said.

"Now, you girls remember what I told you, and let Kate catch her breath," Alice said severely. "You'll not get any presents until Christmas afternoon, and not then, if you don't behave yourselves."

"You'd better do as Mammie says, and try to be patient," Kate said, smiling. "Things are all the better for waiting."

She caught her mother's glance and gave her a reassuring smile. It said that she was well, and recovered, and that there was no need to refer to what was past ever again. Kate knew the unspoken messages would suit Alice, who had always found it difficult to speak of personal matters, and even less to know how to deal with a daughter who had almost committed the sin of marrying a bigamist.

"When will Dad and Donal be back?" she said.

"In a while. They're doing some treecutting in the village in return for a Christmas tree and some logs for the fire. If you want to take your things up to your room, Kate, get the girls to help you."

"I haven't brought very much, except the presents. But I daresay they'll be better off in my room for the time being, before little fingers start poking about to feel the shape of things inside the wrapping paper."

"We wouldn't!" Aileen said.

"Yes, you would," Kate laughed, "so you can just help me carry it all upstairs to my room, then let me unpack my things in peace, and I'll be downstairs again before you know it."

She needed that small space of time to be on her own. The last time she had been in her old bedroom she had been preparing to leave for London. She had been entering the unknown, and it had all turned out infinitely better than she could ever have dreamed it would. But she couldn't quite forget the awfulness of that other morning, here in this bedroom, on what should have been her wedding day, when she had been presented with Walter's cruel letter.

Kate looked around her slowly, gazing through the window at the wintry panorama beyond. The day was drawing to a close, and the fields were spangled with the first hint of evening mist. She could hear the bleating of sheep from a nearby farm. It was reassuring and comforting and familiar. She recognised the rich sense of continuity in the old country ways, more enduring than all the fads of fashionable city life. Everything here was the same, and only she was different. She didn't want to think of herself as not quite belonging any more. It was good to be home, she kept telling herself, even though the very last thing she had thought as she watched Father Mulheeney drive away from the cottage, was whether she would have the nerve to ask him if she could telephone through to a London number on Christmas morning to wish Luke a merry Christmas.

She would never do such a thing, of course, unless they had had a telephone here at the cottage. The very idea of it was so absurd that it lightened the small tinge of unease she felt, imagining the very ordinary Sullivans getting above themselves and owning a telephone, just so she could hear Luke's voice from all those miles away!

It was just as absurd as admitting to herself that she was missing him already.

Chapter Thirteen

Long before Brogan and Donal came home, Kate had begun to feel more relaxed. She could hardly help it, once her small sisters came banging on her bedroom door, begging to see all her new clothes, and to hear all about London.

"Is it bigger than here?" Maura said.

"Much bigger," Kate said, trying to keep a straight face. "It's a very noisy place too, with huge buildings, and lots of motor cars and trams, and a big park where the ladies and gentlemen go walking on Sunday afternoons—"

"And a palace where the king and queen live," Aileen put in. "We learned all about it at school."

"Have you seen 'em, our Kate?" Maura said excitedly.

Kate had to laugh, shaking her head. But Maura was looking so much better these days, no longer so pale and pasty, that she couldn't dampen her enthusiasm.

"Kings and queens don't go walking the streets like ordinary folk, you ninny. They're far too busy doing all sorts of important things."

"What things do they do except kinging and queening?"

"I don't really know." Kate had forgotten how inquisitive they were, and she knew she'd soon be out of her depth. "Anyway, do you want to see the frock I've got for Christmas Day, or not?"

It was easy to divert their attention, and to show off the forest-green, low-waisted frock, with her favourite handkerchief points at the hem. It wasn't as fancy as one of the silkier ones

199

she posed in for the photos, but when she wore it with her long green glass beads, she felt like the proverbial million dollars.

"Mammie don't like us wearing that colour," Aileen said at once. "She always says green's unlucky."

"Well, I like it," Maura said, fingering the soft, warm material. "I wish I could have a new frock for Christmas Day."

Kate didn't answer. Among the Christmas parcels she had brought home were two new frocks especially for the girls. Until now, they had always had home-mades, mostly from left over bits of fabric from Granby's Garments. This year, they would have ready-mades for the very first time in their lives, bought from the bargain basement of a West End shop. It gave Kate a good feeling to know she could do this, even though she had forgotten her mother's aversion to the colour green.

It was all superstitious nonsense, anyway, and any bad luck due to come Kate's way had surely been and gone. She certainly didn't intend to let it bother her.

They all heard the men's voices at the same time, and the girls jumped off Kate's bed, shrieking that Donal would have brought home the tree. They dragged Kate downstairs, where she was enveloped in a bear-hug from her less inhibited father.

He had the whiff of the outdoors about him still, but it was a woody and familiar smell, enhanced by the bits of fir cones and pine needles sticking to his crumpled tweed jacket.

"You'll have our Kate all prickled up, Dada. Put her down and let her catch her breath," Donal said with a grin.

Kate didn't mind that this was his way of greeting her. Suddenly it felt like home. They were all together again; the men were mildly sparring; the girls were squabbling as usual; and her mother was trying to scold everyone at once into taking off boots and washing hands and helping to set the table for the meal.

"So what about this tree I've lugged all the way from

Luxton's Farm?" Donal said. "Doesn't anybody want to see it after all my efforts?"

The girls rushed outside, and Kate followed them, laughing. Christmas was about children, she thought, and families. It was why she had been so glad that Luke had Mrs Wood's all-enveloping household to go to, for he had no one else he could really call his own.

The tree was a splendid one and, as usual, Alice grumbled at the size of it, and said they would never get it inside the house. And, as usual, Brogan and Donal pooh-poohed her and said it would take better men than themselves not to knock it into shape. Everything was back to normal, Kate thought.

After the evening meal, they decorated the tree with fir cones and holly and sprigs of mistletoe and other berries from the hedgerows. And by the time she got into bed that night, Kate was so tired she fell asleep at once, despite thinking that she never would.

She woke early, and couldn't think where she was for a minute. What had always been so familiar was temporarily alien, until she recognised the rose-patterned wallpaper and the picture of the stag at bay in a misty Highland scene on the wall, and the marble washstand in the corner of her bedroom. She was home, and it was Christmas Eve.

She shivered in the chill of early morning, and padded across to the window in her bare feet to stare out at the wintry scene outside. It hadn't snowed, but the hoar-frost was thick on the ground and dripping off the trees. They would be glad of the stack of logs in the yard that the menfolk had brought home. Once the fire was rekindled, and the range warmed through, the whole place would be cosy and warm.

But right now, it was cold. She put on her thick dressing gown and slippers and went downstairs quietly to make a cup of tea. Early though it was, the men had already left the house, but her mother was there, her normally pinned-up hair hanging in wispy strands. Kate felt a litle shock, seeing how grey it was, and wondered how she had never noticed it before.

"Shall I make some tea for us both, Mother?" she asked.

"It's brewing," Alice said.

The small silence between them was as wide as a gulf, and Kate knew she had to be the one to bridge it.

"Everyone looks very well, Mother."

"And why shouldn't they? You've hardly been away so long that you've forgotten what we all look like, I hope."

She had forgotten just how tart her mother could be when she had something on her mind. Kate sighed inwardly, knowing it would be coming. And so it did.

"Your Dada's still not too happy about those pictures you sent home, Kate. He won't say anything, and I've reassured him that they're professionally done . . ."

"But now you need a bit of reassuring yourself, by the sound of it. Is that right?"

Alice eyed her silently, and Kate felt the colour steal into her cheeks.

"Mother, Luke Halliday is a gentleman. Surely Donal told you so after he and Dada met him in London."

"Aye, he told me. But then, he introduced the other one to us as well, didn't he?"

Kate's cheeks burned. "So he did, and I was a fool then, but I won't be making the same mistake again, I can promise you that!"

"Then we'll say no more about it. I've said my piece, and there's an end to it."

It rankled, though. And when the girls came downstairs, and were given errands to run in the village for the last-minute table preparations, Kate refused their insistence that she should go with them.

"Why not?" they howled in unison.

"Because there are people I want to see, that's why," she invented quickly. "I promised I'd call on Vi whenever I came home, and tell her all about London. So that's what I'm going to do this morning. Unless you want me to do anything in the cottage, Mother," she added as an afterthought.

"There'll be plenty for you to help me with tomorrow morning," Alice said shortly. "You go off and show your old workmates what a fine lady you've become."

Kate looked at her, hating the sarcasm with which she peppered her words. Spoiling the homecoming. Spoiling everything.

Vi Parsons opened her cottage door, her mouth dropping open with shock as she saw who was standing there.

"God Almighty, I thought you'd vanished off the face of the earth, duck. But I can see you ain't been doing so badly for yourself these last six months. So are you coming in, or are you going to spend the morning standing on the doorstep lettin' the winter in?"

Kate laughed shakily. Some things never changed, she thought thankfully, and Vi was one of them.

"I'll come in if you don't mind my sopping feet. I'd forgotten how wet the fields get."

"Oh, stop your fussing. Come and warm your toes by the range while we dry out your boots, and don't talk so daft about me minding wet feet, you soft 'a'porth of nuts."

"Is your bloke in?" Kate said, doing as Vi said, and placing her boots on top of the range where they began to exude a familiar smell of damp leather.

Vi snorted. "He's out working in the fields, and he'll probably call back for his tucker sometime, but then he'll be gone again till tonight, so we'll have some cocoa to warm us while we gossip."

"I can't stay too long."

"Why not? We could have a bite to eat later if you don't mind soup made from leftovers. Bert won't miss his share.

Though I reckon you're used to better fare nowadays, by the looks of you," she said, eyeing her up and down.

"I couldn't stay that long, Vi. You know what my mother's like. And don't look at me like that. I'm still the same!"

Vi shook her head decisively. "Oh no, you ain't, my girl, and don't let anybody kid you on that score. You look a darn sight better than before you went away, for a start, and if some bloke hasn't put them stars in your eyes, I'd like to know what grog you've been taking instead."

Kate laughed. "I do work for a nice man—"

"I knew it! And I bet he don't have you stitching half the night away by candlelight for a pittance, neither."

Kate stared for a minute, and then the penny dropped.

"Oh, I'm not sewing garments in a sweatshop any more. I'm a – I work for a photographer. I'm his receptionist." She had nearly said she was a photographer's model, but she knew only too well what Vi would think about that!

"Well, fancy!" Vi obviously didn't know what else to say for a minute. Photographers were completely outside her experience, and Kate had been very cagey about the encounter with Luke in Bournemouth.

"He's very nice, and very respectable. And I've got a room in a boarding house run by a middle-aged lady. There are two other girls lodging there, Doris, who's Irish, and Faye from Yorkshire, and an elderly theatrical man."

"God Almighty, it sounds bloody awful!" Vi said, plonking two mugs of thick dark cocoa and a plate of shortbread biscuits in front of them both. "Does the old girl keep you all in a straitjacket, or do you get the chance to see this photographer bloke of yours outside working hours?"

"Of course I see him, whenever I like, but our association is strictly business," she said, knowing it was far from the truth.

"And if you expect me to believe that, I'll believe in pigs flying over Edgemoor," Vi said dryly. "So are you quite over your other little trouble?"

Kate sipped the scalding liquid and bit into one of Vi's less than perfect biscuits. She had expected the question. Wasn't it really what she had come here for, as a weird kind of exorcism? And to assure herself that Vi had kept her promise never to betray her?

"Quite over it," she said. "It's past and forgotten, and nobody's any the wiser. Nobody but us, Vi."

She held her breath, hoping Vi would understand the unspoken question without taking it the wrong way. The older woman nodded.

"And you want to be sure that I ain't said nothin', is that it?"

"I never thought you would . . ."

"Well, I ain't, and I never would, so you can forget any worries about that. What do you take me for, Kate?"

"A good friend," Kate mumbled, wishing she'd never said anything at all. "I'll have to go soon," she went on awkwardly.

"Not until you've told me about this new fellow! What's his name, and is he going to make an honest woman of you? Oh bugger it, I didn't mean that to sound the way it did!"

She clapped a hand over her mouth, and Kate saw the pricked and sore fingers that came from the constant stabbing of sewing needles at the sweatshop. Her own hands used to look like that, and now they were soft and white, with the nails nicely trimmed so that she presented a very respectable image to the very respectable clients who frequented Luke Halliday's studio. She was so aware of the difference between herself and Vi now, that she felt almost too embarassed to hold the cocoa mug.

"His name's Luke, and we get on very well," she said quickly. "And I don't know if we'll ever have a closer relationship than a business one. Luke would like it, but, well, I'm not sure it would be right, or if I could."

She hadn't meant to say anything at all about her personal

worries, but she should have known Vi would put two and two together quicker than blinking.

"You ain't going to let what happened spoil things for you, I hope! I thought you said you was over it, Kate?"

"So I am, and I never want to see Walter Radcliffe again as long as I live! But you know what he did to me. You know all that happened, Vi. And you know I'm not – I'm not—"

"A virgin, you mean." Vi snorted again. "So you got to use your loaf and pretend, girl. You won't be the first one."

"I don't know how you can pretend about something like that. It's not like you can hide it."

"It's not like you've only got one arm that he can see right off, either! Ain't you never heard of horse-riding women who get broken in from riding before they ever have a man?"

"Of course I have. You can't live in the country all your life without knowing *something*," Kate said crossly.

"Well then, ninny, there's your answer. As far as your fellow's concerned, you've worked on farms and you've ridden horses. You tell him that and he'll get the message."

Kate felt a wild and ridiculous desire to laugh. Vi always had an answer for anything. And she could just see herself, explaining to Luke Halliday that he didn't have to go carefully when he made love to her, because she was already broken in.

"See?" Vi, went on, seeing her red face. "You don't need to be lacking in that department."

That was just where she was wrong, though. It would be one more deception, and the sudden sense of exhilaration Kate felt disappeared as quickly as it had came. She put down the half-empty mug of cocoa and stood up, not wanting to see Vi's knowing face a minute longer.

The back door opened and she heard the sound of stomping feet as somebody kicked off the frost and mud from his boots in the scraper.

"Come and say hello to Kate Sullivan, Bert," Vi yelled, as if he was a mile away instead of in the tiny inside porch.

The florid-faced, beefy-looking man came inside the kitchen, looked Kate up and down and gave her a nod before his mouth widened into a leering smile.

"Well, living away from home's certainly done things for you, girl. I wouldn't have recognised you."

"Seeing as how you've only ever seen me once or twice before, that's not surprising, is it?" Kate said, trying to keep her voice polite since she was in his house.

But she didn't like him, and never had, and she didn't like the way he was ogling her now.It reminded her all too clearly of oily Jenkins at the sweatshop, and the way he'd tried to get her to work extra hours.

"Put your eyes back in their sockets, Bert," Vi said sharply. "Kate's just here for a short visit, and she's got to be getting back to her folks."

"Well, when I've had some cocoa and picked up my tucker I could walk her part of the way back. It's on me way."

"Thanks all the same, but I've got some more people to see, and I should be gone already," Kate said, pulling on her boots and lacing them quickly, trying not to wince at the way they had tightened up by being dried too fast on the range.

"Thanks for the cocoa and the chat, Vi," she said. "It was good to see you again."

"And don't you forget what I told you, will you? There's more than one way of skinning a cat."

She escaped as quickly as she could, breathing in the clear, cold air of the countryside, and wanting to put as much distance between herself and the Parsons as possible. Together, they made her feel cheap and uncomfortable.

Vi had always been crude and outspoken, and although Kate was sure she would never have told Bert about Walter and the miscarriage, she couldn't help wondering if women were somehow subtly marked when something like that happened. As if certain men could see when a woman had been ruined, and saw her as an easy touch. She shivered at the very thought

207

of some oaf like Bert Parsons touching her intimately in the way Walter had touched her.

By the time she had walked aimlessly across the fields towards home again, she knew it had been a mistake to call on Vi. She had needed to know that her secret was safe, but inevitably it had stirred up all the bad memories again. She thought they had been behind her for ever, but they weren't. They were always there, the way a bad penny always threatened to turn up when you least expected it to. Like a bomb that was biding its time to explode.

They all went to church on Christmas Eve, and Alice would have no arguments from Brogan about the annual pilgrimage. To Kate and the girls, it was one of the most beautiful nights of the year, when the entire congregation celebrated midnight mass, carols were sung, and the Christmas crib was displayed in all its glory in front of the altar. The rituals were always the same. Everyone entering the church was handed a candle, and as the first ones were lit, each person touched his lighted candle to the one alongside him, until the whole church was ablaze with light. It was a scene that was always throat-catching.

The Sullivans always lit two special candles for their own wee twin boys who weren't here to share Christmas with them. But once the service was over, and the priest was standing at the door of the church bidding all his flock goodbye and the compliments of the season, they all felt a slight sense of relief.

Father Mulheeny clutched each pair of hands of the Sullivan family, giving Kate's a special squeeze.

"Tis good to welcome you back to the fold, Katie, for however long a time you plan to be here with us," he said. "If you can spare yourself for a longer visit, let me know."

"I can't do that, Father," she said quickly, wondering why he had to make a simple remark sound like a censure. "I can stay a week but no more, so I'd be obliged if

208

you'd take me back to the station next Wednesday as arranged."

"I'll be at the cottage for you to be sure."

He passed his pious, blessing hands along the rest of the congregation, and as the Sullivans snuggled deeper into the collars of their coats and began their procession home, Kate felt Donal's hand press her elbow.

"Take no notice of him, Kate. It's part of his job to make folk feel guilty. If everybody was perfect, priests would have nothing to do."

She laughed ruefully. "He'll never be out of a job, then, since none of us is perfect. We're all blemished in some way."

The rest of the family were ahead of them by now. The small girls chattered excitedly to their parents. Donal spoke more quietly to his sister.

"Whatever happened in the past, Kate, you've come out of it unscathed, and you're making a better life for yourself, so you've got nothing to blame yourself for. I'm proud of you, and that's the last I'm going to say about it."

Her eyes prickled at the unexpected praise. But she knew he only saw what she let him see, the way everybody did. He didn't know the secret shame of her, or how his one-time friend had ruined her. And he never would, she vowed.

"Did you ever see such a bright moon, or so many stars?" Donal went on, as if determined to dispel the sudden charge of emotion between them. "There's snow in the air, and we may yet get a white Christmas to please the girls."

Kate looked upwards. The moon was full and it seemed low enough to touch, and the stars were a brilliant mass of silver against the deep indigo of the sky. She had always thought the sense of infinity was closest right here, where the vastness of the heavens blanketed the gentle hills and fields of the Somerset countryside. The sound of her sisters' laughter brought her back to earth, and she wondered instead just how the sky looked in London right now, and if city folk appreciated its beauty among all those concrete buildings.

Was Luke gazing up at the night sky at this very moment, and thinking of her? Were they watching the same moon and stars, and wishing they were together? The thought overpowered everything else in Kate's head, and she knew instantly how much she loved him. And with that realisation came the certainty that she could never deceive him as Vi had suggested. On this night, especially, it seemed like sacrilege even to consider it.

When they got back to the cottage, Alice made them all a drink of hot Bovril before the girls were bundled off to bed. The adults lingered, talking quietly for a few minutes more as always. The goose was already prepared and in the side oven of the range, to begin its long, slow cooking before morning when the fire would be stoked up, and the winter vegetables had been pulled from the garden ready for peeling.

Kate felt the same sense of anticipation she had felt as a child, when Christmas Day was almost here, knowing there would be a feast of humble proportions to eat, and presents to unwrap, however modest. She felt a wave of love for them all as she finally said goodnight, and went upstairs to bed.

Once there, it was as impossible to sleep as it had been when she was a child. She didn't close her curtains, since she had always loved to watch the sky through the small square of windowglass.

When she had been as young as Maura and Aileen, she had always hoped desperately that when she woke on Christmas morning, the window ledges would be thick with snow, then she and Donal would hurl snowballs at each other and build a snowman, with bits of coal for his eyes, and a carrot for his nose.

Her thoughts now were far from childish. All she could think about, as she gazed through the window, was Luke. And the feelings that flooded into her were ones she recognised all too well. She wanted him to hold her in his arms, kiss every part of her, sweep her off her feet, and overcome all her remaining inhibitions. She wanted him so badly to make love to her, wildly and passionately . . .

She was breathing very fast, and her heartbeats were so erratic they were almost painful. She *wanted* him, in the biblical sense of the word – and in the earthiest way imaginable. Her entire body throbbed with her need for him, and the feeling was all centred in the hot, moist part of her that needed him most. She felt the exquisite pulsing inside her, and squeezed herself together, trying to push the feeling away. She knew instantly why she was rejecting these indescribable sensations. It was because she was alone, and making love was something wonderful to be shared. It was being a part of someone you loved, and not something to experience in the loneliness of a solitary bedroom.

A small sob welled up in her throat, knowing she had so much love to give, and wondering if she would ever know the happiness of it again? Unless Luke could take her as she was, then she never would. And she had no idea how she could ever tell him.

Kate was thankful her two small sisters were up early the next morning and bouncing on her bed the minute they awoke. It helped to alleviate any questions about the look on Kate's face that betrayed a sleepless night. She forced herself to be bright and cheerful, because nobody should be sad on Christmas Day.

She imagined Luke waking up and looking through his window at the cold London streets, and dressing in a leisurely way before going to spend the day at Mrs Wood's. She felt the most enormous sense of jealousy, because Mrs Wood and Doris and Faye, and even the impossible Thomas Lord Tannersley, would be sharing the day with him, and not her. Kate told herself she must be going slightly mad, but then, people in love always were. Everybody knew that.

She defiantly wore the new green frock she was so fond of, despite her mother's distaste for the colour, but she was obliged to cover it with one of Alice's voluminous overalls while she helped with the final dinner preparations. By two o'clock in the afternoon the meal was ready, and as she dispensed with the overall at last, Donal gave a low whistle.

"We've got a real film star at the table today, and no mistake," he said, and as Kate saw her mother's frown, she wished he hadn't said anything of the sort.

"Don't be daft. It's only me inside, whatever the clobber," she said quickly. "And you wait and see how Maura and Aileen will look with what I've brought for them."

It was the nearest she would say about their surprise gifts, but it turned the conversation from her own appearance.

And in the end, the day was as noisy and cheerful as any other Christmas Day. The girls paraded in their new frocks, and her mother was clearly pleased with her warm winter scarf and stockings, and the box of sweetmeats from a posh West End store, and the menfolk appreciated their gloves. Kate had been given little trinkets from them all, that she told them she would always treasure.

There had been only one moment of disquiet, and that was when she had opened all her gifts from her London folk. Most of them were modest enough – a box of hankies from Doris and Faye; a carton of chocolates from Thomas, and a small glass paperweight from Mrs Wood. And then there was Luke's gift.

She had opened the small box carefully, aware that they were all watching intently. It was so obviously a jeweller's box, and men didn't give women jewellers' boxes unless their intentions were honourable. She could read their thoughts so well at that moment.

"Open it, our Kate. Is it a ring or summat?" Aileen shouted excitedly.

"If it is, he'll have to marry her. Ivy Phillips said so," Maura informed her.

"Be quiet, child," Alice said. "It means nothing of the sort, and I shall have words with Ivy Phillips' mother if that's the kind of nonsense she's telling you."

Kate found herself praying that it wouldn't be a ring. But of course it wouldn't. Not unless Luke had decided to choose this way of giving her back the opal ring she had worn on their second Bournemouth holiday. Whatever her mother said to Maura she knew how badly it would look to them all.

She opened the box carefully, and gave a sigh of relief as she saw the delicate filigree brooch inside in the shape of a little bird poised for flight. She knew the significance of it. He had often likened her to exactly that.

"It's very pretty," Alice said, obviously disapproving. Jewellery of any kind between unmarried people was suspect in her eyes, and Kate told her airily it was all the rage in London now for professional people to give small trinkets of this kind to their staff.

By the time the week at home was over, it was something of a relief to hear Father Mulheeney's old car chugging up to the cottage, and to be able to say goodbye to them all. Kate knew it was sad that she should feel that way, when they were her family, but people moved on. Coming back here for the holidays had only proved to her how true that was.

Once she was safely on the return train journey to London, her heart grew lighter with every mile it covered. As the train steamed into the station Kate saw Luke at once, before he saw her. It was always easier to pick someone out on the platform, than for them to find someone in the crowded, swaying carriages, with everyone opening the doors, eager to get out. She felt a searing pain of disappointment that he wasn't alone, Doris and Faye were hanging onto each arm.

She told herself not to be stupid. It was sweet of them to want to meet her and welcome her back, especially as they hadn't had the chance of going home themselves. But she couldn't help feeling less than charitable towards them. Surely they might have guessed that she wanted Luke all to herself, she thought belligerently. But then, why should they? After all, he didn't belong to her.

Chapter Fourteen

It was late afternoon when the train arrived at Paddington, and they all felt the usual strangeness people did after a week apart. But the feeling was quickly dispelled, and she realised that the main object of Doris and Faye's wish to meet her had been for the ride in Luke's Bentley. However, they were relegated to the back seat, while Kate sat in the front with Luke, and they breathed down her neck all the way back to Jubilee Terrace.

"So did you have a nice Christmas among all the hayseeds, Kate?" Doris asked, giggling.

"Very nice, thank you," she said, not rising to the bait. "And I daresay you did too."

"I'll say we did! We got Luke under the mistletoe so many times, it's a wonder his mouth's not permanently swollen," Faye squealed.

"Shut up, you two, or Kate will wonder what on earth went on at Mrs Wood's" Luke said with a grin. "It was all very proper, I assure you, Kate, and they're just having you on."

"I'm sure it doesn't matter to me," she said, wishing their banter didn't make her feel as old as Methuselah.

They were both so bright and breezy, and Luke seemed to be egging them on, despite what he said. She was desperately tired after a train journey with so many stops and starts that she wondered if they would ever reach their destination. All she wanted now was sleep, and that was no way for a twenty-one-year-old to feel.

"Have you done any work since I went away, Luke?" she asked, wanting to bring herself into his world.

"Some," he nodded, keeping his eyes on the traffic ahead. "If you feel up to it when you've had a meal this evening, I'd like to show you the new material I've been working on."

"Oh, let me and Faye come as well!" Doris said eagerly. "You never let us into that studio of yours, Luke."

"That's because Kate and I go there to work, not to idle the days away. If you want to pay for a portrait sitting, that would be a different matter, of course."

"At your prices? We're not made of money. Not unless you're offering us a discount, that is," she added hopefully.

"Sorry, no can do," he said, and Kate breathed more easily. It was bad enough they were here, filling the Bentley with their cloyingly cheap scent; the last place she wanted them was at the studio, which she felt as proprietary over as Luke himself.

She didn't answer Luke about going there that evening. She knew what the new material was, and she was dying to see the new portfolio which he was going to show to one of the major postcard printers in the city.

Once they were all back at Jubilee Terrace the girls disappeared, and Mrs Wood insisted on Kate eating a huge plate of meat and potatoes. After she had protested at the amount, and eaten what she could, Mrs Wood wanted to know every detail of how people celebrated Christmas in the country.

"Pretty much the same as you did here, I daresay," Kate said with a laugh. "We ate too much food, and the men drank too much ale, and we told ghost stories on Christmas Eve, and went to midnight mass."

She paused, because what swept into her mind then was gazing up at the night sky and the moment she had known for certain how much she loved Luke Halliday. And if she dared to look at him now, she was afraid he might see the truth of it mirrored in her eyes.

"It sounds as if you've got a lovely family," Mrs Wood said

approvingly. "But I already know that, from the way your Pa and brother came to see that you were all right."

"And you all had a good time over Christmas here, from what Doris and Faye were saying."

"Those two!" Mrs Wood said disapprovingly. "Chasing Lukey all around the place with their bits of mistletoe!"

"And catching him, I'll bet," Kate forced herself to say.

"Only when he wanted to be caught," Mrs Wood said slyly, "and that wasn't very often."

"If you two have quite finished discussing my amorous encounters, Kate and I want to go to the studio to look over some work," Luke put in.

"But the girl's only just got back. Give her a breathing space, for pity's sake."

"Oh, don't bother about that, Mrs Wood," Kate said quickly. "I love Christmas, but once it's over I'm always glad to be back to normal again. But before we go, I have to give you some carrots and Brussels that my father promised you."

"So he remembered!" the landlady said, pink with delight. "It'll be fresh veggies tomorrow then."

They left her admiring the size and colour of the Somerset produce, and drove off to the studio. Luke glanced at Kate as she snuggled into her coat beside him.

"Did you mean what you said about wanting to get back to normal again, or was it just an excuse to get away from the inmates of Jubilee Terrace?"

Kate laughed. If there was any excuse in her mind at all, it was to be with Luke, but she wasn't telling him that!

"If you mean am I always glad when Christmas is over, in a way I am. I love being with the family, but there's still an enforced jolliness about it all. It probably makes me sound a grouch, but I think I prefer everyday normality."

"You could never be called a grouch, sweetheart, but I'm not so sure about preferring normality. If all our plans come to fruition, I'd say life could get very exciting."

"But that's different. That's a normality we're both involved in."

She could hear the smile in his voice as he answered.

"Hearing you link us together like that is just about the best Christmas present anybody ever gave me, Katie."

"It doesn't take very much to please you, then," she laughed uneasily.

"I wouldn't say that, but it'll do for now," Luke said.

They pulled up outside the darkened interior of the studio, and Luke told her to stay where he was until he opened the door for her, since the roads were quite icy now. He gave her his arm, and they went inside the studio together.

The blinds were drawn down, but before he even turned on any gaslights, Luke pulled her into his arms.

"God, but I've missed you," he said simply. "This past week has seemed like years, Kate. And I'll agree with you in one thing. If you can't spend Christmas with the one you want to be with the most, it's just not Christmas."

"I don't remember saying that," she murmured.

"But I did."

Luke kissed her with unrestrained passion, and she kissed him back.

When they broke apart she spoke shakily, not trusting the depth of her own feelings. "I thought we were here to look over some work."

"Is that what you want to do?" he said, demanding.

"Whether I want to or not, I think it's what we should do," Kate said. "I shouldn't stay out too long, either, Luke. I really am tired from the journey, and I need a good night's sleep before starting work properly tomorrow."

She listened to herself, sounding more like an old woman who couldn't cope with a train journey than a young and nubile woman alone with her lover – she flinched at the word. Luke wasn't her lover, not yet, and maybe not ever.

He sensed her mental withdrawal, and gave a small sigh.

"You win. But we're not starting tomorrow. It'll be New Year's Eve, for God's sake, and then it'll be the start of the weekend. If a man with a successful business can't give himself and his assistant some time off when it pleases him, what's the point of working at all? We'll start again in earnest on Monday, Kate. But come through to the back room and take a look at the portfolio. I've set up a couple of special appointments for next week, by the way."

"So soon!"

"Of course. We don't want other photographers to hit on the same idea, do we, and get in before us?"

It hadn't occurred to Kate that they might, and she knew it would be a real body blow to Luke if that happened. She followed him through to the back room, and saw the large portfolio on the desk. Her interest quickened, knowing he would want to display some of the best of her poses. She was eager to see them and she sat beside him as he opened the folder.

"I hadn't expected you to do this!" she exclaimed.

"It seemed the obvious way, in order to get my point across. I've had some new thoughts since last week, Kate," he said, and she could hear the underlying excitement in his voice. She could sense that there was more to come.

The photos he'd already taken of her were already reduced to postcard size instead of the usual portrait-sized ones the clients paid for. It didn't detract anything from the poses, and even Kate could see the attraction for folk who wanted to send something different from the usual seaside or country scenes. Though why anyone would want pictures of an unknown girl . . .

"Do you think it will work?" she said at last, struck by doubts again, and trying not to let Luke see it.

"This will be no more than a novelty," Luke agreed, to her surprise. "I wrote to my old buddy a while ago to ask him to send me any more postcards of a similar type, and the package arrived this week. It was a real eye-opener, Kate. What sells is not only glamour, but advertising."

"Advertising?"

"It's becoming big business in America, and it's the way of the future. Here, take a look at these."

He pulled out a large envelope from one of the desk drawers, and spilled the contents out in front of her. There were several dozen postcards inside, some portraying a new face cream that was supposed to transform the skin into satin, but the majority of them depicted new makes of cars or motorcycles with a few lines of basic statistics printed on the reverse side of the cards.

"Do you see? Such postcards are printed in their thousands, Kate. Now, here's my idea. Imagine the same cards with a woman's face included. For instance, try to see Kate Sullivan lounging against the bonnet of a new Rover, or Kate Sullivan's smiling face above a bar of soap, or any other commodity!"

She wasn't slow to grasp what he was saying, but when she didn't speak he went on enthusiastically.

"What we have to do first of all is sell the idea, and provide the photos for the original cards, like the ones in the portfolio. Once we've got a printer interested, we can contact motor manufacturers and other companies, and present them with the idea of increasing their advertising potential."

The magnitude of the idea took Kate's breath away and she couldn't think sensibly for a moment. She stared at the various postcards.

"Have you had any kind of Christmas break at all?" she said at last. "Or have you spent the entire week dreaming up all this?"

"I've spent a lot of time dreaming," he said, "and not just about work, Katie. But you're right. I've also been preparing the way, and this is the result."

He turned to the back of the portfolio, where there were half a dozen different postcard samples. Somehow Luke had

220

superimposed her poses onto the advertising cards. Just as he had suggested, there were several of her with a new bar of soap, but far more of her in full-length poses standing beside the newest motor cars. It certainly enhanced the glamour of it all, she thought, if glamour was what people wanted.

"How on earth did you produce these?"

"With a lot of headaches and re-photographing and sleepless nights," he said. "But these are only suggestions of course. We'd need to get backing from the commercial firms concerned otherwise the question of copyright would come into it, and I've no wish to have a law suit on my hands. But these cards would appeal to a vast range of people, including collectors, and with the manufacturers to commission us, we could make a fortune."

She was totally caught up in his excitement now. "It's a marvellous idea, but it's also a bit scary."

"Why? Because you'd have to pose in different locations with the products? You needn't let that scare you, since I would be still be the photographer."

"Different locations?" she echoed.

"Well, obviously. We could hardly wheel the new cars into the studio to do it, could we? And any manufacturer who commissioned us would have their own ideas about portraying their products to their best advantage."

It was all starting to get far too technical for Kate. She could feel the panic inside her gut now. She had a sudden urge to tell Luke that she couldn't do any of this. That she was just a simple soul, a country girl, who couldn't cope with all this talk of big business and commissions. And if she did that, she knew she would be dashing his dreams.

"So what do we do next?" she asked huskily.

Kate found it hard to sleep that night, even though Luke had told her to sleep on it and think how rich they were going to be. She crossed her fingers, thinking about that. He had already set up appointments for next week, which he was sure was going to bring them luck. She was glad of the breathing space and, as if aware of how momentous all this was for her, Luke restrained himself from mentioning it any more than was necessary. Even though it was on his mind night and day, almost as much as Kate Sullivan was herself. It wasn't until New Year's Eve, when they joined the entire Jubilee Terrace household in the festivities in Trafalgar Square, that he mentioned it seriously again.

As the chimes of Big Ben roared out into the night and the cheering of the crowds followed, Luke pulled Kate into his arms and kissed her long and hard.

"Here's to us, Katie, and to our success in all our future ventures. That's one of my dearest wishes for 1926."

"Only one of them?" she said, knowing she shouldn't ask, but being swept up in the magic of this night along with everyone else.

"I think you know the other one," he said, seconds before Doris and Faye dragged him away from Kate and plastered him with New Year kisses.

And since the flamboyant Thomas Lord Tannersley was bearing down on her now, after enveloping Mrs Wood in a bear-hug, Kate had no option but to be soundly kissed by him too.

On Monday, January the fourth, Kate went to work. She and Luke were taking the portfolio to a printer in the city who had already shown interest in Luke's proposals. Then they would drive out of London to visit the car manufacturers, and then maybe onto other companies.

What Luke didn't want, was any delay in getting all parties interested in his ideas at the same time, and Kate could see the sense in that. But she was very nervous as they arrived at the big printing works north of the river for the appointment with Mr Ronald Clarke.

The girl in the small outer office showed them into a much

plusher one, and brought them tea. The smell of paper and printing ink wafted up from the large printing works alongside, and Kate was so nervous by then, she prayed they wouldn't be kept waiting. When the owner came in, she was relieved to see a big, bluff man who seemed to have a permanent smile on his face.

"Good morning to you both," he said. "I'm Ronald Clarke, and you are Mr Luke Halliday, and . . . ?"

"This is my assistant and model, Miss Kate Sullivan," Luke said for her.

"Charmed," Clarke said. "I see you've been given tea, so shall we get down to business right away, Mr Halliday?"

He nodded towards the portfolio, still smiling as if he'd made some witticism. Kate wondered if he took anything seriously, but presumably he did, if the size of his organisation was anything to go by. Luke put the portfolio on the desk and opened it at the original postcard samples.

For a few moments she felt hugely embarrassed at seeing so many of her photos displayed like this to a stranger, but she would have to get used to it if her picture was to be on postcard stands in hundreds of newsagents. It was a frightening thought, but Ronald Clarke was quickly becoming businesslike now; the geniality simply a façade. Where business was concerned, she could tell he wouldn't suffer fools or time wasters.

"These are very good, and the little lady does you credit, Mr Halliday. And I agree that it could be a good proposition, providing the British public are prepared to buy postcards of the glamour variety as I understand the Americans are. That's the only thing I have reservations about."

Kate felt her heart sink. Luke had been so sure about this, and she wanted his success so much. But he wasn't prepared to be put off easily.

"I understand perfectly, Mr Clarke, but an American friend has sent me some advertising postcards that I think might interest you. I've prepared some samples of what could be achieved in conjunction with various British manufacturers, and I'd like you to take a look at them."

He opened the further pages of the portfolio, where the superimposed advertising samples were mounted, and Clarke studied them in silence for a good few minutes. He nodded slowly.

"I think we may have something here, my dear sir," he said. "Have you contacted any specific firms yet?"

"I have my first appointment with Wesley's Motors today, but I wanted to get your approval as to printing."

Clarke's hand shot out across the desk.

"And you have it, sir! I'm more than willing to do a small print run of the little lady's pictures alone, but you've obviously already seen the potential of combining the sight of a pretty girl and advertising. If you can get the backing of whatever firms you have in mind, then I'd say we could be in business on a large scale. You have my card, and I'll wait to hear from you as soon as possible."

They left the printing firm, walking on air, having promised to telephone Ronald Clarke the minute there was a chance of a meeting between all parties concerned.

"We're made, Katie!" Luke said jubilantly. Then he caught sight of her pale face as they went out into the cold January morning. Every breath they took sent a small cloud of vapour into the air. "Are you all right?"

"I think so, though everything seems to be happening so fast now, it makes my head spin."

"Well, just hold on to your head until we've got everything signed, sealed and settled. And then you and I are going to celebrate tonight by sinking a bottle of champagne – or maybe two."

"Good Lord, how extravagant!" Kate said, laughing, knowing that champagne would really make her head spin.

"You'd better get used to it, Katie. From now on, I can

see us living the high life," he said, opening the door of the
Bentley for her with an elaborate flourish.

She couldn't hide her smile at that. Kate Sullivan, living
the high life, indeed, and drinking champagne for a pastime!
It was a far cry from a country girl scraping a pittance of a
wage packet at Granby's Garments.

By the end of the afternoon, Luke was more jubilant than
she had ever seen him. They had driven to the address
in Hertfordshire where Luke had an appointment with a
progressive motor manufacturer by the unlikely name of
Theodore Wesley. From the size of the place, and the gilt
lettering announcing Wesley's Motors, it was clearly a growing
concern.

Wesley himself was a dapper, cigar-smoking man in his
late sixties. Luke went through the portfolio samples again,
explaining his ideas, and Wesley wasn't slow in showing
his interest, frequently nodding and glancing at Kate, and
repeating that he knew a potential money spinner when he
saw one. Finally, he gave the desk a decisive slap.

"You've got a good business head on your shoulders, young
man. If everyone concerned is in agreement regarding financial
and contractual terms, I'd be more than happy to set up a
trial run for the postcards with Miss Sullivan draping herself
prettily over the bonnet of my motors."

She wasn't sure she cared for the way he described it, but as
the two men continued to discuss the project, she realised how
carefully Luke had thought it all through during the Christmas
holidays. Wesley listened attentively.

"Subject to your approval, sir, I suggest that Kate poses
in a variety of outfits, which would go on sale according to
the season, although they could all be photographed now,"
Luke said. "For example, for this time of year, a fur-collared
coat and smart cloche hat would attract winter sales. In the
spring and summer the poses could be more carefree with

light summer frocks, especially for your sporting cars. Then
there's more glittery evening wear, which would attract the
more discerning and wealthier clients."

"Say no more, boy," Wesley said. "You've put up an excellent
case for business, so get back to your printer and let's all get
together as soon as possible. We won't want to waste time
and let other competitors get hold of a similar idea."

"My feelings exactly, Mr Wesley," Luke said, hardly able
to believe his luck at finding such a kindered spirit.

"My business associates and board of directors will obviously
need to be consulted," Wesley went on, "but I'd say we're all
onto a winner, thanks to this little lady's pretty face. Now then,
if you want to use the phone to get back to your printer, feel
free to use the office while I show Miss Sullivan some of the
models she'll be getting to know."

Kate looked startled for a moment, then realised he was
referring to his motor cars, and not models of the human
variety. She went outside with him, glad to breathe fresh air
after the staleness of the cigar-filled office as they walked
towards the huge doors of the manufactory.

"Are you and and Mr Halliday closely connected, girlie?"
Wesley said, eyeing her gloved hand and detecting no tell-tale
bulge from a ring.

"We're just business colleagues," Kate said, thinking how
grand it sounded.

"Ah. Then if you're unattached, perhaps you'd do me the
honour of having dinner with me one evening very soon,"
Wesley said smoothly.

At once, Kate wished she had said she and Luke were closer
than colleagues. It wasn't too late. She gave a small, rueful
laugh, as if needing to cover her mistake, and felt her cheeks
colour.

"Oh dear, I'm afraid I've given you the wrong impression,
Mr Wesley. Mr Halliday and I are in business professionally,
but we also have a more personal relationship."

"I see. Oh well, you can't blame an old roué for trying, can you?" he said, chuckling quite blatantly.

Kate laughed back, thankful that he hadn't taken offence at being rebuffed. Though what her father would have said if he'd heard a man of Wesley's age asking to take her out to dinner, she didn't care to think. Especially one who referred to himself as an old roué! Young girls who accepted dinner invitations from wealthy, cigar-smoking gentlemen of advancing years would definitely be branded as scarlet women in Brogan Sullivan's eyes.

But no thoughts of home or anything else could dampen the way her spirits soared now, as Wesley showed her around what looked like hundreds of motor cars in various stages of production. The noise from the machinery inside the plant was deafening, but at least it prevented the necessity of having to talk too much as Wesley pointed out the different models of cars. It was clear to see his love for his machines, and she warmed to his enthusiasm.

When they went outside, it was to see Luke coming towards them, a broad grin on his face.

"Can we fix a meeting for the end of this week, sir? Ronald Clarke suggests this Friday afternoon, but he's willing to fall in with whatever arrangements you prefer."

"Friday will suit very well, and the meeting will take place in the boardroom here, naturally, so shall we say two o'clock sharp?"

He still spoke pleasantly, but Kate could sense the subtle change in his manner. He was at once the businessman, taking control; holding the reins of power and dictating the terms. It didn't matter, and she was sure Luke would feel the same, just as long as they were going to be set up in the business they had set their hearts on.

"I'll inform Mr Clarke as soon as I get back to my studio," Luke said.

"Then we will all meet again on Friday afternoon. I

227

guess you won't want to leave your portfolio here until then?"

"You guess correctly," Luke said, with a firm smile. "It belongs at my studio until we have a firm contract. I'm sure you understand."

"Just testing that you've got your head screwed on the right way, boy, that's all. Until Friday then – and you be sure to bring Miss Sullivan along. The board will want to see what an asset we have in her in selling our product."

For the first time, Kate began to feel less than pleased. She pulled the car door shut behind her, and sat with folded arms as Luke backed it out of the company car park.

"He made me feel cheap with that remark!" she said explosively. "What does he expect me to do – parade up and down on the boardroom table for them all to ogle me?"

"Calm down, Kate! It's just his way, and he didn't mean anything by it. He wasn't flirting with you."

"No? He's already asked me out to dinner!"

Luke had started up the engine, and now he turned it off again. "You didn't accept, did you?"

"Would it bother you if I had?"

"Yes, it bloody well would. Kate—"

"Don't worry, I didn't accept," she said, shaken at his vehemence. "I had to tell a white lie, though. I said we had a more personal relationship than just a professional one, and that put him off."

Seeing her flaming cheeks, Luke laughed out loud, his good humour restored. He put an arm around her and kissed her.

"Well, we both know I'd like it to be the truth, don't we? And if you want to impress on the old boy that we're more than friends, you'd better smile, Kate, since he's watching us from his office window."

For Kate, it wasn't in the least difficult to pretend they were more than friends for Wesley's benefit, since it was what she also would dearly love to be. But she smothered such thoughts, knowing that a professional relationship was going to be far easier on her nerves.

It was late in the afternoon when they got back to Jubilee Terrace, where Luke waited for Kate to change her clothes for something suitable for dining out.

"We're celebrating a special deal with a client," was all that Luke would tell the landlady.

"Is it royalty?" Mrs Wood said eagerly. "I bet it is!"

Luke laughed. "No, it's not, so you can put your tiara back in the closet, my old dear. But we're both feeling chipper about it, and we're celebrating with champagne, so Kate might very well be back late tonight."

"She has her own key, and she's over twenty-one, and I know she's safe with you, Lukey," Mrs Wood said complacently.

Once they arrived at Luke's apartment for him to change his own clothes, he brought out a bottle of champagne and poured them each a glass.

"Here's to us, Kate. And you know my feelings on what I told Mrs Wood, don't you? If I had my way, you wouldn't be returning to Jubilee Terrace at all tonight."

Despite her determination not to let this evening get out of hand, Kate felt a wild thrill run through her veins. She didn't doubt what he meant, and they were both already so high on excitement she knew they hardly needed the added potency of champagne. She also knew very well that the mood they were both in was heady – and dangerous.

"And you know that no matter what Mrs Wood said, Luke, she'll be noting the time I get back, and you wouldn't want my reputation to be in shreds, would you?" she said, as lightly as she could.

"No. I just want to make love to you," he said.

Kate drew in her breath. She knew that the sooner they left the apartment for a restaurant where there were plenty of other people, the better it would be for her peace of mind.

"Please don't say that," she said in a low voice.

He tipped up her chin, forcing her to look at him.

"Is it so very abhorrent to you, Kate? Or do you really think you can go through the rest of your life without love?"

"I don't think any such thing!"

"Then why won't you let me love you?"

She shook her head, taking fright at once as his voice became far too demanding for comfort.

Luke took the champagne glass from her hand and drew her into his arms. At the look in his eyes, her heart began to beat so erratically she thought she might faint.

"You're wrong if you think all men are the same, Katie," he said gently. "Haven't I proved to you all these months that what happened to you in the past has nothing at all to do with the present or the future?"

She bit her lip. No matter what he said so unwittingly, Kate knew the past had so very much to do with her future. Walter had seen to that.

"You've been a real friend to me," she said unsteadily. "And that's what I hope you'll continue to be. Now that we've got this exciting business future ahead of us, it would be a shame to complicate it with something else, wouldn't it?"

He looked at her without speaking for a minute. "Are you trying to tell me you're as ambitious for the good life as Doris and Faye, all of a sudden? If so, it just won't wash."

"Why shouldn't I be?" she said, seizing the chance to turn the conversation. "I'm no different from any other girl in wanting nice things for myself."

"Funny, but that's just what I always did think you were, Kate. Different, I mean. It's what attracted me to you in the first place. I can't believe you've changed that much."

"But you don't really know me, do you?" she said, feeling

230

ominously close to tears now. "You only see what you want to see in me, and I'm not a saint, Luke."

It was the nearest she could come to saying what a sinner she really felt she was.

"You're everything I ever wanted," he said simply. "But since it's obvious that you still don't want me in the same way, then we'll concentrate on establishing our new working arrangement and making our fortune. But I won't wait for ever, Kate. When the anniversary of our first meeting comes around, I'll be asking you the same question again."

He disappeared into his bedroom to change, while Kate stood looking dumbly at the closed door between them.

How could he possibly have forgotten that the anniversary of their first meeting was also the day Walter had jilted her – the day she had expected to be married?

But why should he remember such a detail? It was only important to Kate – and only if she let it be.

Chapter Fifteen

From the outset, it was clear that the advertising postcards were going to be a roaring success. The enthusiasm of the photographer and his lovely model, coupled with that of Theodore Wesley's keen eye for the potential for increased sales, saw to that. And with the large fees the magnanimous Wesley was prepared to pay, Luke abandoned any idea of approaching other companies for advertising for now. Even though Wesley hadn't stipulated in their contract that his motor company was to have exclusive rights to the postcard advertising, Luke saw the ethics of it.

The cards began flooding the market at the end of February, showing Kate snuggled into a fur-trimmed coat and matching cloche hat, and looking appealingly into the camera as she leaned against the bonnet of the gleaming car. Wesley was delighted with the image. Kate looked the epitome of the rich young woman about town, he told her approvingly, and it was an image that was definitely going to promote car sales. There was a set of six different winter poses, and he thought that folk would start collecting them.

Later, once the new spring batch of postcards appeared, showing Kate in flimsy, fashionable summer frocks and smiling that glorious smile, other companies began approaching Luke.

Kate was settling a client's account in the studio one Monday towards the end of April, when Luke answered the phone, and put his hand over the receiver for a second.

"It's Pollard's," he mouthed at Kate.

Her eyes sparkled. They were one of the big new soap companies in the area. She didn't mind posing in front of the motors, but it was a man's world, and in Kate's mind there was something infinitely more feminine in advertising soap.

When she had sent the first batch of motor cards to her family, there had been all the disapproval she had expected.

"Your Dada's not so sure he likes the thought of all and sundry seeing your face on these cards, our Kate," her mother had written. "And Donal says you should have told us what you were doing before now. There's even a few of the cards on sale at the village shop. That nasty little gossipy person, Violet Parsons, stopped Donal the other day and told him to pass on her best wishes to you, and to say she always knew you'd come up smelling of roses, and not to worry if the priest thinks it's wickedness gone mad."

Kate could just imagine how Donal would hate to be approached by Vi in that arch voice of hers which always intimated that she knew something he didn't.

And so she did, in this case, Kate thought, with a shiver. But Donal never did have time for Vi and would have dismissed her words as just her usual gossipy nonsense.

Kate had written straight back home again, reassuring her family that everything was respectable, and enclosing an amount of money that must have made their eyes pop out. Since then, she had heard nothing more about the wickedness of the postcards, from the priest or anywhere else.

She ushered out the client from the studio, while Luke was still talking on the phone. But once they were alone, he grabbed her hands.

"We're going to see the managing director of Pollard's tomorrow afternoon, Kate, but there's no doubt that he intends to offer us a contract."

"That's marvellous," she said, with genuine delight. "But do you think Mr Wesley will have any objections?"

"I'll phone him right away, but I can't see why there should be. He keeps boasting that we've increased his car sales, and your face on different cards will only endorse the importance of it."

"It's not just my face, Luke," Kate protested, not wanting to take the credit or the responsibility of it all. "It's your photography that's at the heart of it."

"You're wrong, sweetheart. It's *you* who's at the heart of it all. Without you, none of it would be possible."

She wasn't sure about that. He could always get another model, but at the thought, her heart froze.

There were already a couple of other photographic firms jumping on the advertising bandwagon, but they were the first, and the most successful. Kate Sullivan was just what Luke had intended her to be. Even if she wasn't his, by now she was the nation's postcard sweetheart.

Luke put through the call to Theodore Wesley, and he was smiling at the end of it.

"He was perfectly all right when I pointed out that your face was obviously the one destined to launch a thousand different advertising ships, Kate."

When she looked totally blank, he laughed.

"It's literature, darling. Marlowe wrote that Helen of Troy had the face that would launch a thousand ships."

"Oh, I see."

But she didn't, not really. All she saw was that Luke was well versed in the classics, while she didn't have a clue what he was talking about. There were times, and this was one of them, when she was sharply reminded that she was still little Kate Sullivan, country girl; despite the new, smart clothes and bobbed haircut, and the fashionable places where she and Luke were seen in the city, and where her face was occasionally recognised. She brushed the feeling aside, knowing it was silly to feel inadequate when the girls at the boarding house were almost in awe of her now, telling her she had the world at her feet, and Thomas Lord Tannersley was forever booming at her that she should be on the stage with her looks.

"And there's only one thing wrong with that," she always told him. "I can't act!"

But she had acted a part at the Charlton Hotel all those months ago, and she was still acting a part now, she sometimes thought uneasily.

"I keep wondering when you're going to move out of here and get your own place," Doris said one night, quite tartly.

Kate's eyes widened. "Why on earth would I want to do that?"

"Well, with all the money you're making now, and the posh clothes you're buying, don't you want to act the way the model girls do and have a flashy apartment overlooking the river?"

"No thanks," Kate said. "I'm perfectly happy here with Mrs Wood. She hasn't said anything about wanting me to move out, has she?" she added as the sudden thought struck her.

"Course not," Doris said with a shrug. "Me and Faye just thought you'd want to. Either that or move in with *Lukey.*"

"Luke and I are business colleagues, and nothing more," Kate snapped. "How many more times do I have to tell you?"

"You're more of a fool than we took you for then – unless you've got some other well-heeled gent on the horizon."

"Sometimes, Doris, you really disgust me."

"Yeah, well, that's because I ain't got your looks or your money, or your chances," she said sullenly.

Kate put it all down to jealousy and tried to ignore it. Though it didn't help the occasional frosty atmosphere between them to know that Mrs Wood had the complete collection of postcards pinned up in her kitchen for all to see.

Luke had also sent them all off to the American friend who had put the idea in his head in the first place.

Pollard's Soap Company wanted to hire Luke and Kate immediately to help promote a new pink facial soap they were in the process of putting on the market. Their artists had already drawn up sketches showing how they wanted Kate smiling into the camera in a head and shoulder pose, holding a pink rose to her cheek, with the bar of soap behind her and a suitable caption beneath.

"Why should we argue, since they've already formed their own ideas?" Luke said to her, when the deal was settled. "It will be a completely different angle from Wesley's, and it'll do us no harm to show our versatility."

"Whatever that is," Kate murmured.

"Come on, you're not that dumb," Luke said with a smile. "In fact, you're not dumb at all, so don't pretend that you are. You put across some very pertinent points at the meeting with Pollard's, about make-up and flattering necklines."

"Oh yes, I'm learning," she said.

He glanced at her as they drove back to the studio.

"What's wrong?" he asked.

"Good Lord, nothing at all. Whatever could be wrong with the glamorous and successful – and almost disgustingly rich – Kate Sullivan!" she said.

"Well, something is. I know you too well, and sarcasm doesn't become you. So get it sorted out in your head, and when we get back to town you can tell me all about it."

Oh yes, of course she could do just that! She could tell him that she was feeling increasingly restless of late. That success didn't always equate with happiness. That she loved him, and wanted him, and that frustration was a word she was beginning to know all too well.

There was also the certainty that as the months went by Luke increasingly wanted more from their relationship. It couldn't be long before he was going to demand an answer from her, and she couldn't hold him off for ever. He'd been far more patient than Walter had ever been.

She rarely thought about Walter these days. If ever his name reared up in her consciousness it gave her a nasty little lurch in her stomach. And that in turn reminded her of what he'd done to her, and how her life had been ruined because of him. She tried to push all such thoughts away as they returned through the congested streets of London.

"If the general strike goes ahead, as it surely will, the streets won't be busy like this for very much longer," Luke observed. "With all public transport out of action, and industry grinding to a halt, London will be in chaos."

"It won't really be that bad, will it?" Kate said, thankful to be talking about something else, something that had been the main topic of conversation in the city for days now, ever since the miners had called their strike for the first of May. The Trades Unions had decided to join their cause and decreed that from May the fourth there would be a general strike throughout the country. The date was drawing near, and nothing had been done to resolve matters.

"Things have gone too far now for it to be averted," Luke said. "Don't you read anything in the newspapers?"

"Of course I do, some of it, anyway," Kate said defensively, "but if the miners want more money than they're already getting, it seems even dafter to go on strike and not get any pay at all."

"You try telling that to those poor devils who can't make ends meet already, and are now being expected to accept lower wages. People have to stand by their principles, Kate, and the government should listen to their views."

Kate hadn't read the newspaper reports in any great detail, and it was mainly due to Thomas's ramblings on how he'd run the country if it was left to him, and Mrs Wood's arguments on behalf of the miners' plight, that Kate knew as much as she did. But Luke took a fairly keen interest in political matters, especially those that affected business.

"There's rallies being held everywhere, by militant leaders and anybody else who wants their voice to be heard, all trying to inform the public of what's going on, and getting their support," he went on. "I'm going to one up west tomorrow night, if only to be better informed from the horses' mouths, so to speak. Do you want to come along?"

"All right," she said, having no idea what would be involved, but not wanting to appear a complete ninny. "Though if everything's so settled already I can't see what help a lot of shouting and arguing is going to do."

"The miners and the union men will still want to know that people are behind them. God knows how long the strike will last, but it's going to cause disruption everywhere. Vehicle owners will suddenly find themselves very popular when trams and buses are no longer available to get people to work, which is why I'm thinking of locking the Bentley safely away out of sight as soon as it starts."

"Why would you do that?"

"Because I'm not so public-spirited that I want to see my motor crushed by a frenzied crowd of people trying to get a free lift to work, or anywhere else. Selfish or not."

"I don't think it's selfish to want to keep something you've worked for. It's not as if you need the car for work yourself, and I can walk to the studio from Jubilee Terrace."

"Or you can move in with me until all the fuss is over."

Kate's face flamed. "That's not an option, Luke."

"I didn't think it would be. But you can't blame a fellow for trying," he said teasingly.

They joined the crowds at the evening rally in the park on the following night, where a hoarse young man with a heavy Welsh accent was ranting and raving at some hecklers in the front, asking how they would care to try and survive on the pittance he and his wife and family had to exist on.

"He'll be just a token speaker," Luke said in Kate's ear, "a poorly-dressed miner put up by the union men to get the initial sympathy vote in the crowd. The real heavy speakers will be on later, and the hecklers are probably planted there as well to make the miner's plight sound even worse."

"How cynical you make it sound!" Kate said. "I can't believe it's like you say, Luke."

"Then keep watching. When the miner moves away into the crowd, he'll be slipped a few coppers from a well-dressed man who'll be the next speaker."

Kate watched, disliking the falseness of it all, but still fascinated by the implied machinations. And that was about all. If this was politics, you could keep it, she thought. In fact, you could keep all of it. It just seemed like a lot of shouting; like kids at school. She had every sympathy for those who couldn't support their families, and indignation against a government who gave with one hand and took away with the other. But she had never understood the devious workings of politics, and if all this bawling and yelling was an example she didn't really want to start now.

She was only here in the park listening to the men on their soapboxes because Luke had suggested it, but as the noise in the crowd grew louder she couldn't even make out any sensible conversation among all the shouting and rabble-rousing, and she quickly became bored. They had been pressed ever more forward into the crowd when some ugly scuffling broke out among those at the front, and by then Kate decided she had had enough.

"Luke, can we go now? I really don't like the way things are going here."

He saw her pale face and nodded. He'd willingly gone to war for his country, but he had no intention of getting caught up in an angry civil mob. The constables had little chance of controlling the crowd, and once the strike began in earnest, even they would be off the streets, with only the special volunteers and the troops enlisted to try to keep order and distribute the lorry loads of food that would be taken to a huge central dump in Hyde Park.

A Different Kind of Love

By the time they decided to leave the scene, there were more people behind them, and they were somehow in the middle of it all. They had to fight their way through, and more than one elbow and boot found its way into Kate's body, until she thought she would be black and blue by tomorrow. But at last they left the park and reached the end of the road where the Bentley was parked. As she slid inside it, Kate was fervently in agreement with Luke, to keep the car off the streets for as long as the strike lasted.

She gave a grateful sigh as he started up the Bentley's engine, relaxing against the leather upholstery and feeling more than thankful to be heading back towards the comparative sanity of Jubilee Terrace. But if she hadn't had her eyes closed for those few blissful moments, all her complacency would have disappeared in an instant.

The man in the smart striped suit with wide lapels, and hair slicked down with oil, was wandering aimlessly aroud the West End to fill in time before making his way back to the hostelry where he had temporary lodgings. He didn't really care for London all that much, although there were rich pickings in the markets for a go-ahead travelling man with goods to sell and a ready patter for the ladies. He especially didn't care for the gap in the evenings, when work was over, and the night-time activities hadn't yet got going. He wasn't particularly interested in this bloody strike which was going to paralyse the country, either, and he was already thinking he'd do best to get back up north where he belonged, before he was left here like a stranded fish.

He was on the edge of the crowd, craning his neck to see what the belligerent speaker was on about, when he suddenly stood perfectly still, stopping so quickly that people cannoned into him, cursing his stupidity. He hardly noticed. He was too busy staring after the green Bentley disappearing around the corner, wondering if he'd been seeing things.

It couldn't really have been Kate Sullivan, all dolled up and

241

looking fancier than he'd ever seen her in his life before, a world away from the frightened-eyed country girl who'd begged him to marry her.

Walter Radcliffe frowned, unwilling to have too many reminders of that time, almost a year ago now, knowing full well what a bastard he had been. He frowned again, as his memories forced him into thinking about something else. Something he'd pushed squarely out of his mind all these months when he'd been so neglectful in sending money home to Kate, like he'd promised. Money for the kid.

His eyes narrowed. From the look of her, sliding into that bloody flash motor car and looking like Lady Muck, she wasn't short of money. The car was far more swanky than the piddling thing he drove, spluttering around the country.

If it *was* Kate, she'd come up trumps all right, and he'd like to know just how. And more than that, he'd like to know just what she'd done with the kid. Her kid. His kid.

All the talk back at Jubilee Terrace was about the strike. Luke stayed long enough to join in the discussion with Thomas, who was sounding off as usual in his booming voice, while Doris and Faye made themselves scarce. Even darling Lukey's presence couldn't make them interested in politics.

"I say give the miners what they deserve," Mrs Wood said stoutly. "A man has a right to a living wage, and if those poor buggers ain't getting it – pardon my French – then the government should be ashamed of itself."

"No government was ever ashamed of itself, dear lady," Thomas said.

"Then it's time we got 'em out! It's up to people like us to vote for the other lot when the time comes, ain't it? The Tories have had things their way long enough, always on the side of the toffs and not the workers."

"Providing you think the other lot would do things any better, Mrs W," Luke said, as she got into her stride.

"They couldn't do no worse, could they?" Mrs Wood retorted. "We always did differ on this one, Luke, and I daresay we always will, and I ain't going to spend the rest of the night arguing about it. So who's for cocoa and a piece of my seed cake?"

"That sounds a marvellous idea, dear lady," Thomas said soothingly. "And I'm sure things will go ahead in the way it's been ordained. What do you say, little lady?" he asked Kate.

She jumped as he directed his penetrating gaze on her. He had such a theatrical presence, she thought fleetingly, she could see just how he would captivate an audience, but she hardly knew how to answer him.

"I'm not sure what you mean," she murmured.

"Oh, come along, I'll bet my Hamlet boots that you believe in destiny and fate and a greater order of things beyond our understanding! You're a far deeper-thinking girl than our twittery young things upstairs!"

"I'm not sure whether that's a compliment or not," Kate laughed. "It makes me sound pretty dreary!"

"You're anything but that, sweetie. Right, Luke?"

"Oh, Kate knows what I think about her," Luke said with a smile. "And I refuse to be drawn on that, you old rogue."

"Well, if you've both finished sorting out my character, I think I'd like to go to bed," Kate said, pink-faced. "And I'll see you tomorrow, Luke."

She fled from the room, hearing Mrs Wood chide the pair of them for making her feel embarrassed and chasing her away. But Kate knew it was more than that. It was what Thomas had said about believing in destiny and fate.

In her more receptive moments she definitely believed that fate had sent her to Bournemouth on the day she had been jilted. Fate had sent Luke Halliday there at the same time, and destiny had brought them together. And that was where the fantasy ended, because her own stupid conscience wouldn't let it go any further.

If she was a different sort of girl – maybe the sort of twittery young thing in the way Thomas had described Doris and Faye – she would do as Vi Parsons had suggested. She would concoct some story about how she was no longer a virgin because of a horse-riding escapade or accident. She could blame it all on nature.

But she was too honest for that. Her mouth twisted at such a bizarre thought, when she was guilty of such lies and deceit. Even letting Walter go on believing she was pregnant, when she wasn't. But she was more than thankful that he'd never lived up to his promise of sending her any money after he had deserted her. She could never have used it, despite the fact that his failure to provide for her and the child just proved what a rat he really was.

She undressed quickly and crawled into bed, shivering. She had never thought her association with Walter would have such far-reaching effects. He had ruined her life, but she had naively thought it could be put together again, and that one day she would find a kind, honourable, loving man. Now that she had, she was too afraid to let him love her, because she couldn't bear to see the shock and disgust in his eyes if he ever learned the truth.

She turned her face into her pillow, feeling the tears squeeze through her tightly closed eyelids. Wishing for the hundredth time that she could change the past, and most of all that she had never met Walter Radcliffe.

Walter was contemplating his third jug of ale in the hostelry he was staying in and deciding what to do with the knowledge he'd obtained that evening.

All around him there was political talk, with loud-voiced Londoners putting the world to rights, some for, some against, the imminent strike.

It was all getting out of hand in the public house, just as it had done in the park, and he was tired of it all. His plan had been to get out of London before it all began. He'd done enough business to see him right with his boss, and he'd far rather be back in his own territory than stuck in a city where nothing was going to move for God knew how long.

But all that was changed now. He'd got a glimpse of Kate Sullivan, and he was damned if he was leaving here until he knew what she was up to, and what she was doing with his kid. He felt a unexpected spurt of filial pride at the thought, wondering if it was a boy or a girl. He had to know, and the more he thought about it, the more he knew he had to find her.

"What about these special constables, then?" he asked loudly, when there was a small break in the other drinkers' conversation. "Can anybody volunteer?"

"Course they can, brother," one of the men said. "You just report to any police station and they'll issue you with an arm band and baton to say you're now a special going about official business. You'll report back to them and they'll let you know where there's trouble to be sorted out."

Walter wasn't interested in sorting out trouble. He'd kept well enough out of it in the trenches, and he didn't aim to be in the thick of it now. But it could be useful in finding his way around London and having a legitimate reason for staying here. It seemed unlikely that even street traders would be welcomed if the strike went on for any length of time, so he might as well be seen to do his bit.

He discovered his mistake once the strike began to take effect. Anyone trying to do an honest day's work was blackballed by picketers, and those trying to get into their regular places of business were called scabs and worse. After a week of chaos, troops and volunteers were being stoned by regular workers thinking they were taking their jobs, however temporarily. Walter decided that London was not the place to be after all.

He'd had his car put out of sight in a lock-up, so at least that was safe. But after he'd got hit in the face at one demonstration, he'd had enough, and he told his group of volunteers he had urgent business elsewhere. The leader looked at him sourly, menacingly slapping his baton into the palm of his hand.

"Oh yeah? Getting lily-livered, are you? Well, you ain't getting out of it that easily, boy. We've had a call to get round to Lombard Street to break up a fight. We ain't losing one of our number now, so get moving, you yellow bugger."

He was pulled along with the rest of them. They were passed by a food convoy on its way to Hyde Park escorted by troops, and Walter dearly wished he could have leapt onto the truck and got away from these bloodhounds.

Once they reached Lombard Street he was again in the thick of it, and it took a good hour before they were able to break up the demonstration that had been blocking the streets stopping vital services getting through. By the time order was restored, there were several men lying on the ground with bleeding heads.

"They ain't hurt bad," one of the specials growled. "Somebody get 'em onto the pavements and off the streets, and the rest of you come with me."

Walter began to drag the wounded men into the nearest shop doorway. All the shops were closed, and no business had been done here or anywhere else for a week. All the same, it seemed as if support for the miners was beginning to fade, and everybody said the static situation couldn't last much longer. People were simply tiring of the incovenience. By now the trains had begun to run again, the timetables announced on the wireless. If all else failed, Walter thought savagely, he'd get on a bloody train and get back where he belonged.

And then, just as surely as a moth was drawn to a flame, his eyes were drawn to a wire display stand inside the shop where he was standing. A display stand holding birthday cards and postcards. And there, staring out at him on a postcard demonstrating a luxury motor, and smiling the voluptuous smile he remembered, was Kate Sullivan's face. The shock was so great that Walter almost staggered over the prone shape of the one wounded man left in the doorway now. The man groaned in protest, but since he wasn't dead Walter didn't give him another second's attention.

"Bugger me!" he said out loud. "The bitch has got it made all right. First I see her living it up in some fancy man's Bentley, and now she's making a mint of money, I'll be bound, from some motor firm paying her oodles of cash for this lark. She don't look like no innocent no more, and Walter, lad, this takes some thinking about."

His eyes narrowed as he studied several more postcards showing Kate Sullivan posing against different motor cars, her eyes lustrous and wide, her curvaceous shape shown to best advantage. He felt the lusty urges stir in his crotch, remembering . . . he heard the man at his feet groan again, complaining that the least he could do was to get him to a hospital.

"You'll not be hurt that much. It's no more than a scratch," Walter snapped. "But I'll give you a few coppers if you'll tell me what I want to know."

The man perked up a little. "Make it the price of a pint and I'll tell you anything you want. I've had enough of demonstrating for a lost cause, and I'm off home to my missus as soon as I can stand," he muttered.

"Well then, what do you know about these motors?" Walter said, stabbing his finger against the shop window.

The man looked at him as if he was daft.

"Do I look as if I'd know anything about motors like that? I ain't got two ha'pennies to rub together on a Sat'day night, let alone owning a fancy motor or any other kind. If you want to know more about 'em you'd better go to one of them car showrooms once they're open for business again."

Walter could hear the bitterness in his voice, and he flung him the coppers anyway, watching him tip his cap in gratitude and slink away. His type probably didn't even know what he'd been demonstrating about, but at least he'd given him an idea. Tomorrow, he'd find a car showroom and knock up the proprietor.

Or better still, he thought suddenly, he'd come back to this shop or some other newsagents, and persuade the shopkeeper to open up so he could buy a couple of postcards. It would be easy enough to show the armband and pretend he was here on official business, warning shopkeepers of potential trouble in the area. There'd surely be some detail about the motors or the model girl on them, or even the firm printing the things, and then he could track Kate down. It would be a laugh to have her picture in his wallet – providing he remembered to keep it well out of sight before he got home to his old woman.

Chapter Sixteen

The general strike lasted all of nine days before it was called off, although the miners doggedly refused to give in, and declared their intention to remain on strike for the foreseeable future. But London and all the major cities breathed a collective sigh of relief, and got back to normal.

"What disruption it caused, and for what?" Mrs Wood observed over the evening meal with her lodgers. "The poor devils are no better off now than before. Lord knows how long they'll have to stay out without the support of the country."

"They must feel the country has let them down," Kate said.

"More likely the government, as usual," the landlady said keenly. "Still, you and Luke will be glad to get back to proper work, I daresay. I wonder you didn't take the chance to go home to your folks for a while, Kate."

"I couldn't do that while the trains weren't running," she pointed out, "and I wouldn't have asked Luke to take me. Besides, there was plenty of work we could do at the studio, even though we were officially closed."

"Oh aye, in that mysterious darkroom of his, I'll bet," Faye put in jealously.

"That's right," Kate said, deliberately leading her on. "You'd be surprised what wonders go on in there."

"Now then, you two," Mrs Wood said. "I'm sure it's all perfectly innocent and above board, and I won't have my

Lukey's name slurred, miss," she added to Faye.

"Nor Kate's neither," she added as an afterthought.

The post had begun to be delivered again, after being held up all this time, and Kate had an anxious letter from her mother. The village of Edgemoor didn't experience much day-to-day difference during the general strike. In farming communities cows still had to be milked and pigs and hens still had to be fed, and big business and trades unions were just words.

But Alice was concerned for Kate's safety, and she made it plain in her letter to Kate that her father wanted her to come home to the safety of the country. Even as she read the letter, and understood their concern for her, Kate knew she couldn't go back, at least, not for ever. She would always think of Edgemoor as a haven, and she loved her family, but she had moved on and away from them. It was sad, but inevitable, she thought. Everybody had to establish a life of their own eventually. She wrote back to her mother straight away to reassure her.

Dear Mother,

We've all been perfectly safe here, and Luke and I have been able to continue working behind closed doors, getting the new batch of photos ready for the autumn set of postcards. It seems odd to think of autumn already, but in the advertising business you always have to be thinking of the season ahead and not the present one. I've learned a lot about it these past few months. Don't worry about me. It's pleasantly warm here in London now, and I'll bet the country around Edgemoor is looking lovely.

She paused in writing the inane words about the weather, but she knew how much Alice always wanted to know if the city was full of fog, even in summer. As she paused, Kate remembered with a burst of nostalgia just how lovely the countryside around the village would look now, with the summer blossom filling the hedgerows, and the fields and hills so green, busy with the hum of bees and the drone of insects. And the white-washed farm buildings and thatched cottages.

She smiled ruefully, knowing that part of her would always belong to Somerset, no matter how far she travelled. It was home, and sometimes you had to go away from it to appreciate how much it meant to you.

"What a profound thought for a Wednesday," Kate said aloud. She continued with her letter, not wanting to let sentiment get in the way of what she had to tell them. It was something private as yet, but there was no harm in letting her folks know, since they were hardly going to spread the news, and they never gossiped.

Luke had some important news this week, once the post got through again. He was approached by an American company, showing some interest in his skills as a photographer for some advertising postcards over there. It's all hush-hush at present, and I'm telling you this in confidence. I don't know whether he'll do anything about it. It all came about because he sent our postcards to his American friend, who showed them to the company concerned, and this is the result.

She didn't tell them any more, because she didn't really know any more, and Luke had been unusually casual in telling her. She had expected him to be over the moon with excitement at the prospect of such a commission, but he hadn't seemed to be. Knowing him as well as she did, his reaction had puzzled her. It would be marvellous for him to be known internationally, but it had to be his decision, of course.

She finished her letter, sending lots of love and kisses to her sisters, stuck the stamp on the envelope, and decided to go down to the posting box with it right away.

Writing home had reminded her of walking in the country, where you could walk for miles without seeing anybody and just revel in the solitude. She found herself thinking she'd like to do that right now, and wished Mrs Wood had a dog she could exercise, since it always seemed less aimless than walking alone. But why not take a walk on her own? Plenty of people did on such a warm, mellow May evening.

There was a small park not far from Jubilee Terrace. One of the things that had pleasantly surprised Kate when she first came to London was the number of small parks there were between the mass of buildings.

With his knowledge of the city, Luke had told her it went back to ancient times, when London was as countrified as anywhere in England, full of lush meadows instead of being packed with buildings. And many of the small, enclosed parks and copses remained. He'd shown her an illustrated book about London the way it used to be in times past, and she had been charmed by it all.

There weren't many people about now, but being alone had never bothered Kate. Once or twice lately, a few folk had stared quite hard at her as if they recognised her and it had made her more uncomfortable. She would rather be an anonymous face in a crowd. It was the price of fame, Luke had told her. It came from having her face displayed on all the postcards, and she should learn to accept it and enjoy it. She smiled ruefully, wondering if she ever would.

Walter Radcliffe prided himself on having done a good bit of detective work. He had gone to the nearest newsagents and bought up all the postcards with Kate's face on them, and studied them minutely at his hostelry lodgings. She had always been a good-looker, but by God, she was even better now.

His idea of tracking down a few car showrooms to find out the origins of the cards was quickly abandoned as he discovered that it wasn't necessary. All the statistics of the cars

were on the reverse side of each card, together with the name of
Luke Halliday, photographer. There was no mention of Kate's
name, but as far as Walter was concerned, there didn't need
to be. He'd have recognised her full, obliging mouth and that
seductive, willing little body, if it was hidden inside a sack.

He'd thought hard about what he was going to do. If Kate
had come into money, he wouldn't mind a sub. It might be worth
it to her to keep him out of the picture, especially if the kid was
calling some other chap daddy by now. He felt a surprising stab
of jealousy at the thought. If she had a kid, then it was his,
and he had a right to see it, at least. But he decided not to act
hastily. That had always been his downfall in the past.

He found Luke's business address from the telephone book,
and bided his time sitting in his car at a convenient vantage
point from the studio, watching the comings and goings of the
rich clients who frequented the place. He also knew the time
that Kate arrived there each day, and when she left, either on
foot or in the Bentley, and he frequently followed her back to
Jubilee Terrace at a safe distance.

He was tempted to go brashly into the tall house while she
was out at work and demand to see his kid, since presumably
somebody there was looking after it. He even toyed with the
idea of kidnapping, but quickly forgot that, since it was an
encumbrance he didn't want. And his old woman would be
none too pleased at seeing another woman's brat, either, Walter
thought feelingly.

So he had decided against storming the house, and waited
until he could confront Kate on her own. His chance came
when he saw her leave the house early one evening, walking
towards the posting box with a letter in her hand, and then
going towards the local park.

"Hello, Kate."

She heard the voice, and for a split second refused to believe it
was the voice she detested most in all the world. She turned very

slowly and her heart beat sickeningly, knowing very well who she was about to see. It confirmed what had been nagging away at her lately, when she'd been eerily convinced that someone was watching her. It also confirmed what she had always known – that for every sin, there had to be a reckoning.

But for the moment her mouth dried completely, and she couldn't speak as she looked into the bold eyes and fleshy mouth of her one-time lover. Walter was as nattily turned out as ever, his hair slicked back to a glossy sheen. As he smiled arrogantly, the feeling of hatred in her soul for him shocked Kate to the core.

She stepped back clumsily, almost stumbling, and Walter's hand shot out to steady her.

"Don't you dare touch me, you bastard," she said venomously, shaking him off.

His eyes widened a little at the unexpected expletive. Coming from quiet little unassuming Kate, it was quite something. But there was nothing quiet and unassuming about her now.

"Well, well, it's easy to see you've come out of your shell since the last time we met," he said, sneering to cover his feeling of surprise. "Is this new air of confidence to do with the new boyfriend with the swanky Bentley, or the new successful artist's model you've become? I suppose it'll be nude pictures next. And to think you played the innocent with me for so long, darling."

Kate felt as if she'd been punched in the stomach. How the devil did he come to know so much about her? And how dare he demean the work she and Luke did so successfully? Her eyes filled with furious tears, and she blinked them quickly away.

"You're scum, Walter, and you always were. How my brother ever befriended you I'll never know. I wish to God I'd never set eyes on you."

"But you did, darling, and we both know it was more than just our eyes that got together, don't we? So where is the little brat?"

254

Kate stared at him, not understanding, and after a moment his hand shot out to grip her cruelly around her wrist, making her gasp with the pain of it.

"Or are you going to deny me access to my own kid, on account of I never sent you any money for its upkeep? Let's see, it must be three or four months old now, by my reckoning, and I must say you've still managed to keep that luscious shape of yours, Katie girl. I still have a taste for it . . ."

"Keep away from me, you bastard!" Kate screamed as his face came nearer to hers, and the meaning of what he was saying dawned on her.

There was no time to think. All she wanted was to get him away from her, and she said the first words that came into her head, just to be rid of him.

"There's no baby. There never was, at least not by the time you were supposed to marry me."

The second she had spoken, she clapped her free hand to her mouth, seeing the murderous look in his eyes. His face was almost purple with rage.

"Are you telling me, you bitch, that you tried to get me to marry you under false pretences?"

Kate gave a hysterical laugh. "Well, that's bloody rich, coming from you! You led me on, and you were the one ready to commit bigamy, and you didn't even have the guts to tell me to my face about the wife at home."

She screamed again as he struck her on the side of her head. Her senses spun, and for a few moments she was totally disorientated. He shook her until her teeth rattled. She wished desperately that someone would come and end this terror, but it seemed now as if the park was deserted except for themselves.

"And what if I'd gone through with the bloody wedding?" he shouted. "Then I'd have been in real trouble, wouldn't I? I told you at the time it was best for all concerned if I simply disappeared."

"It's a pity you didn't do that before you ruined me," Kate sobbed, stiff with the pain in her cheek, wondering how many of her teeth had been loosened by his rough handling.

"Aye, perhaps it is," he sneered. "All right, so there's no kid. Whether or not there ever was one is beside the point now. So what happened to the money I left you? Did you do as I said and go to Bournemouth and find some other sap who was taken in by those innocent blue eyes and all your play-acting? You certainly fooled me, bitch."

She stared at him. He was unbelievable. But he wasn't going to deprive her of all her dignity. She lifted her chin and stared him out.

"Yes, I went to Bournemouth, and I enjoyed it, too," she almost spat at him. "I put your nasty little letter in the fire where it belonged, and I spent all your money on having a bloody good time."

She shrieked as he grabbed her to him, his eyes hardening. He pushed her back towards the bushes, and she was more frightened than she had ever been in her life. This was not the sweet-talking seducer of women she had once known, but a potential rapist.

"Walter, for God's sake, don't do this."

"Don't do what? Take my pleasures the way I used to do, sweetness? I'd almost forgotten what it was like to fornicate with you, but by God, I intend to revive my memory now."

He pushed her towards the bushes, and it was only because they were so thickly meshed that she managed to stop herself falling flat on her back. Once she did that, she knew she would be at his mercy. So, still on her feet and before she gave it a second thought, Kate drew back her arm and clenched her fist, and then rammed it with all her might into his crotch.

"You stinking whore!" he gasped, bent double and clutching himself. His eyes filled with tears of pain. "I'll have you for this!"

"You'll be lucky to do anything with that thing for a while

256

yet," she shouted. "Don't you ever come near me again, Walter Radcliffe. If you do, I'll have the law on you."

Somehow, while he was still cursing her and nursing his tender, throbbing parts, she twisted away from him. She ran as fast as she could, out of the park and along the road, sobbing and gasping, brushing past the few passers-by who tried to stop her and ask what was wrong.

She couldn't face anyone. She couldn't let Mrs Wood see that she was so upset, and she certainly didn't want Doris and Faye interrogating her. And the last person she could bear to see right now was Luke.

She walked the streets for what seemed like hours, until it grew dusk and darkness fell, and only then did she return to Jubilee Terrace. She called out goodnight to anyone who might be in the parlour, and went straight up to her room. She made herself a hot strong cup of tea on her little gas ring, lacing it with brandy to counteract the shock, and drank it down without ever noticing how it scalded her mouth.

In minutes, Walter had brought back all the horror of the past to the surface. It was never going to go away. He had shamed her for ever, and if she ever thought she could keep it hidden away indefinitely, she knew differently now. She sobbed long into the night.

She hardly slept. Her nerves were so ragged that she jumped at the merest sound of traffic outside the house, and the alarm made her heart pound so fast she thought she was going to die.

Maybe it would be better if she did die, she thought, at her lowest ebb. She had thought so before, when Walter deserted her, and everything had seemed so hopeless, but she had overcome it all. She had met Luke, and because of him she had come to London and taken the first step in making a new life for herself and re-establishing her self-esteem.

Because of Luke, she had found the kind of modest success

she had never even dreamed about. And because of him, she knew how desperately she had never wanted to see or hear of Walter ever again. Luke would totally despise her if he knew her past history, and she couldn't bear to see that dawning look in his eyes when he knew she was little more than a slut. She didn't hide from the word. It was what everyone in Edgemoor would have called her, if they had known the truth. Small communities didn't take kindly to one of their number playing fast and loose with travelling men. She condemned herself more with every thought, as if it would help to cleanse her soul.

"Kate, have you got a bar of soap I can borrow?" she heard Doris's voice say, followed by the hammering on her door. "I know Pollard's have given you some samples, and I've just run out, so I have."

Kate wasn't even out of bed, but irritably she flung off the bedcovers and called to the girl to come in while she fetched the soap from the box the company had given her. Doris and Faye had mocked that it was a pity she hadn't been given a complimentary sample from Wesley's motors instead.

"Here you are. I don't want it back," she said, handing Doris the bar of soap, knowing she would never have intended replacing it anyway.

"Merciful Mother of God, what's been happening to you?" Doris exclaimed.

"What do you mean?" Kate snapped.

"Take a look in the mirror, for the Lord's sake, and don't tell me you're after forgetting how you got that shiner! It was never Lukey that did such a terrible thing, was it?"

Kate rushed across to the mirror.

Her face still felt so stiff with crying and tormenting herself, that she had completely overlooked the real reason for it. Looking at herself, her heart jumped. One side of her face was swollen and distorted where Walter had struck her, and all the skin around her left eye was a fine mixture of reds and purples. There was a cut on her lower lip, and now she moved her jaw a litle more carefully, she felt how tender it was. But not as tender as Walter's nether regions, she hoped savagely.

"What happened?" Doris said, flopping down on Kate's bed as if she had no intention of moving until she heard it all, her concern mixed with avid curiosity. "Did you and Luke have a fight? Was he trying it on after all? I never really thought he was that kind, but a bloke's a bloke—"

"It wasn't Luke," Kate snapped. "Don't be so daft, nor always so quick to jump to conclusions, Doris."

"Well, don't try telling me you fell against a door, me darlin', because we can all recognise the lies behind that one. Somebody hit you, and hit you bloody hard, by the looks of it. Have you reported it to the police?"

The last thing Kate wanted to do was report any of it to the police, or to have Walter investigated. Her vivid imagination soared wildly, Vi being dragged up as a character witness, and hearing the woman being scared into revealing far too much. It would be the worst humiliation of all, especially if it all came out, about being seduced by Walter, and the miscarriage, and the almost bigamous marriage, and her own deceit in not telling him there wasn't going to be a baby after all. When it was all boiled down, she didn't know which of them was worse.

"I haven't reported it to the police, because I've got no idea who it was," she invented quickly as Doris impatiently waited for information. "Somebody jumped out on me in the park and knocked me out, and the next thing I knew I came round and it was dark."

"Did he tamper with you? You know! Down there." She nodded to Kate's lower regions. "You'd be feeling bloody sore if he did, Kate, and I reckon you should get yourself off to see a doctor because you might have caught something. You never know with tramps or fly-by-nights."

Kate swallowed. The girl was only trying to help, but unwittingly she had said something Vi would surely have

259

latched onto. She could pretend it had been an appalling attack, and she'd been the victim of an unknown rapist . . . But she couldn't add more lies to all the others. Anyway, what doctor was going to look at her and say she had just been interfered with? There would be physical evidence of such a thing . . . her mind veered away from the distasteful thought. Even more so, from the indignity and shame of being examined by a stranger.

"Nothing like that happened, Doris," she said huskily, "I know I'm still the same as before."

"Well, you'd better have some witch hazel for your face," Doris said practically, clearly disappointed that there was no juicier piece of gossip to pass on. "I know Ma Wood's got some, so I'll fetch it for you. There's not much point in going to work today with a face like that, is there? Lukey won't want to be taking pictures of it, unless it was for the coppers' identity files."

She giggled at her own joke, and before Kate could protest that cold water would be good enough to reduce the swelling on her face, she was gone to fetch the witch hazel. As expected, when she came back, Faye and Mrs Wood were with her, exclaiming in horror at the state of Kate's face.

"You'll definitely not go to work today, my dear," Mrs Wood declared at once. "Your mother would never forgive me if I didn't do my duty by you and insist that you stay in bed."

"I'm not ill, Mrs Wood, and Luke will be expecting me."

"Don't you worry none about that. Thomas can go down there and tell him what's happened. I'm sure he can manage without you for one day, and you wouldn't be able to pose for your soap pictures now, would you?"

"We've done all we were commissioned to do for the present."

"Well then, that's that. Now, you just dab your poor face

with this magic stuff and get yourself back into bed, and I'll bring some breakfast up to you."

"Honestly, it's not necessary!"

But she was weakening. Mrs Wood was acting like a mother hen, shooing the curious girls out of the room and taking care of her. And she needed so much to be taken care of right now. All her carefully built-up confidence had been shattered in one brief meeting with Walter. And if she had ever believed in fate, she believed in it now. Fate was paying her back.

"She's been *what?*" Luke almost shouted, as Thomas delivered his message at the studio, and looked around him with interest, and he thought it a pity he'd never had more professional photos done for posterity.

"Now calm down, my dear sir, she's not badly hurt," Thomas said, putting on his best soothing face. "The poor little lady was attacked while out walking last night, and suffered some swelling to her face and a bruiser of an eye. But it's nothing that won't heal of its own accord."

"But who did it? Does she know? And more to the point, has she done anything about it?" In his agitation, Luke grabbed Thomas's lapels, and the man shook him off carefully.

"I gather she had no idea who attacked her, and nor does she want any fuss. She was most adamant about it. All she wants is to be left alone to recover, and she begs you to forgive her absence here today."

Luke looked at him as if he was demented. "For God's sake, man, do you think I care about that if Kate's hurt?" he snapped. "I'll cancel all today's sittings, and go to her at once."

"I'm sorry, my boy, but she doesn't want that. She sent you a note, explaining."

He handed it over, and Luke ripped open the envelope. Kate's usual neat, square handwriting was less than tidy today, and he guessed the note had been hastily written.

261

Please Luke, give me a few days to be alone. You wouldn't want to see me now, anyway, with my face such a sight. But I'm all right, really, and Mrs Wood is taking good care of me. Please don't cancel anything on my acount.

She had signed it, and Luke's mouth tightened as he saw how it was scrawled, as if even that had been too much of an effort. But she knew him too well, anticipating that he'd close the studio for her.

"Is she really going to be all right?" he said at last.

"Of course she will. It was a nasty shock, I guarantee, but you have to understand how she feels, wanting to hide herself away for a while, just like a wounded animal would. Let her have some dignity, Luke."

After a minute Luke nodded slowly, and drew out some money from his wallet. If time was what Kate needed, it was what she must have.

"There's a flower seller at the end of the street, Thomas. Will you buy the biggest bunch of red roses you can find and take them to her for me with my love?"

"Gladly, dear boy."

Luke watched him go. He'd far rather be taking the roses to Kate himself. But he knew, as well as she did, that there was a busy schedule today. A titled lady and her children were to have their portraits done, and it would have been awkward, to say the least, to have cancelled it. He would have done so, though, even if he risked losing the commission.

New propositions were coming his way all the time, and many of them he simply discarded. But there were others that needed a lot more consideration. He'd been going to talk to Kate about them when the right opportunity arose, but now certainly wasn't the time. She would be feeling as fragile and vulnerable as she had been when he first met her a year ago.

He cursed the unknown attacker for destroying all the self-confidence he had seen grow in her over the months.

She had always been a stunningly pretty girl, but lately she had grown into a lovely, sophisticated woman, while still managing to retain her air of innocence. A look that was enhanced by that provocative smile which had wound itself around his heart for so long.

And the year since he met her was up. He'd held off all this time, when his dearest wish was to make her his wife. He wasn't prepared to wait much longer. He had all the natural urges of a virile, red-blooded young man – and he simply wouldn't think about what to do if Kate finally refused him.

There was only one thing he was sure about – if she ever gave him that ultimatum, then he couldn't go on seeing her day after day. Their relationship had to be resolved, one way or another. He was her friend, and glad to be so, but this assault on her only made him more sure that what he wanted most out of life was to be her protector, her husband and her lover.

Chapter Seventeen

Kate knew Luke wouldn't stay away for long. When Mrs Wood brought the huge jug full of red roses to her room and told her Luke had sent them, she knew she couldn't hide behind closed doors for ever. The roses filled her bedroom with their heady scent. They were the colour of love and passion, and she knew it was what Luke wanted from her, just as much as she longed to give it. If only there had been no Walter.

She insisted on coming downstairs for the evening meal, even though the others hardly knew how to talk to her without embarrassment. The swelling on her cheek had gone down considerably, but the skin surrounding her bruised eye had changed from red and purple to a lovely shade of midnight blue, Faye told her.

"Thanks for being so complimentary," Kate retorted. "That makes me feel a whole lot better!"

"I only meant it was a lovely colour, and it matches your eyes," Faye said. "There's no need to be so snappy."

"Leave Kate alone and get on with your food," Mrs Wood said. "It's bad enough for the poor girl to have the bruises without being reminded of them all the time."

It didn't help, either, to listen to Faye's nasal Yorkshire tones, with their similarity to Walter's. It had never bothered Kate before, but every little thing seemed to be magnified in her mind now.

Both the other girls were meeting young men that evening, and Kate and Mrs Wood were being treated to one of

Thomas's endless theatrical anecdotes when Kate's acute hearing registered the sound of the Bentley outside. A few minutes later Luke was inside the parlour, coming to sit beside Kate and taking her cold hands in his.

"If I knew who had done this to you, I'd kill him with my bare hands, my love," he said roughly.

Her eyes filled. She wasn't sure she could cope with his kindness right now, and she tried to laugh off his words.

"And a fat lot of good that would do, since it would only land you behind bars!"

"I'd far rather see the villain behind bars," he agreed. "Didn't you get even the briefest glimpse of him?"

"I've already said so a million times. Didn't Thomas tell you?" Kate said jerkily.

"Just the bare essentials," Luke said, thinking that the assault had left her far more disturbed than he had imagined. She looked pinched and drawn, and he was reminded of how she had looked when he had first seen her on her balcony at the Charlton Hotel.

"You've got to put it all behind you, Kate," he went on firmly. "You musn't let it prey on your mind."

Her eyes flashed at him. "That's easy for you to say, isn't it? But not so easy for me to do!"

"I'll go and make us all a nice cup of tea," Mrs Wood said, when it looked as though they were going to get heated. Thomas got up as well, muttering something about having things to do, and Kate and Luke were left alone.

"Do you want to talk about it?" Luke said.

"No, I don't want to talk about it," she snapped at him. "I was attacked, and I just want to be left alone to get over it in my own time, that's all!"

"He didn't hurt you, did he? You know what I mean."

Kate felt her face flame. It was one thing to ward off Doris's salacious questions, but it was something else when it was Luke.

"He didn't hurt me. Now can we forget it, please? And you won't mind if I don't come into work for a couple of days, will you? I don't feel I'm the best advertisement for you at the moment."

"Stay off for as long as you feel the need. You must take care of yourself, and Mrs W. will be sure to look after you."

Kate knew it wasn't just the embarrassment of the way she looked, and the lingering bruising in her face that was filling her with misery. She and Luke were talking to one another like strangers; it was a gap that neither of them seemed able to bridge.

She was thankful when Mrs Wood came back with a tray of tea and biscuits, calling out to Thomas that if he wanted some he'd better come downstairs pronto. Even so, the usual easy chatter between them all seemed to have temporarily deserted them. When Luke said it was probably time he left, even the adoring Mrs Wood said she thought it was best, and that Kate needed her rest. All of it was her fault, Kate thought desperately. Because of her problems, everyone was finding it hard to be themselves.

"I think I'll have an early night," she said a little later, thought it was barely nine o'clock, and very early for anyone to retire in this bohemian household. "I've got a couple of letters I want to write."

It wasn't strictly true, though she thought vaguely that she might write to Donal if she could think of anything to tell him that wasn't too personal.

In the end, she decided to write to her brother, because in doing so, she would feel a sense of normality again, even though the main thing she had to tell him about was the general strike. He'd want to know, and she hadn't cared to tell her mother too many details.

You wouldn't believe the numbers of people crowding into the streets, Donal. It was unnerving to walk about with all the demonstrators and militants shouting and arguing the toss.

Ordinary folk were never in any danger, though. Luke took me to a rally in one of the parks, and it just sounded like a lot of silly men behaving like children. I know it wasn't really like that, and I felt enormous pity for the miners, and still do. But if they thought this was the way to go about getting a bit more money, it didn't work.

Mrs Wood thought I might have wanted to go home for a while, but for a start nobody knew how long the strike was going to last, and for another, there weren't any trains running. Anyway, it didn't seem quite the thing to do to run out on Luke, when we still had plenty of work we could do.

She chewed the end of her pen, wondering what else to tell him. Not about the encounter with Walter, that was for sure. Just like Luke, Donal would be ready to tear the city apart until he found Walter and dealt with him. Jerkily, she screwed up the letter and threw it in the bin.

She shivered. All she wanted was to forget his assault had ever happened, and to put him out of her life. She had never imagined he'd want to see his child, since he'd never struck her as having paternal tendencies. She knew it was wrong that she had never put him right about her miscarriage, but, never expecting to see him again, she had let the fact slip conveniently to the back of her mind.

Now she knew how foolish that had been. But, praying that she wasn't being hopelessly naive again, perhaps now that he knew the truth, he wouldn't want anything more to do with her.

By the end of the week, when make-up hid most of the bruises and swelling on her face, Kate felt marginally better able to put things into a more reasonable perspective, and of course

Walter wouldn't bother her again. Why should he? He would never dare, when she could produce all the witnesses she would need to denounce him for breach of promise, which would also bring to light the fact that he was already married.

If only she had thought about that in the park, she could have threatened him with exposing his nasty little game, because now that she had had plenty of time to think about it, she knew she had all the trump cards in her hand.

It didn't matter that in her heart she was sure she could never do such a thing with all the publicity it would arouse, especially with her new status as what Luke teasingly called the nation's postcard sweetheart. At least it helped her recover a little of her feeling of self-worth by remembering that Walter had done far more wrong to her than she had ever done to him. He had promised her marriage long before she had become pregnant, when he was in no position to do so.

But by Monday she was feeling just as uneasy as ever. Luke hadn't been to the house all weekend, and she could only assume he was taking her at her word and leaving her strictly alone while she recovered from her attack. He'd expect her to report for work today, and she knew it was the best thing she could do. She couldn't stay moping around the house, with Mrs Wood's sympathetic gaze following her and making her feel even more guilty.

"There's a letter for you, Kate," the landlady said cheerfully at the breakfast table. "There's no stamp on it, so it must have been shoved through the letter box by hand. It's from one of your adoring fans, I've no doubt."

The second Kate saw the handwriting, she knew it wasn't from any adoring fan. She felt physically sick as she snatched it up, as if she thought Mrs Wood might see right through the envelope and the filthy words she knew would be inside.

"I'll read it later," she said, her voice scratchy. "I don't feel like breakfast, just a cup of tea, Mrs Wood."

And no matter how much the woman protested, Kate knew

she would never be able to eat a thing. As soon as she could she went back to her room to get ready for work, and then tore open Walter's note. There was no preamble.

Don't think you can get away with it, you bitch. I wonder how your new fancy man will enjoy hearing about his slut of a model. He should be willing to pay a pretty penny to keep the scandal quiet from his respectable doors.

That was all. Kate hadn't thought he would resort to blackmail . . . when was it ever going to end? If Walter went to the studio today and told Luke everything, how was she ever going to face him? She should have told him the truth first – and she still could – but her nerve simply failed her. It was too late, and he would always wonder if she had intended keeping it a secret for ever if Walter hadn't turned up again.

She left the house as if she was going to work, but instead she wandered around the streets for an hour, her eyes straining for a glimpse of Walter's car. He must have been following her, stalking her. Every thought sickened her more. She couldn't even be certain he'd really go to Luke and tell him everything, but she couldn't take the risk. She had to get away.

The idea was in her head before she could stop it, and once there, she thought rapidly. Mrs Wood always went to the market on Monday mornings, and the house would be empty by now. By the time the landlady returned, Kate would be gone, and no one would be any the wiser. Luke would simply assume she hadn't turned up for work because she still needed time to recover, and she wouldn't be missed until evening. Once she decided what she had to do, Kate didn't waste time. She went back to Jubilee Terrace, bundled all the clothes she needed into her travelling bag, and left a short note for Mrs Wood on her pillow, saying she'd send for the rest of her things later. She didn't say where she was going, but there was only one place, of course.

"Paddington Station, please," she gasped out to the cab driver who pulled up alongside her at her wild waving.

"Got a train to catch, duck?" he said agreeably.

"Yes, so please hurry."

"Right you are, lady," he said, and drove at hair-raising speed towards the huge façade of Paddington Station.

"One-way or return fare?" the bored clerk at the ticket counter asked.

"Just one-way, please," Kate said in a choked voice.

He suddenly gave her a harder look. "Don't I know you from somewhere? Your face looks familiar . . ."

"No. You don't know me," Kate said, and fled down the platform to wait for the train that was scheduled an hour from now. It seemed like an endless wait, but once the train drew into the station, she sank into a corner seat in an empty carriage. And once the wheels began to move and the platform was temporarily enveloped in steam and smoke from the engine, the tears flowed, her nerves as shattered as they had ever been in her life.

Walter Radcliffe was still undecided what to do. His note to Kate had been no more than a spiteful bluff at first, just to make the bitch squirm. But his own words had given him an idea. Why not go to this Halliday bloke and offer to tell him a juicy bit of gossip about his precious model girl, for a price? Why not? He decided to put his new plan into action, even though he'd sized up Luke Halliday by now. From his age and stance Walter guessed he had also been in the army during the war, and that he'd be able to hold his own if it came to a fight.

But Walter wasn't banking on anything like that. He just wanted a few quid for providing information and that would be that. By the time the bitch turned up for work again, she'd be in for a real shock when her lovey-dovey bloke turned on her, he thought viciously.

It should all be so easy. He sat in his car in his usual vantage point from the studio on Monday morning, noting that Kate hadn't turned up. She'd still be nursing her wounded head and pride, he thought, without a second's compunction, and probably snivelling over the note he'd delivered late last night. But it was time he made his move.

His heart stopped as a large black car drew up outside the studio, and two uniformed men got out. He couldn't tell from here what the uniforms were. He only knew that the less he came into contact with uniforms, the better he liked it. He'd had enough of their bombastic bullying in the trenches. He wondered furiously if Kate had been here all the time. Maybe she'd found his note last night and come rushing over here to warn Luke. Maybe she was even shacking up with the bloke, and they'd decided to notify the police of his blackmail threat.

Whatever the truth of it, Walter wasn't waiting to find out. He cursed himself for ever writing the note at all; but he hadn't signed it, and they wouldn't know where to find him. The thought of being investigated and banged up behind bars – and even worse, the thought of his old woman finding out about Kate – was enough to make his veins fill with ice.

His time in London was long since up, and his boss was already braying for him to get back on the road. The sooner he did so and went back up north where he belonged, the better. In a blind panic, Walter started up the engine of his car, sent the tyres squealing and headed as far away from the capital as possible.

Luke had expected Kate to turn up for work, but he wasn't unduly worried when she didn't. It would need time for her bruises to settle down, and he didn't blame her for not wanting curious eyes to wonder how she had got them. On Monday the only scheduled business was for the two officers from the Fire Brigade who were due to have their portraits done for the company records, for whom he gave a generous discount, and he could manage the details on his own.

It was mid-afternoon when the door of the studio opened and a flustered Mrs Wood came inside. Since she had never been here before, he knew something bad had happened, even before she spoke.

"She's gone, Lukey," she gasped. "She left the house sometime today without saying a bleedin' word, and it looks as if she's taken half her stuff with her."

Since it was so unlike her to swear, Luke knew how shaken she was, but his attention was caught by the last part of her garbled sentence.

"You mean Kate, I suppose," he said, steering her towards a chair before she collapsed, and smiling at her melodrama. "But if she's only taken half her stuff as you say, she hasn't gone for ever. Are you quite sure she's gone at all?"

"See for yourself." She thrust Kate's note at him. "She says she's sorry for causing any fuss, and would I say sorry to you as well, and she'll be in touch when she can sort herself out. The attack must have affected her more than we thought. And that letter she got this morning might have had something to do with it as well," she added.

"What letter?" Luke said sharply.

"It was shoved through the letter box sometime in the night, I suppose, and she went as white as a sheet when she saw the writing on the envelope, as if she knew who it was from, but she wouldn't read it in front of me."

She paused for breath, but Luke didn't need to question her any further. Nor did he need to be a clairvoyant to guess who the letter was from, nor why Kate had become so secretive and unnerved since the attack in the park. It could only be one person. It was the swine who had jilted her, come back to try his luck with her again. He clenched his fists, wishing he had the bastard's neck between them.

"What do you think she's done?" he heard Mrs Wood's

voice say fearfully. "She wouldn't have done nothing stupid, like throwing herself in the river, would she?"

"Of course she wouldn't! She'll have gone home to her family for a few days, that's all. You sit there while I close up and then I'll make you some tea and decide what to do."

He put up the closed sign on the studio door, took her up to his flat and brewed the tea while she hovered behind him as if unwilling to be in this strange environment alone.

He already knew what he had to do. He was going to do what he should have done long ago. First thing tomorrow morning he was going to drive down to Somerset and find Kate Sullivan, and demand that she came to her bloody senses and marry him.

Kate hadn't bothered telephoning Father Mulheeny from Temple Meads Station. She couldn't have borne his probing questions. She had money, and she had recklessly jumped into a taxi cab outside the station and asked the driver to take her all the way to Edgemoor.

Her mother's face was filled with shocked surprise when she rushed inside the cottage, throwing her arms around her and sobbing and shaking uncontrollably.

"What's happened, Katherine?" she said sharply. "What's got into you, girl? Has someone hurt you?"

At the innocent question, Kate saw her sisters' small, scared faces as they clung to their mother's skirt, and mentally thanked her lucky stars that her menfolk weren't home at this moment. For now that she was here, how could she possibly tell them all of it? How could they understand the way their girl had believed that lust had been love, which had set her on a trail of near damnation?

"I'm not hurt, Mother," she mumbled into her mother's shoulder. "I'm very tired from the travelling, that's all, and I needed a rest away from London."

Alice held her away from her, and looked deep into her

274

daughter's eyes. Kate prayed she couldn't see the guilt and shame there.

"I don't fancy that's all there is to it, girl, and your face don't look too chirpy, but at least you know the place to come to when you're in trouble."

"There's no trouble, Mother," Kate said huskily. "I had a bit of a fall last week and hurt my face, and I'm sorry to have frightened you and the girls."

Brogan and Donal arrived home soon afterwards, their faces a mixture of astonishment and delight at seeing her. Somehow the awkward moments passed, even though Kate knew that Alice's female intuition told her there was far more behind this visit than a healthy young girl needing a rest.

"Did you bring us anything, our Kate?" Maura said.

"Not this time, pet. I only decided to come home on the spur of the moment."

"Leave your sister alone and let her catch her breath. She can't always be bringing you presents," Brogan said, glad enough to see her, although by now he had registered her guarded eyes.

He might not be the brightest of men, but he also guessed there was more behind this visit, and that Kate would tell them in her own good time. But she looked so exhausted now, that they all knew they'd get nothing more out of her.

Only Donal pursued her up the stairs when she pleaded with them to let her get a good night's rest, and that she'd feel more like talking tomorrow. Not that she expected to sleep.

"Why are you here, Kate?" he said at her door.

"Aren't you glad to see me then?"

"Don't talk daft, of course I am, but I know you better than the old 'uns do. Has your man been giving you trouble?"

She didn't pretend not to know what he meant, and her eyes scalded, knowing what a champion Luke had always been, and still would be, given the chance. She put her hand on Donal's arm.

275

"Luke's never been anything but a gentleman to me, Donal. It's got nothing to do with him."

She bit her lip, knowing it had everything to do with him, but she couldn't tell her brother any of it. Nor could she imagine what Luke might be thinking of her now, if Walter had carried out his threat and betrayed her again. She gave a convulsive shiver, knowing she had lost everything.

"I can't talk any more, Donal. I've got a terrible headache after the train journey, and I can't even think straight at the moment," she said.

"All right," he said reluctantly. "But Katie, whatever it is, you know you can rely on me."

She knew that, and it was the reason she was here; she knew she could rely on her family, even if she couldn't tell them why. They were family, and families could always be counted on in a crisis.

If she had expected it to be easy to slip back into her old life, she very quickly found out how wrong she was. The girls went off to the village school next morning, and the men went to their work. Nobody roused her, assuming she needed to sleep, although she had tossed and turned half the night. When she finally went downstairs, there was only her mother and herself, and the atmosphere between them was as stiff and awkward as it had ever been.

"I'm sorry to have landed myself on you like this, Mother," Kate said, over a cup of tea and a thick wedge of dripping toast.

"This is your home, the same as it's always been, and when did a daughter ever have to excuse herself for coming home?" Alice said crisply.

But it wasn't the same home for her as it had been when she was a child or an adolescent, and they both knew it. She was a woman now, and she had inevitably grown away from them, and the old saying that you could never go back was never more poignant to Kate than now, when she and her mother simply couldn't find anything to say to one another. Home had seemed the only place to go, but right now she felt as though she didn't belong anywhere.

By the time the interminable morning had ended, and they had eaten a scrappy midday meal together, Kate decided to go for a walk. The futile attempts at conversation had led nowhere, and she began to feel more upset than ever, totally in limbo and adrift. She struck out across the fields without any real sense of direction, but well away from the village. She needed to be alone, and to think. Eventually she arrived at the old sea wall that held back the high tides of the Bristol Channel, and sank down on one of the grass-covered banks that had always been her favourite haunt.

How long she stayed there, sitting with her arms clasped around her knees, she didn't know. The sun was warm on her head, and the sea was tranquil. This place had always calmed her, but she was too immersed in trying to sort out her own tangled emotions to notice any of it. If only she had told Luke everything from the start, and taken her chance on whether or not he would have turned against her. Many men would, but she had never given him the chance . . .

She felt a sob rise in her throat and dashed the mistiness from her eyes as she stood up to turn back. Unsteady for a moment, she wondered if she was seeing a mirage as a tall figure came striding across the fields towards her. Her heart surged uncomfortably. It couldn't be him. He was back in London, where he belonged.

When Luke reached her, he pulled her into his arms without ceremony and gave her a none-too-gentle shake.

"What in God's name do you think you're playing at?" he said angrily.

Kate stared at him, thoughts milling around in her head so fast she almost stumbled as she tried to get out of his embrace, but he wasn't going to let her go. He must have been to the cottage, and her mother would have told him of her old favourite haunt for thinking. She felt physically sick, knowing there could be no more secrets between them now.

"You know, don't you?" she whispered. "Walter did what he threatened and told you everything. Well, now you know the kind of girl I am, and the kind of home I come from. I wonder why you even bothered to come after me."

"What the hell are you talking about?" Luke said, still angry. "I came after you because I love you, and because of this American deal that involves us both."

"What American deal?" Kate said faintly, thrown completely off balance now.

"I tried to tell you God knows how many times, but I got cold feet." He gave a short laugh. "Funny, isn't it? I faced death a thousand times in the trenches, but I was too afraid to ask you to marry me and come to America, because I couldn't bear the thought of your refusal."

Kate couldn't speak. She could only look at him dumbly, trying to register what he was saying. But Luke's mind was also working, and he slowly pulled her down beside him on the grassy bank and held her hands tightly.

"I don't know why you thought I should give a damn what kind of home you came from. And what does Walter have to do with it? I thought he was out of the picture for good. If he's not, don't you think it's about time you told me what it is that keeps holding you to him?"

"Haven't you seen him, or heard from him?" she said.

He stared at her, and then gently touched her bruised eye and ran his finger down her cheek. "He did this to you, didn't he? Why on earth didn't you tell me?"

"How could I?" Kate said, suddenly brittle. "I was hardly proud of the fact that my ex-lover thought so much of me that he could hit me and try to rape me!"

"Your ex-lover?" Luke said.

She felt angry and defensive now. "Are you going to make

me spell it all out for you in all the gory detail? I thought Walter would have done that already!"

"Kate, I've never seen the man in my life, and I've no intention of moving from this spot until you tell me what the hell has been making you act like a frightened virgin since the day we met."

She flinched again, knowing she had been hardly that. But Walter's threats had all been empty after all, and there had been no need for her to run away and hide. If all Luke said was true about the deal that was being offered to him in America, they could have gone there together and started a new life. But she knew it could never have happened like that. When she began to speak, the words came out in a gasping rush.

"I've never been honest with you, Luke. There are a lot of things about me that will shock you, and I can't even pretend I've wanted to tell you many times before, because I never wanted to tell you at all, nor anyone else. I wish none of it had never happened, but it did, and I can't change it."

"Try me. You'll find me pretty unshockable."

"Please don't be kind to me before you know the truth, because I can't bear it. Just listen, and then make up your own mind about the kind of girl I am."

It was the hardest thing in the world to tell him, but she knew she had to do it. She told him about her head being turned by Walter, and loving him so recklessly, and innocently believing he would marry her when she became pregnant. And then about the horror of that morning when his cruel letter came telling her he was already married.

"You're not the first girl to get into that situation, Kate," Luke said quietly. "The man was a rat and you're well rid of him. And since I presume you were mistaken about being pregnant, you can thank God for that."

She closed her eyes. Beads of sweat trickled down her back and between her breasts. Now was the moment she had always dreaded, and she shook her head slowly.

"I *was* pregnant, Luke, but I lost the baby very early on. By then, the wedding was going ahead, and I was too frightened to stop it." She swallowed thickly. "So I never told Walter I had lost the baby. He betrayed me, but I was as much to blame for trying to deceive him into marrying me. Now do you see why a decent man like you shouldn't have anything to do with me?"

When he didn't say anything, she knew she had lost him.

"But then he sought you out you again," he stated.

"He wanted to see the baby he thought I must have had by now," Kate said in a high, cracked voice. "After the way he jilted me, it seems incredible that he'd even care about it, because I'm damn sure he never really cared about me."

"But I do."

She had been gazing out to sea, not wanting to see the derision in Luke's eyes, but now he forced her to look at him.

"Kate, what's past is past, and I know we can't change it. You had a terrible experience, but you came through it, and in the year that we've known one another, do you think I don't know the sweet girl you really are? What happened in the past doesn't have to ruin the rest of our lives, unless you let it. We can have a wonderful future together in America, if you'll just say you'll marry me and come with me."

She gave him the first small smile she had been able to smile that day, trying to tease him as her voice wobbled. "Are you sure you don't just want me to be your model on the advertising commissions?"

"I'm damn sure what I want you for," he said, masculine and arrogant. "I could always get another model, but there's only one girl I want for my wife. So what do you say? Do we take America by storm, sweetheart?"

She moved closer into his arms, loving him so much, and pressing her mouth to his in a long, sweet kiss that gave him all the answer he needed.